THE MIXER

*

'The Mixer' was the Underworld's name for an elegant and ruthless operator who, like some modern Robin Hood, preyed only on those who had enriched themselves at the expense of honest men....

Also in Arrow Books by Edgar Wallace

The Avenger
Big Foot
Flat 2
Room 13
The Twister

Edgar Wallace

The Mixer

ARROW BOOKS

ARROW BOOKS LTD
3 Fitzroy Square, London W1

AN IMPRINT OF THE HUTCHINSON GROUP

London Melbourne Sydney Auckland
Wellington Johannesburg Cape Town
and agencies throughout the world

First published 1927
New edition (reset) John Long Ltd 1966
Arrow edition 1966
Reprinted 1973

Made and printed in Great Britain
by The Anchor Press Ltd,
Tiptree, Essex

ISBN 0 09 908070 2

Contents

	Introduction	7
1	The Outwitting of Pony Nelson	11
2	The Great Geneva Sweepstake	20
3	A Speculation in Shares	29
4	The Bank that Did Not Fail	37
5	Mr. Limmerburg's Waterloo	47
6	A Close Call—and its Sequel	55
7	How a Famous Master Criminal was Trapped	62
8	Mr. Sparkes, the Detective	70
9	The Naval Coup	79
10	A Strange Film Adventure	87
11	The Girl from Gibraltar	94
12	A Gambling Raid	106
13	The Gossamer Stockings	115
14	The Case of Donna de Milo	124
15	The Seventy-fourth Diamond	133
16	Film Teaching by Post	142
17	The Billiter Bank Smash	152
18	The Spanish Prisoner	159
19	The Crown Jewels	168
20	The Professor	175

Introduction

By PENELOPE WALLACE

Whoever reads a book by Edgar Wallace has the feeling of knowing him, for he puts so much of himself into every page—his beliefs, his likes and dislikes and perhaps, above all, his sense of humour.

It was his contention that the writing of an author must be backed by experience and during his life he achieved experience in such varied fields as newsboy, printer, milkboy, medical orderly, publisher, special constable, war correspondent, journalist, racehorse owner, film director, playwright and author.

He was born in Greenwich on the 1st April, 1875. His father was an actor, his mother an actress—they were not married. When the boy was nine days old he was adopted by a Billingsgate fish porter and grew up in Greenwich and the surrounding parishes. Intelligent and observant, and having that quality of humanity which enabled him to understand as well as to observe, he acquired in his boyhood the knowledge and love of London and her people which can be felt in so many of his books.

After he left school he tried a variety of jobs ranging from printing to plastering. At eighteen he joined the Army. In 1896 his regiment was transferred to South Africa. Here he wrote a poem in honour of the arrival of Rudyard Kipling, *Good Morning Mr. Kipling*; he was hailed as 'The Soldier Poet' then in 1898 a book of his poems was published under the title *The Mission That Failed*. This was the first of the 173 books which were published in the following 34 years.

In 1899 he bought himself out of the Army and was engaged as a correspondent to cover the South African War for Reuter and later for the *Daily Mail*. By an ingenious scheme he scooped the signing of the Peace Treaty. The *Daily Mail* was delighted;

Lord Kitchener was furious and permanently banned him as a war reporter.

With the war at an end he became the first editor of the *Rand Daily Mail* but later returned to England to the London *Daily Mail*. Here as a reporter he covered crimes, trials and hangings. He stored up knowledge of crime and criminals and he learnt two practical lessons—economy of words and the ability to meet a deadline; and, later as racing correspondent for various papers, he acquired his affection for racing which proved invaluable for his books but highly detrimental to his bank balance.

His first novel *The Four Just Men* he published himself in 1905 but his success as an author stemmed from the stories of Africa which he wrote for the *Tale Teller* and which were later published as *Sanders of the River*.

During the years that followed he wrote books, plays and articles. His success and his enormous output—in 1926 he had 18 books published—enabled him to live in a far different way from the early days in Greenwich; he was never ashamed of his early poverty but rightly proud of his achievement.

Edgar Wallace had a remarkable memory which enabled him to work out the complete plot of a new book without making notes; invariably he wrote the first page in longhand, dictating the rest to his secretary or into a dictaphone according to the time of day—for sometimes he would work far into the night and sometimes he would begin extremely early in the morning always fortified by half-hourly cups of tea and with a plentiful supply of cigarettes to be smoked in his long holder. His powers of concentration were immense; his young children could go to his study at any time with their problems; sleepless guests would call in for a cup of tea—but these interruptions had no effect on his chain of thought.

He worked hard and almost his only relaxation was racing and, in the summer, a journey up the river to Maidenhead in his motor launch the *Miss Penelope*.

In November, 1931, Edgar Wallace took up yet another profession, he went to Hollywood to write film scripts; he worked at his usual speed and in nine weeks he had written four scripts including *King Kong*—this in addition to alterations to a play short stories, articles and the long letters to his wife which were later published as *My Hollywood Diary*.

He planned that his family should join him in Hollywood before his return to England in April, 1932, but early in February he developed a sore throat; this was no ordinary sore throat for rapidly it became double pneumonia and within three days he died. He died but his books have lived; fast moving and vital they have taken countless readers out of their ordinary lives and into the world of master criminals and little crooks; or murder and robbery. A world where right triumphs and a world which confirms that it is impossible not to be thrilled by Edgar Wallace.

The Mixer was first published in 1927 and it reflects the author's belief in justice; that wrongdoers should not escape merely because they are within the letter of the law. This is a light-hearted book and the punishment meted out to the evil-doers is usually financial.

1: The Outwitting of Pony Nelson

Pony Nelson had clicked, and it was the biggest click of years. It was a click that gave him precedence over all his contemporaries. It is a long story, and has little to do with this narrative, but some £35,000 was involved, and Pony, who was the prince of confidence tricksters and the greatest and most amazingly clever card-sharp that ever handled the 'boards', made a clean job of it. There were sharings, of course, but Pony had had a good season, and could afford to behave handsomely to the rest of the gang.

He had planned a summer of idleness, a car tour in the West of England, a few weeks up the river, and he was actually negotiating for a shoot in Scotland, when Bradley, of the Central Police Investigation, gave him the office that big trouble was brewing. The indefatigable Detective Sennet, who gave his whole time and attention to such crimes as were Pony's speciality, was hot on his track and needed only another scrap of evidence to put Mr. Nelson where the dogs wouldn't bite him or the cats disturb his slumbers.

Whereupon Pony passed the word round, announcing that his passport was in order and that he was leaving at an early date for the South of France, his plans having undergone revision; and there assembled at the Seven Feathers in Soho all that was best and brightest and most dexterous in what was colloquially known as the 'Nelson Push'.

Simmy Diamond, Colethorpe, May Bluementhal and Chris O'Heckett were present at the sumptuous repast which Pony gave, and the wine passed freely. I give these names, few of which need be remembered, since the majority subsequently sank their identities in numbers. But the names are emphasised for the moment so that the reader may realise that The Mixer was not present. He was not a member of the 'Nelson Push', though it may be said that he had very excellent information about Mr. Nelson, his habits, his weaknesses, and his plans.

'Lucky you!' said May, who sat at Pony's elbow.

Pony chuckled.

'Well, things might be worse,' he answered complacently, 'but I hate going abroad with the season opening up, and money for nothing waiting to be picked up.'

He shook his head with well-simulated regret, or perhaps his regret was not wholly simulated. Pony was a *poseur*, as all great artists are. He responded to the atmosphere of adulation in which, for the moment, he had his being or, vulgarly speaking, Pony was showing off.

'Yes,' he went on thoughtfully, 'there's lashings of money for you boys and girls and, though you're welcome to it, I hate the thought of being out of the running.'

He stopped, and a new light dawned in his eye.

'I'm leaving tomorrow,' he said slowly, 'by the eight o'clock train. My bag's packed and at the station.'

He paused again and the adoring company listened breathlessly, for Pony was a man of genius and at times gave vent to memorable sayings, which were repeated even in the lower strata of rascaldom.

'This is going to be an expensive trip for me,' said the whimsical Mr. Nelson, his eyes smiling mischievously. 'By the time I get through, what with the railway fares, crossing the Channel, my expenses in Paris, tipping porters, etc., I reckon this trip will cost me a hundred pounds.'

The statement was received with sycophantic smiles, for had not Pony the greater part of £40,000 stored away in various pockets, secret and open?

The girl was the first to divine his meaning.

'Don't be a fool, Pony,' she said seriously. 'Leave well alone. You go home and have a sleep and get away to France. I know what you're thinking about.'

'What?' challenged Pony.

'You're going to do a job to bring you in your fare,' she said. 'You'll have all the busy-fellows in the world waiting for you tomorrow morning at Victoria Station. Sennet's after you, and maybe a fool slip tonight will get you a lagging.'

Pony laughed.

'The splits have been after me for years,' he said, 'and they haven't got me yet, have they? And is it likely that I should go and ask for it at the last minute? No, May, if I do a job tonight it'll be a safe one, and I'm going to do it.'

It was Simmy who added his warning to the girl's.

'It's asking for trouble, Pony,' he said, shaking his head. 'I've seen some of the best men in the business put away because they weren't satisfied with a lot, but wanted a bit more. It isn't as though you are unknown, Pony. Why, even the copper on his beat knows that you're mixed up in these jobs, and it's only because they haven't proof that you haven't been pinched. Wherever you go you're watched and, what's more, it isn't like you to do a job without a lot of preparation and fixing. How can you cover yourself when you don't even know the kind of job you're going to do?'

The logic of this appealed to the professional instincts of the company, and there was a murmur of approval. But Pony Nelson was full of good vintage and was, moreover, excited by the prospect of his holiday. It was true he had made a good picking—incidentally ruining one man and two women in the process of his enrichments. It was true that he had enough money to last him for two or three years, and that before him lay leisure and opportunity for planning still greater coups.

But he felt he had a reputation for daring and ingenuity to sustain, and he had great faith in his star.

'I think some of you people want holidays, too,' he said sarcastically. 'What's biting you all? You don't suppose I'm going to walk up to a goldsmith's shop, smash the window and pinch a handful of watches, do you? Or do you expect me to go into Piccadilly, where the flatties are as thick as flies in a dustbin, and knock some old josser over the head? I tell you I'm going to get a hundred pounds to pay my expenses, and I'm going to get it easy.'

He had no definite plan in his mind, but he was chockful of wine and optimism.

'What you want,' growled Simmy, 'is a blinking miracle.'

And then the miracle happened.

The Seven Feathers café and restaurant occupied the ground and first floors. Pony had chosen the ground floor for his dinner, because it gave him opportunities of observation. The little dining-room was, in fact, a curtained recess, where there was only room for three small tables or, as in the present case, one large one. The main room was occupied by a small bar, which had an excellent reputation amongst connoisseurs.

Moreover, from the ground floor there were three exits, which was also a consideration with Pony who, despite his apparent recklessness, was in reality a very cautious man. From where he sat he commanded, through a slit in the curtain, a view of the café, and even as Simmy growled his sardonic comment there passed before the field of Pony's vision two young men who were making an unsteady way from the café entrance to the bar. Had he not seen them he must have heard them, for one of them at least was verging on the noisy. Instantly alert, Pony reached out and increased the gap in the curtain. He was an opportunist to his fingertips, and somehow he sensed, in these new arrivals, a manifestation of the miracle at which the sceptical Simmy had scoffed.

He raised his hand for silence, but this precaution was unnecessary, because his guests had interpreted the look on his face.

The noisy one of the pair of newcomers was arguing loudly with the bar-tender, his companion acting as echo. It was not unusual for the gilded youth of London to drift into the Seven Feathers, for the fame of its liquor was widespread. These newcomers were in evening dress. They were not only well, but expensively attired. The noisy one was young and good-looking. His companion was slightly older, less handsome, less boisterous, but obviously was not less inebriated.

'Wait,' said Pony softly, and slipped out, for he saw his click.

He also was in evening dress, and wore it so well that he could never be mistaken for a waiter. He walked across the café floor in a leisurely way, his hands in his pockets, a long cigar in the corner of his mouth and, making no attempt to introduce himself to the strangers, addressed the barman.

There was no need to address the others, for the youngest lurched towards him and laid a genial hand on his shoulder.

'Have this one with us, dear old boy,' he said. 'We've yards of money, and the night's young.'

Pony returned an affable smile.

'I don't as a rule drink with strangers,' he said.

'Forget all about that, old chap,' returned the other. 'The night's young, and it's my birthday.'

'So it is—let's celebrate,' added his friend, waving an unsteady hand.

Pony demurred, but accepted. There was a solemn drinking of healths, and then the first man who had addressed him thrust his hand into his pocket and pulled out a bunch of banknotes of such respectable thickness and of such denomination—Pony saw out of the corner of his eye that they were all tens—that the clear-headed man made his plan on the spot.

Conversation was easy. The handsome young man did all the talking, echoed enthusiastically by his companion, and he talked about himself and his friend. He did not say as much, but Pony gathered that they were sons of men who had recently acquired their wealth. He gathered, too, that they had both been in the Army, but what interested him more than anything else was a little gamble which they conducted between themselves.

The process was simple. One young man put a folded note on the counter, and asked the other to guess whether the final number inscribed at the head of the note was odd or even. Pony left them to this interesting occupation and went back to his friends.

'The miracle has happened, Simmy,' he said in a low voice, and then with a nod to May Bluementhal, 'I shall want you, May. Is your flat in Albany Street available for visitors?'

She pursed her lips in doubt.

'You're not going to take them there, are you?'

He nodded again.

'I only want a hundred out of it, you understand,' he said. 'These kids have got a thousand, if they've got a penny.'

The girl's face changed.

'That's a little different,' she said. 'What do you want me to do?'

Pony outlined his plan briefly. Presently he rejoined the boys at the counter.

'I'm afraid I must leave you, boys,' he said. 'I hate to do it, but I am dining with a lady, and if she sees you tossing she'll never leave you, because she's an inveterate gambler.'

'That's the kind I like,' said the boisterous one, but Pony shook his head.

'I'll tell you what I'll do,' he said, as though a sudden thought had struck him. 'Let's see her home, and then I'll introduce you to the best night club in town.'

The proposal was received with a howl of joy. Pony, going into the recess, reappeared presently with May, a diffident, modest young lady, who had no other anxiety than to get home.

The young men, whose names Pony had not troubled to secure, had a taxi waiting at the door, and the four drove off through the squally night, watched by the remainder of the gang.

'He's asking for trouble,' said Simmy, coming back to the table. 'I don't like it a bit. How do we know those two chaps aren't splits?'

'Splits!' sneered another of the gang. 'Did you ever know a split that didn't look like a split? These are mugs!'

Beyond the fact that the young men insisted on singing all the way to Albany Street, nothing extraordinary happened, but as they approached her flat (in reality it was a very long way from her flat) May expressed a desire to stop and walk the remaining distance, even though a thin drizzle of rain was falling. The young men might be oblivious in the morning to all that had happened, but the taxi-driver, at any rate, was sober, and he could give information which would be distinctly uncomfortable.

The young men readily agreed to her suggestion, stepped out, paid off the taxi and, four abreast, they walked along the deserted sidewalk until they reached the doorway, through which May passed, followed by the others.

The visitors found themselves in a very handsome apartment, but apparently they were not impressed. Pony managed to get the girl aside and spoke to her in a low voice. He returned to the roisterers.

'Miss Johnston doesn't want you boys to go until you've had a drink,' he said, 'but I think you've had enough already, haven't you?'

'Not a bit,' said the talkative one, 'and thank Miss Johnston on our behalf.'

Pony hesitated.

'She wanted to know if you would play "chemmy",' he said, 'but I shouldn't if I were you. She's awfully lucky and, as I told you before, gambling is a passion with her.'

'Chemin de fer,' roared the younger, 'is my long suit. Produce your cards, my lad.'

'I don't want to play,' said Pony, shaking his head. 'As a matter of fact, I don't approve of gambling.'

They smacked him on the back and dug him in the ribs and generally gave such evidence of their good spirits that he was prevailed upon to play.

The girl produced the cards from the box, and the game began.

At first the young men won, but thereafter began a very steady decline in their fortunes. They paid up uncomplainingly, and the pile of notes under May's hand grew steadily; and Pony, making a mental calculation of his winnings, saw that not a thousand but two thousand was coming into the pool, and mentally resolved to amend his arrangements with May.

Presently came the inevitable moment.

'I'm broke,' said the elder of the two. 'Lend me fifty, Anthony.'

But the other shook his head.

'I've got this twenty pounds left and I'm going to play it.' he said.

He played and lost, and for a while there was a deep silence, broken only by the rustling of the notes as the girl counted them with skilful and rapid fingers.

'Bad luck,' said Pony cheerfully. 'Now you boys must have a drink. Are you quite broke? I can lend you fifty to go on with.'

But the young men waved aside his generous offer. May prepared the drink at the sideboard and put it on the table. The young man who had done least of the talking walked slowly to the door, his hands in his pockets, whilst the other lifted his glass and sniffed it.

'Chloral hydrate!' he said pleasantly, and Pony stared.

He stared more open-eyed when the other offered the glass to him.

'Drink that!' he said.

'What do you mean?' asked Pony.

'Drink it!' said the youth, and at that moment came the click of the door being locked.

Pony swung round in time to see the elder of the two take the key and put it in his pocket.

'What the deuce is the game?' he asked.

'Big game, Pony,' said the man with the glass. 'Drink this, or I'll drill your stomach full of rivet holes.'

The girl made a dart at him, but the young man who had locked the door sprang to her and caught her in his arms.

'Let me go,' she cried fiercely. 'I'll scream for the police! Pony, what are you doing standing by and letting this——'

'Calm yourself,' murmured the young man who held her.

'Yes, calm yourself,' said his friend, 'and whatever you do, don't send for the police. Pony will tell you why.'

'Now what's your game?' asked Pony.

He was quiet now, and every sense awake.

'First of all,' said the other, 'let me relieve you of this money which you have so inhospitably taken from us by means of a stacked deck of cards.'

He took the roll of notes from the girl's hand and put it in his pocket.

'You can have a long look at that drink, Pony,' he continued, indicating the wine. 'It has a knockout drop and the effect is very quick. Will you allow me just to outline your little plan of campaign with us? Having relieved us of our money, you were going to give us a little dope, strip us of all our possessions—that is to say, all the possessions you have not already taken—and leave us in some nice back street—I presume that you could have called all your pals to your assistance by telephone. And when that was done, Pony, you were going off to France by the eight o'clock train tomorrow to spend your ill-gotten gains in riotous living. As a matter of fact, you've got your passport in your pocket but, which is more to the point, you have the necessary funds to give you a jolly nice time.'

'Well?' said Pony.

'Well?' drawled the other. 'Before I make any request of you, allow me to introduce myself. I won't tell you my surname, because that would not interest you. Familiar as it may be, you can call me Anthony. Or you can call me The Mixer. My friend here is Paul. The third member of my company is at present sitting outside waiting patiently for our reappearance.'

'Is that a bluff?' asked Pony.

'Not at all,' drawled Anthony. 'Sandy is the taxi-driver. You could say that he works for me. I've promised him that one day he shall retire rich: and I mean it, too. Also he deserves it, but I'm afraid you wouldn't appreciate his good qualities, if I told you about them. As for myself and my friend here, you understand, Mr. Nelson, we are not young heroes who find ourselves slighted by an apathetic world. We have been heroic enough,' he said modestly, 'and we have decorations which we would scorn to mention in view of our present nefarious employment. Paul there is an officer of the League of Honour, aren't you, Paul?'

Paul nodded.

'It is perfectly true that our lives are made more difficult by the fact that we both left the Army in unpleasant circumstances. Paul left hurriedly owing to the fact that he remained seven days in town longer than his leave allowed—and I was kicked out of the Army most ignominiously for punching in the eye a young person who well deserved it.'

'And now what is the game?' asked Pony again.

'I am out to make money,' said Anthony. 'I am the Invincible and Incomparable money-maker, and that is my motto. And I've discovered that the easiest way to make money is to take it from men of your kidney. That is why Paul, who is an extremely moral man, consents to act as my secretary, companion, and general assistant when required. In fact, if it wasn't that he lacks initiative and loves ease, he would have taken to rascal-skinning on his own account, being very unwilling to return to humdrum pen-driving, and very tired of looking for it, when I met him. As it is, he is good enough to lend me his support and assistance in relieving people like you of their wealth, fellows who can't squeal and who have grown rich on robbery.'

'You won't take anything from me,' said Pony between his teeth.

'On the contrary,' said the polite Anthony, 'I shall take all I want from you, and all I want is all you have.'

'By God, I'll get you for this!' hissed Pony, and again Anthony smiled, but a little wearily.

'You've got to realise,' he said gently, 'that we have taken bigger risks than your vengeance represents for considerably less money. There is nothing you can do to me that I can't do to you, and do it a little better,' he explained. 'I daresay you have a gang behind you who would lay for me one night and kick me to death if they ever caught me unprepared. They never will catch me unprepared and they'll be wasting their time and labour and laying up a whole store of disappointments if they try that little game. Now then, Pony,' his voice rang sharper. 'Shell out!'

'I refuse—yes, point blank!' exclaimed Pony, and sprang at him.

His whirling arms struck into the empty air, then the heavy barrel of a Browning crashed down on his skull, and Pony Nelson crumpled in a heap.

The girl had watched this scene in silence, her face white as death. Now, as Anthony leaned over the insensible figure and began searching the pockets, she spoke.

'I shall remember you,' she breathed.

'What a pity!' murmured Paul, as he held one of her arms.

'I should be extremely disappointed if you did not remember,' said Anthony, politely.

There was another silence, then:

'What are you going to do with me?' she asked.

'I am just going to leave you here,' said Anthony. 'That is the delightful thing about my method. I don't have to bind you or gag you or poison you or dope you, I just leave you to carry on. You can't shout for the police, because the police will come.'

'Do you call yourself a man?' she asked softly.

'I call myself a gentleman,' said Anthony with great solemnity.

The search was brief but lucrative. He piled six thick wads of notes on the table, slipped a big rubber band about the whole, and pushed them into his pocket.

He glanced round.

'I think we can go now, Paul,' he said. 'Sandy will be getting anxious.'

He nodded pleasantly to the girl, who stood stock still, and passed down the stairs with his companion.

He opened the door and stepped back, for three men stood upon the doorstep, whilst a policeman waited at the foot of the steps. Only for a second did he hesitate, then he moved out, was pushing past the waiting men when one of them caught his arm, and a torch was flashed in his face.

'Hello,' said a voice, 'who the devil are you?'

'And who the devil are you?' asked Anthony.

Then a voice in authority said impatiently:

'This is not the man. Who's his pal?'

The torch was flashed on Paul.

'That's not him either. What are you gentlemen doing here?'

'Before we go any farther,' said Anthony, falling at once into the grave tone of an argumentative drunken man, 'may I ask if there is any law which prevents me coming out of this door in the middle of the night?'

There was another awkward pause, then Detective Sennet, of Scotland Yard, said:

'All right, let them pass. They probably live in one of the flats above. You're sure this is the place?' he asked one of his companions.

'Certain, sir. I know May is in, because I saw the lights go up on the first floor.'

'All right,' said Sennet, then to Anthony. 'Is that your taxi, gentlemen?'

'That's my taxi,' answered Anthony.

'Well, good night,' said Sennet, and passed into the hall and up the stairs.

A few minutes later he dashed down again in search of the taxi, but The Mixer had disappeared.

2: The Great Geneva Sweepstake

Graeside is a very pleasant house in a very pleasant road in the pleasantest suburb of a North of England town. It may be mentioned in passing that the owner of Graeside suffers from some chronic chest trouble and spends the greater part of the year in the high Alps. Artistically and even comfortably furnished, with an acre or so of excellent garden, it was the source of some bitterness to its wheezy owner that he found difficulty in letting Graeside furnished at seventeen guineas a week.

He confided this much to Mr. Burnstid over an after-luncheon cigar in the lounge of the Hotel Bellevue, at Interlaken. The emptiness and desolation of Graeside, the meanness of prospective hirers of furnished houses, and his asthma were Mr. Ferguson's main themes, and Mr. Burnstid, who had listened drowsily to a long dissertation upon what Dr. This had said and Dr. That had advised, and had taken a yawning interest in the various symptoms of the disease which assailed Mr. Ferguson, woke up suddenly when the virtues of Graeside came to be discussed.

Burnstid was a very stout man, with a large, healthy face and a large, healthy nose. He was always well-dressed and even better than that. He wore across his yellow waistcoat an immense chain of gold, and on his plump fingers sparkled and scintillated the products of Kimberley.

'Nice house, eh?' he asked. 'Good neighbourhood, and all that sort of thing?'

'The best,' said Mr. Ferguson emphatically.

'In a road or standing by itself?' asked Mr. Burnstid, and Mr. Ferguson explained that it was detached, that it was not overlooked, that it was luxuriously furnished and had bathrooms of transcendent beauty, that it was honestly worth seventeen guineas of anybody's money, and that a spirit of meanness and parsimony had swept over the whole of the North Country.

'H'm,' said Mr. Burnstid, and sucked at his cigar, looking at the floor through half-closed eyelids. 'Are you letting this place yourself or have you got an agent? You always ought to have an agent, you know.'

'I've got an agent,' said the melancholy Ferguson, and gave his name.

At Mr. Burnstid's request, he added the address, and remarked in parentheses that he was probably the most inefficient agent that any house-owner ever had.

Mr. Burnstid grunted, and a little while afterwards went to his room, where his first act was to write down the name of the agent and the place where he was to be found. He did not mention Graeside to Ferguson or show the slightest interest, and when, eight or nine days later, the delighted Mr. Ferguson heard from his agent to the effect that Graeside was let, Burnstid was not at Interlaken to hear the good news, or to receive the congratulations and thanks of Mr. Ferguson, even supposing that Mr. Ferguson had been aware of the fact that it was due to his stout and amiable companion that the letting had been effected.

Mr. Burnstid had indeed gone across country to Lausanne, and thence by boat to the Lake of Geneva, for he had an appointment with his two partners, also stout men who smoked expensive cigars and were girded with large gold cables.

The meeting took place in an airy office on the Rue du Mont Blanc, and was wholly informal. Mr. Epsten and Mr. Cowan were present in addition to Mr. Burnstid.

'Well?' was Mr. Epsten's first greeting, and he was apparently a person of some importance. 'What's the prospects?'

'The prospects is pretty good,' replied Mr. Burnstid, who was superior to the rules that governed the speech of his adopted country. 'I am sending three-quarters of a million circulars, and they will all be posted in England. We are certain to get in two hundred thousand from our old clients, the fellows we had for the Cesarewitch sweep, and a lot more besides. I haven't wasted the winter.'

'That's good,' said Mr. Epsten, nodding. 'Then you think the Lincoln sweep is going to be a success?'

'Think?' scoffed the other. 'I know. It will be like shelling peas. We ought to get at least £100,000.'

'What prizes are you offering?' asked Mr. Cowan.

'First prize £20,000,' said Burnstid promptly. 'Wait a bit. I'll give you the full particulars.' He took from his pocket a slip of paper, adjusted a pair of gold-rimmed glasses, and looked down his nose at the document. 'First prize, £20,000,' he read. 'Second, £10,000; third, £5,000; fourth, £1,000; ten consolation prizes of £600, and £500 for every other horse drawn.'

Mr. Cowan nodded, satisfied.

'That ought to bring 'em in,' he said, 'but wouldn't it be well to make the first prize £40,000?'

Burnstid shook his head.

'You'd scare 'em at £40,000,' he said. '£20,000 is a reasonable sum. You see, the public argue this way: They think we are making a bit out of it, and they don't mind so long as it isn't too much. If we offered £40,000 they would smell a fake, because the people who go in for sweepstakes know very well that there ain't a great deal of money going for the Lincolnshire Handicap anyway. No, we want to put a reasonable prize list out, and I think this will do.'

'That's all right,' said Epsten. 'Now what about money for preliminary expenses?'

'I reckon it will cost £10,000,' said Burnstid, 'not reckoning my own personal expenses, if I am going to stay to work it as I did last year. I'll put up £2,000, and you two others put up £4,000 each, and we'll split three ways.'

There was some argument as to this division, because it was not in the nature of either Mr. Epsten or Mr. Cowan to agree readily to any proposal which involved the putting down of hard cash, but eventually the agreement was made.

'What about a staff?'

'I've got that fixed,' said Mr. Burnstid. 'In fact, I have been very lucky. I have taken a lease on some old offices at a reasonable figure, and I have engaged a bright young man to run the whole thing.'

'A bright young man?' said Mr. Epsten suspiciously. 'Where did you get him?'

'He's very well connected, by all accounts,' explained Mr. Burnstid, 'very smart, and willing to do anything. He speaks French, German and English, and he is well in with the authorities here. I am going to fix it up so that if any trouble comes he will be the mug.'

Mr. Epsten smiled and Mr. Cowan smiled, and Mr. Burnstid smiled in sympathy.

'Is he straight?' asked the virtuous Mr. Epsten. 'We don't want any crooks in this business, you know, Burnie. I mean, suppose he finds out that none of the big prizes are paid?'

'Leave that to me,' said Mr. Burnstid with confidence. 'I tell you, this lad will do anything for £1,000, and, besides, I can always fake the draw; and, in fact, I have made arrangements already for the awarding of the first prize.'

He did not explain what the arrangements were until later. but his companions were satisfied.

They left that night for Paris, leaving Mr. Burnstid to carry out his plans. Mr. Burnstid did not exaggerate the qualities of the young gentleman whose services he had secured. They had met one day on the boat to Ouchy, and Mr. Burnstid, who never lost an opportunity, nor failed to diagnose the financial conditions of those with whom he was brought into contact, had, as he was subsequently satisfied, accurately placed the bright and talkative young man whom he met in the smoking-room of the boat.

He saw his friends off from the station, and then went to the little Café du Planet, where he had arranged to meet his new

assistant. The new assistant was sitting disconsolately gazing a
an empty coffee cup, but brightened up at the sight of his nev
patron.

'It's all right, Stevens,' said Mr. Burnstid jovially. 'I've fixe
up your job with my partners.'

'Oh, I say,' said the grateful young man, 'that really is joll
good of you. You are most kind. Really, you are a perfectl
wonderful old boy.'

'Not so old,' growled Mr. Burnstid, with whom age was
sore point. 'Now, you understand I am putting a lot of confi
dence in you. This business of ours is not exactly—er—business

'Quite so, quite so,' said Mr. Stevens chirpily. 'I think you'r
a jolly good chap, and don't worry about my conscience be
cause I haven't one. Now let's hear what I've got to do.'

Mr. Burnstid told him. Apparently Stevens had to do nothin
but to sit in a luxurious office and keep an eye upon innumer
able other men and women who were opening envelopes con
taining currency, which would be sent from Britain by eve
larger numbers of other young men and women, desirous o
getting rich quick by drawing the winner of the Lincolnshir
Handicap.

'You will take charge of all the money and be boss. If any
body comes and wants to know who is running it, remembe
it's you. You will sign all the cheques.'

The young man purred.

'After I have initialled them,' said Mr. Burnstid. 'I have ar
ranged with the bank manager that no cheques will be cashe
unless my initials are on the left-hand corner.'

'Very proper, very proper,' said the young man.

'Now you understand'—here Mr. Burnstid became mor
careful than ever, and spoke slowly and with emphasis—'tha
it often happens that we do not get in enough money to pay th
big prizes. In that case the prizes are reduced. That's fair, isn'
it?'

Stevens agreed.

'And sometimes,' explained Mr. Burnstid further, 'even whe
there is a lot of money the expenses are so heavy that we hav
to knock off the first prize to pay our way.'

'I see,' said Stevens thoughtfully.

'When I say knock off the first prize,' said Mr. Burnstid, '
don't mean that we go and tell the people that we've had t
knock off the first prize. We award as though we hadn'
knocked it off, if you understand.'

'That's a jolly good idea,' approved Stevens. 'I suppose th

poor chap who gets it doesn't get it at all. Is that the scheme?'

'Not quite, not quite,' Burnstid rubbed his nose and hesitated. 'Well, you've got to know this, as you are in the game, and you're going to draw £1,000—a whole thousand Jimmy O'Goblins—as your share of the——'

'Loot?' suggested Mr. Stevens.

'That's the word, loot. We may have to plant somebody to take the first prize. You see, strictly speaking, the draw occurs the day before the race, and the holders of the various horses are advertised. Well, you can't do that, because if you planted a man with the favourite, the favourite might lose. So what we do is to announce the names of the people who have drawn the horses after the day of the race and then the thing is simple.'

'Simplicity itself. My dear fellow, I understand the business quite well. What you mean to say is that we're running a commercial concern, and we cannot afford to take uncommercial risks, ha! ha!'

Burnstid smiled in sympathy.

'Now,' Mr. Burnstid continued, 'I've taken a house called Graeside, in the North of England. I'm going to get somebody I can trust to live there till the draw. I need hardly tell you that the first prize is going to the tenant at Graeside. If inquiries are made there, he will be as large as life, ready to answer any questions. Now, I'm sending my son, Barney, there. Nobody knows that I am connected with this—this——'

'Swindle?' suggested the other innocently, and Mr. Burnstid frowned.

'That is not the word,' he said sharply; '"enterprise" is a better one. Anyway, he will be there. Now you know the whole run of the game. If we have a very successful sweep I'll give you a little more than the thousand for the season—you'll find me pretty generous. If there's any kind of trouble, don't forget that you're the man in charge, and you've got to take whatever medicine is coming to you. That is why I'm paying you so high.'

The young man known as Stevens light-heartedly brushed aside the possibility of there being any trouble. If there was, he was quite prepared for all eventualities.

For the next few weeks Mr. Burnstid lived a contented life. He saw his office coming into shape, and was more than satisfied with the adept way in which this young man handled his staff. The sweep had been well advertised, and the fruits of the circulars were beginning to appear. The stream of money orders and postal orders and banknotes—the promoters of the Great

Geneva Sweepstake accepted no cheques—grew in volume, but never in the busiest time was Mr. Stevens snowed under. Then, when all things were looking serene, a blow fell.

One day Stevens was summoned to the Bellevue Hotel, and found his employer pacing the ante-room of his elegant suite.

'Here's a pretty mess,' he said. 'Somebody in England has discovered that Barney is my son, and has advertised the fact—and after Barney had moved into Graeside with his wife!'

'That's pretty bad. You can't award him the prize now.'

Mr. Burnstid did not answer. He was completely occupied in cursing the interfering busybodies of the British press who had stuck their noses into business which did not, from his point of view, concern them.

'This is pretty bad, pretty bad,' he said, shaking his head. 'It's too late to plant another winner.'

'What are you going to do?' asked Stevens.

'Well,' said Mr. Burnstid, controlling himself with an effort, 'my partner, Mr. Cowan, has got a plan, and it's a very good idea too. Have you ever heard of The Mixer?'

'The Mixer?' asked Stevens with a smile. 'I've heard of more than one.'

'I'm talking about the famous one,' said Mr. Burnstid impatiently. 'There was a bit in the paper about him. He fooled a crook in London, and pinched his money.'

Stevens shook his head.

'No. What is he?'

'Well, according to the newspaper,' said Mr. Burnstid, 'he's a gentleman who is out on the make. He is getting rich by robbing crooks—not,' he added virtuously, 'that crooks shouldn't be robbed. I think it is a very good idea. People who steal money don't deserve to keep it.'

'Well, where does The Mixer come in?' asked Stevens.

'Sit down and I'll tell you.'

Stevens took a seat in a big bow window overlooking the lake, and Mr. Burnstid let himself carefully into another chair.

'Suppose after the draw me and you go to London by the longest route with all the stuff we have collected in a bag?'

'Stuff? You mean money?'

Mr. Burnstid nodded.

'And suppose between Folkestone and London the bag's pinched by The Mixer?'

'Not being pinched at all, but being planted by us at Folkestone or somewhere?'

'That's the idea,' said the admiring Mr. Burnstid. 'My word, you have got a brain! And suppose we put it out that The Mixer has taken it, and left a note to that effect, and then me and my partners offer to pay out half the prizes out of our own pockets?'

'Talking of brains,' said Mr. Stevens, no less admiringly, 'what a head you've got!'

'You see,' said the flattered Burnstid, 'that wouldn't be a bad advertisement for the next sweep. Shows our honesty, and all that sort of thing, and at the same time saves us a matter of about £50,000, which ain't to be sneezed at. To make it more proper, we will have the press over to see the draw.'

'And to make things more lifelike,' chuckled Mr. Stevens, 'what about getting a couple of detectives from London to accompany us on our way? I know a man who is in that business, and he could supply us with a couple of guards.'

To this suggestion Mr. Burnstid at first demurred, but eventually consented, and things fell out as they had planned. There was a draw, conducted with great solemnity, in the presence of representatives of the sporting press. There were two solemn young men brought from London by Mr. Stevens who guarded the treasure; and after the men of the press had been sent on their way rejoicing and announcements had been sent on to London to the effect that the money would be distributed in person by the promoter, Burnstid, his assistant, and the two detectives boarded a through train from Basle to Boulogne.

'To minimise the risk,' said Mr. Stevens in retailing his plan to the last of the pressmen.

The scheme as the two had arranged it was simple. The big bag containing the money was to be handed to one of the partners on their arrival at Folkestone. He would give in return a bag of similar size containing old newspapers and would then make his way into the town and on to London by car. The boat came into Folkestone harbour at dusk. There was certain to be a great deal of confusion as the passengers landed and, anyway, Stevens undertook to allay the suspicions of the detectives.

Everything went without a hitch except that one of the detectives was so overcome by seasickness that he could not come on from Folkestone. Outside Charing Cross Station Mr. Burnstid opened the bag in the presence of the remaining detective and, with a simulation of horror, which was very well done, discovered the substitute.

'We've been robbed—robbed!' he said. 'Look!'

He drew out a card from the top of the bag inscribed:

'With compliments and thanks.—The Mixer.'

'This is terrible!' moaned Mr. Burnstid.
'This is horrible!' moaned Mr. Stevens.
There was a small crowd of reporters waiting at Charing Cross Station; for the arrival of a gentleman with £100,000 in banknotes and postal orders was, in the romantic circumstances, an event. To them Mr. Burnstid unfolded his terrible tale of pillage, and the faces of some of the prizewinners who had gathered to get as near to their money as was possible fell in ratio to their hopes.
'But,' said Mr. Burnstid, addressing his small audience in a voice broken with emotion, 'I am not going to let the prize-winners lose. Out of my own pocket I am going to pay fifty per cent of the money due, and you gentlemen of the press can take that as official.'
They got to their hotel and, locked in their private sitting-room, Mr. Stevens and Mr. Burnstid exchanged happy smiles.
'That's all right,' said Burnstid. 'They took it very well, and it's a good ad. for me, old man.' He looked at his watch. 'In a couple of hours I'll stroll across to Ealing. Cowan will be there with the money.'
On his arrival at Mr. Cowan's beautiful dwelling the latter gentleman greeted his partner on the doorstep with a look of surprise.
'Have you got that bag?' asked Burnstid without ceremony.
'Bag?' roared Cowan. 'You cabled me not to meet you until the next day.'
'What!' yelled the other. 'You weren't at Folkestone station?'
'Of course I wasn't,' said Cowan. 'I tell you, you cabled me——'
But Burnstid was making tracks for his taxi, and a second later was being whirled back to his hotel, for he had a few questions to ask Mr. Stevens.
But Stevens, who was called Anthony by those who knew him, was at that moment in company with one of the two pseudo detectives, sorting the ill-gotten gains of Mr. Burnstid. The Mixer, with the aid of the gentle Paul and the trusty Sandy, had turned the pious fraud of the Great Geneva Sweepstake promoters into reality.
'Paul,' he said, 'you count the tenners; I'll make a heap of the money orders—I'll send them on to old man Burnstid. They don't amount to much, anyway, but they will help to pay that fifty per cent which he has promised—officially!'

3: A Speculation in Shares

In one of the most fashionable hotels at Brighton, and occupying the most expensive suite in that hotel, lived temporarily a young gentleman described in the hotel register, in an unimaginative manner, as Mr. Smith, with his secretary, Mr. Robinson. Mr. Smith's valet also accompanied him.

It is true that these names had as yet made so small an impression upon their owners that when a waiter carried to their comfortably-furnished sitting-room a telegram, and announced that it was for Mr. Smith, neither the young gentleman nor his secretary immediately answered to the name, and the one whom the waiter knew as Mr. Robinson opened it. As he was Mr. Smith's secretary, doubtless that was quite in order.

Mr. Robinson read the long wire until the waiter was out of the room, then passed it to the other.

'Does he bite, Paul?' asked Anthony, as he took it.

'I think he does,' answered Paul, in his rather prim manner.

'He's going to make me rich,' said Anthony. 'What I love about this Ali Baba life is its glorious certainty. I was reading in the paper this morning about a fellow who held up a bank cashier and got away with two pounds and a thick ear. That's no life for a gentleman.'

'No, certainly not,' agreed Paul, sinking into a chair by the fire. 'I saw a reference to you, by the way, in one of the papers. They call you The Mixer.'

'And a jolly good title, too,' said Anthony complacently. 'Really, though,' and his voice had a more serious note, 'I am a public benefactor. In the first place, I confine my depredations to the crooks, and in the second place, I have rescued you and Sandy permanently—trust to me—from a life of drudgery: always supposing you weren't driven to a life of crime.'

Paul ran his hand over his lank smooth hair.

'I don't know that I should have gone in for a life of crime,' he demurred, 'but I was certainly getting fed up with applying for jobs. As for Sandy, rather than go back to his dim and draughty warehouse—well, it's possible he might have taken a six-shooter and held up the Bank of England. I don't know. But I certainly can say that you have not yet done anything to trouble my conscience.'

'And never will, Paul,' Anthony assured him. 'Hasn't every

gentleman I've relieved of his surplus wealth been a villain of the deepest dye?'

'They all certainly have.'

'Well, Mr. Mothenstein fulfils that description too. He has been a pretty difficult gentleman to counter. The police have been trying to get at him for years, and he isn't going to be an easy job for me.'

'Why not?' asked Paul, looking over the paper he had picked up.

'In the first place, Mr. Mothenstein is warned.'

'About you?'

Anthony nodded.

'I've been working at him for a week,' he said, 'but all the time I came up against his nasty suspicious mind. In fact, you've got to realise that there isn't a crook in London who isn't on the look-out for my unassuming self.'

'Perhaps if I knew Mr. Mothenstein's offence against society . . .' suggested Paul.

'You would be nerved to lend me any assistance I might require in the pursuit of my depredations,' supplemented Anthony.

'Quite so,' said Paul.

'It happens that I don't require your assistance in this little matter,' returned Anthony, filling his pipe as he spoke. 'It's too delightfully simple. Mothenstein is an outside broker carrying on a very respectable business. He advertises pretty extensively and gets most of his clients from those innocent people who think it is as easy to make a hundred into two hundred as it is to turn twopence into fourpence, which, as a matter of fact, it is not. Naturally, they're all shy of outside brokers, particularly as one of the journals who make a feature of looking after the interests of the investor has issued a warning against Mothenstein. But Mothenstein's first act reassures them. He writes them a long and fatherly letter, telling them that he does not think it advisable to risk all their capital in speculative investments and, if they don't mind, he would rather deal with a much smaller sum than they propose investing. Naturally this gladdens the hearts of the innocents and fills them with joy and gratitude. And when the small investment is made, and little cheques for little profits begin to trickle in, they rise on their hind legs and bless the name of Mothenstein.'

'What happens next?' asked Paul, curiously.

'The innocents write saying that they have so much confidence in Mothenstein that they would like to invest a larger sum. He writes back saying that he cannot possibly handle big accounts, because if they lost money it would lie on his conscience and keep him awake at night. He then recommends the firm of Alexander McDougal, Mackintosh & Glenstuart, an eminent firm of Scottish outside brokers, who do a conservative business at a very conservative address up North.'

Paul nodded.

'The firm of Alexander, etc., being Mothenstein, I presume?'

'Got it first time,' said Anthony. 'This conservative firm have no scruples. They urge the confiding lamb to raise every bean, sell the wool off their backs and put it into Waggerfontein Gold Fields, or some such stock, which is going sky high between now and Thursday of next week. And usually the poor dears fall for it, in spite of the fact that Mr. Mothenstein writes to them begging them not to be rash. Do Waggerfontein Gold Fields go up to £9 7s. 3d.? No, sir. They go down to 3d. A gloom falls upon the shorn lambs, and Mothenstein buys a new car.'

He puffed at his pipe reflectively.

'And your intentions are?' asked Paul.

'Well,' said Anthony, speaking slowly, 'I will tell you the weak point in Mothenstein's scheme. He has to have a real genuine stock to off-load upon his victims. Otherwise, very naturally, he is guilty of fraud to the *n*th degree, and he is a stout and respectable man who has no desire to breakfast at Wandsworth off skilly *au naturel*. And there aren't a large number of these dud companies going. He bought up Waggerfontein Gold Fields when the shares were about 2d. net, and he has managed to off-load nearly 200,000 shares at prices between 8s. 10d. and 19s. 6d. And I've had the quiet tip that the eminent firm of Alexander, etc., are on the look-out for a new bargain—and I've found one.'

He walked to his desk, unlocked it, took out a steel box, and put it on the table. When it was opened the other saw that it was full of beautifully engraved script.

'Here,' said Anthony, with the air of an exhibitor, 'are 200,000 shares in the West Australian Lead and Spelter Syndicate. I am sorry it isn't gold, but it is the best I could get. I bought them at the rate of a penny a share, which was exactly one penny per share more than they are worth. The company's rights run out in a month's time, and the property goes back to its original owners unless a new vein is struck. As the mine is situated in the desert and has broken the hearts of its proprietors years ago, the vein is likely to remain unstruck.'

'Where did you get these?' asked Paul.

'From an Australian I knew, a nice lad, who was given the

shares by a man who had borrowed twenty pounds from him and couldn't pay it back. Now, the exact value of these shares nobody knows, and my scheme is to sell these to Alexander, etc., at two-and-sixpence per share. That will get me roughly about twenty-five thousand pounds. Alexander, etc., will jump at these shares, which aren't quoted on the Exchange, and about which nothing is known. They will be able to market them at anything from five shillings to ten shillings profit.'

'Which hardly seems fair to the people who buy,' demurred Paul. 'Forgive me if I seem to interfere in your affairs, but I was brought up in a vicarage.'

'Now if you will possess your moral soul in patience for a while, Paul! I'm telling you. The moment these shares are sold I shall write to all the financial papers, not necessarily in my own name, telling them the true state of affairs about the West Australian Lead and Spelter Syndicate. Another point is that I propose dividing the loot with my friend the Australian, who is down and out.'

'Good,' said Paul, approvingly, and listened whilst Anthony gave him details.

The firm of Alexander McDougal, Mackintosh & Glenstuart occupied a very small cubic area of a large and pretentious building. The manager was known as Mr. Alexander in the North, but as Mr. Mothenstein, Junior, in London. There came to this large young man, whose face was sallow and perennially damp, such an offer from a recently returned Australian that he left urgently by the night train, and breakfasted the next morning with his parents in their stately ancestral palace at Hampstead.

Mr. Mothenstein was very stout and very unemotional, but the news his son brought to him roused him to something near enthusiasm.

'I remember the shares years and years ago,' he said. 'They used to be quoted on the Stock Exchange.'

He rose heavily and went to his limited library, which consisted of many brown volumes of the Stock Exchange Year Book, and took down one dated 1890 and turned the leaves.

'Yes, here they are,' he said. 'Capital, £300,000. Directors, h'm, ha, h'm. This fellow offers you 200,000 which means you've got control of the mine.'

'Mine!' laughed his son. 'That's good, Father. If there was any mine you wouldn't have them offered at two-and-sixpence a share.'

Mr. Mothenstein, Senior, turned upon his progeny with a frown.

'There's a mine,' he said emphatically. 'Please understand we do not deal in properties unless they exist. That would be fraud. And with fraudulent propositions I will have no truck.'

'I'm sorry, guv'nor,' said the youth, abashed, and pulling his face into an appropriate expression.

'Yes,' Mr. Mothenstein went on, putting back the book and returning to the breakfast table. 'It sounds good to me. They ask for half a crown. I suppose they'll take a bob a share?'

Mr. Julius Mothenstein shook his head.

'Not they,' he said. 'Here's the letter. Not a penny less than half a crown a share.'

Mr. Mothenstein nodded heavily.

'Well, we want some shares,' he said, 'and we want them badly. All the shares of the Baltic Trading Syndicate are disposed of, and they are simply clamouring for investments.'

'They are also clamouring for those bonus shares you promised them when the Waggerfontein turned out bad,' said Mr. Julius significantly, and his papa sniffed.

'Perhaps one of these days we will get hold of something that is worth nothing,' he said, 'and then we will fire them along, but at present I am not feeling in a philanthropic mood, my boy. The expense of this house is . . .'

And he launched forth into a lecture upon the high cost of living, the rising prices, the unreasonably exorbitant staff, and Mr. Julius, who had endured all this before, listened without hearing.

On the following morning Mr. Julius Mothenstein was waiting in a friend's office in Birching Lane. It was an office in which he had previously negotiated many interesting sales, and it was admirably suited, for there was a small room leading off, behind the door of which his father sat and listened, and could, by a judicious signal of coughs, agree or disagree with the proposals which his son made on his behalf.

Presently a visitor came, a tall, bronzed young man in a grey suit and a blue shirt. He was, explained Mr. Julius, a typical Australian, though exactly what distinguished an Australian from other members of the British race he might have found a difficulty in explaining.

'Mr. Samuel Soames,' said the cheerful visitor, though his Christian name happened to be Anthony.

'You have some shares you wish to offer us,' said Mr. Julius in his best judicial manner. 'Of course, I understand that these things are comparatively worthless, but my firm likes to make a speculation now and then.'

'So I understand,' said Anthony, producing from a black brief-case a large wad of share certificates.

Julius took the first of the bundles, read the top certificate, and shook his head with a pitying smile.

'West Australian Lead and Spelter,' he read. 'I don't think they are very much use to us, Mr. Soames.'

'Then we won't discuss it any more,' returned Anthony, reaching out for the bundle.

There was a warning cough from the next room.

'Of course,' said Mr. Julius, 'we are always prepared to take a risk. What were you asking for these?'

'Half a crown a share.'

Mr. Julius shook his head.

'Too much,' he said. 'Those shares are absolutely unmarketable, and they would cost us twenty-five thousand pounds. Now, I'll tell you what we will do, Mr. Soames. We'll buy these, which are so much waste paper, at a shilling a share.'

'You will buy them for half a crown,' said Anthony, 'or not at all.'

'Very good,' said Julius, with a shrug. 'Good morning.'

'Good morning,' came the cheery response, as Anthony dropped the shares into his brief-case, snapped the fastening, and rose.

There were two urgent coughs from the next room.

'Now, why not be sensible?' said Mr. Julius, obeying the signal. 'Why not compromise? Suppose we offer you eighteenpence a share?'

'It's half a crown or nothing,' said Anthony, firmly. 'I have already been offered two and threepence by the Thames Investment Trust.'

Now, the Thames Investment Trust was Mr. Mothenstein's most deadly rival. The Thames Investment Trust also appealed to the confiding small investor who wanted to find the royal road to riches, and there broke from the next room a most violent fit of coughing.

'Very good,' said Julius, resigned. 'Now suppose we give you a cheque dated next Monday week?'

'Suppose you give me a cheque dated last Monday week?' said Anthony. 'Look here, Mr. Alexander, you either take these shares at the price I offer them without any monkeying about payment, and you either give me an open cheque which I can cash on my way home, or there's no deal.'

Julius waited. There was a painful cough from the next room, and he took his cheque-book and filled it in carefully.

'You nearly lost us business,' grumbled Mr. Mothenstein, when the visitor had left. 'And you could have got 'em for eighteenpence if you'd gone the right way about it. However, let's get out the letter to the clients. The sooner we get rid of them the better. I have an idea they will fall for this, because there's a big rise in lead and spelter just now.'

For three hours he and his son were engaged in literary composition, which made up in beauty of language for all that it lacked in accuracy. East, north, south and west went these compositions, beautifully printed, expensively enveloped, and then the blow fell.

Mr. Mothenstein, Junior, and his father were working together in their London office, and had just received by telephone the gratifying news that orders were pouring in. No sooner was the trunk call discharged than the telephone rang violently once more.

The speaker proved to be the editor of a small weekly financial paper of great instability and promise, who had reason to be grateful to Mothenstein the elder.

'We have just had a letter come in,' he said, speaking rapidly. 'It looks like a circular letter that's been sent to all the financial papers.'

'What's it about?' asked Mothenstein with a frown.

'It's about some shares that you're handling, some lead and spelter shares. The company's lease of the ground expires next week, and the fellow who's written this letter says they aren't worth the paper they're printed on.'

Mr. Mothenstein turned very white.

A loss of twenty-five thousand pounds was not sufficient to ruin him nor, for the matter of that, ten times the loss, but it was quite sufficient to break his heart.

'We've been 'ad,' he said when he broke the news to his son. 'I ought to have known it. It's that Mixer what I've been warned about.'

'Julius, my boy, we are going to get into trouble over this. This fellow will blow the gaff and make our names smell.' (He did not say 'smell', but employed a much more vulgar word.)

Mr. Mothenstein paced his office in an agitated condition of mind.

'It ain't the money, it ain't the money,' he kept on repeating, 'but this will mean ruin to the firm. I'd give him Mixer—I'd give him ten years! I'd hang him, the dirty low thief!'

Mr. Mothenstein rubbed his nose as he sought vainly for a way out.

'Father,' said Julius suddenly, 'I've got an idea.'

Mr. Mothenstein growled something derogatory to his son's idea, but listened.

'Why not?'

'Why not what?' said his father.

'We can stand the loss,' said Julius. speaking rapidly, 'but we can't stand the injury to the firm. That's the idea, isn't it?'

Mr. Mothenstein nodded.

'Well, why not send out these shares tonight to all our old clients? Tell 'em they're bonus shares. Distribute them all over the country, and pretend that they're going to go sky high. It will get the firm a good name, and get rid of any idea that we are swindling 'em.'

'That's an idea,' said Mr. Mothenstein slowly, 'a grand idea. Get in the clerks.'

The firm of Mothenstein worked very hard that night, and it was near midnight when the last of the bonus shares were posted, accompanied by a heliographed letter which breathed the spirit of benevolent affection which the firm of Alexander McDougal, Mackintosh & Glenstuart held for their clients.

• • • • •

The Mixer heard the news of this free distribution, and laughed softly.

'The old beggar was too wily for me,' he said. 'It must have broken his heart to have distributed two hundred thousand shares, even though they were worth nothing. But, at any rate, he saves the reputation of his infernal bucket shop. I wonder what wild dreams the innocent recipients have about the West Australian Lead and Spelter Syndicate and its future?'

'Dreams that look like becoming realities,' returned Paul. 'Have you seen the papers?'

'What papers? What's in them?' asked Anthony suspiciously.

Paul left his game of patience, which Anthony's entrance had interrupted, picked up a newspaper, folded it with a particular heading uppermost, and handed it to the other, who read:

WESTERN AUSTRALIA SENSATION

RICH VEIN OF GOLD FOUND IN DERELICT LEAD MINE
'WORTHLESS' SHARES NOW SELLING FOR £3

The message was dated from Western Australia, and read:

'Prospectors who have been working on mines belonging to the West Australian Lead and Spelter Syndicate have struck gold and shares which yesterday were hardly worth the paper they were written on, are selling freely today at £3.'

Anthony whistled.

'Well, I've got my share of the swag, anyway,' he said.

'And I mine,' murmured Paul, returning to his game of patience, for he and Sandy were never forgotten when their employer brought home the plunder.

'And there will be some happy hearts among Mothenstein's clients this night, Paul,' said Anthony complacently.

4: The Bank that Did Not Fail

The Mixer walked aimlessly along the Strand. Untidily dressed, with a bundle of books under his arm, he looked like a not too well off student who had strayed out of King's College and found time hanging on his hands.

He stopped at every other shop and looked in the window, and once as he moved on, he collided with a girl who had come out of a doorway leading to one of the upper storeys of a tobacconist's. He smiled an apology, but the girl hardly looked at him. Her face was white, and evidently she had been crying, and Anthony lifted his gaze from her face to the doorway where, on a decorous brass plate, was inscribed the name of Mr. Oliver Digle, financier.

Oliver Digle, financier, was not unknown to The Mixer. His name had figured in more law cases than had that of any other moneylender, and Anthony's natural antipathy to the class was quickened by the sympathy he felt towards the girl.

He followed her, quickening his pace. He thought she was going to Charing Cross Station, but she turned down Villiers Street, crossed the road at the bottom, and entered the Embankment Gardens. She seemed to be seeking for some quiet spot where she could sit, and Anthony kept his eye upon her until he saw she was seated. Then, without any word of apology, he sat by her side, opened a book, and was apparently engrossed in his studies.

He saw out of the corner of his eye the quick resentful glance the girl gave him, and her hesitant movement, as though she were going to move to some other seat.

'One moment, please,' he said quietly. 'And would you be good enough to believe that I do not wish to be offensive?'

She looked at him in alarm.

'I know it isn't the thing for a strange man to address a girl in a public place,' said Anthony with a smile, 'but you needn't worry. That quiet-looking gentleman over there, reading the afternoon paper as though he had no interest in life but the winner of the two-thirty race, is an eminent detective from Scotland Yard. and you can see the uniformed attendant from where you sit. If I in any way annoy you, you can always call on them for assistance.'

She smiled a little against her will.

'I don't want to be rude, either,' she said, 'but I must tell you that I have no desire to enter into conversation with anybody, whether it is a stranger or a friend.'

He nodded.

'That I can well understand,' he said, 'but I rather fancy that you need a friend outside the circle of your acquaintances. You've had trouble with Digle?'

She looked startled.

'How did you know?' she asked.

'I guessed,' he said. 'Has he been putting the screw on you?'

She frowned at him.

'Were you there?' she asked quickly. 'Do you know Mr. Digle? Has he sent you?'

He shook his head again.

'No, I don't know Mr. Digle personally, but I know something of his amiable character. I gather that you're one of the unfortunate people who have got into his clutches, and my only object in speaking to you is to ask whether in any way I can help you.'

It was her turn to shake her head.

'No,' she said, curtly. 'I'm afraid you can't help me. Oh, I've been such a fool!'

'We've all been fools more or less,' he said cheerfully, 'at some time in our lives. Now won't you, as a great favour, tell me just what your trouble is?'

She was silent for some time.

'I don't know why I should tell you,' she said, 'but I've done nothing which the world cannot know, and won't know in a few weeks' time.'

She told him that her husband had died recently after an illness lasting several months. He had left her the small house in the country and a few hundred pounds in the bank.

'Poor Ted was a good husband but he was very careless,' she said, 'and I hadn't the slightest idea that he owed money to Mr. Digle. But apparently he borrowed a thousand pounds a few weeks before he died. I knew nothing of this until one day I received a visit from one of Mr. Digle's agents, he produced the promissory note and demanded payment. I feel I must honour my husband's debt, but it will mean that I shall be left penniless.'

'How much did your husband owe?'

'He borrowed a thousand and he had to repay two thousand,' said the girl. 'It's absolutely wicked!'

Anthony was jotting down a few particulars on the fly-leaf of his book.

'Perhaps you wouldn't mind telling me where you live,' he said, 'the date the bill was drawn, and what your husband borrowed the money for.'

She shook her head and, after giving her address, replied helplessly:

'I'm sorry I can't supply the particulars. They're as much of a mystery to me as they are to you. When Ted borrowed that money I know he had a balance at the bank, and why on earth he should have gone to a moneylender I don't know. Of course, he may have had responsibilities which I didn't know about, but I can't imagine that he wouldn't have told me.'

'Thank you very much,' said Anthony. 'Now I won't bother you any further. I have an idea at the back of my mind that you are being swindled, and my advice to you is not to pay a penny until you hear from me. Have you got a lawyer, by the way?'

'No,' she said, 'I haven't.'

'Well, you'd better start,' said Anthony bluntly. 'I suppose you know that a man who conducts his own case has a fool for a lawyer, and though I wouldn't be so ungallant as to say the same of a woman'—he smiled—'you can't have too much professional advice.'

'Where shall I let you know?'

This was a question which considerably embarrassed The Mixer.

'I'm staying with some friends at the Hotel Rex in Brighton,' he said. 'Perhaps you would send me a telegram there.'

The interview had made a deep impression on him, and he missed the train which he intended taking to Brighton, and made a call upon a private detective agency, which had done very useful work for him without being aware of his identity or the nefarious character of the undertakings which he had carried out.

'Oh yes,' said the cheerful head of the detective bureau, 'I can tell you a great deal about Digle. He's been in pretty low water lately.'

'Stock Exchange?' asked Anthony.

'No, sir,' said the detective. 'No, sir. It's betting. They tell me he's lost nearly a hundred thousand pounds in two years. You wouldn't think that a stout old buffer like Digle would go in for that kind of nonsense, but such is the case.'

'Is he straight?' asked Anthony.

'As straight as the majority in some things.'

'That means to say,' said Anthony, 'that he's as crooked as blazes. Have you heard any complaints about him?'

'No,' said the detective, after a moment's thought. 'Of course, he's had several cases that have nearly gone into the Courts, but he's settled them. They were occasions when the client had died.'

'That's all I want to know,' said The Mixer, and went to Brighton.

The next day he called at the girl's little cottage at Chorley, and heard more of her husband's life.

'Tell me,' said Anthony, 'when your husband was ill did he receive any mysterious letters?'

The girl thought for a while.

'There was one,' she said, 'it was from a lady in Pimlico who said that she'd heard how cheerful Ted was in spite of his illness and would he please write a few words of encouragement to her niece who lived at the same address and who was greatly depressed by her own illness although it was not serious. Ted wondered how the woman had heard of him but he thought the least he could do was to write to the girl. If you'll wait a moment I'll look through his correspondence. I kept all the letters he had during the last year of his life.'

She was gone some ten minutes, and then returned with a bundle, and from this she selected a letter written in a sprawling hand. It was addressed from Pimlico Road, and this address Anthony jotted down. He did not bother about the letter itself, but noted that the lady had signed herself 'Caroline Smith', and referred to her niece as Carol.

The next morning he was at the address, to find, as he had expected, that it was a boarding-house. Mrs. Caroline Smith was apparently an elderly secretary, who worked in the City, and had long since left the establishment—of her niece they had no knowledge.

'Do you know where Mrs. Smith works?' asked Anthony.

Yes, they knew she worked for a Mr. Digle.

That night Mr. Digle's office received a visitor. Mr. Digle was not waiting to welcome his caller, because he was at home, sleeping the sleep of the almost just.

The time was 1 a.m., and the visitor came through a back window and began a most workmanlike survey of Mr. Digle's office. He broke open nothing and apparently he disturbed nothing, yet for two hours he pored over papers which he took from a large safe in Mr. Oliver Digle's private office. Just before daybreak he turned out the lights, took down the blanket which covered the window, selected his notes, replacing the documents in the order in which he had found them, locked up the safe, and went out by the way he had come.

A car was waiting for him on the Thames Embankment, and a quarter of an hour later, driven by his secretary—who looked the last man in the world to be driving one fresh from a burglarious entry into private premises—he was on his way through Balham, following the Brighton Road.

It was at East Grinstead, where they pulled up for an early breakfast, that he gave Paul an account of his night's work.

'The thing is clear to me,' he said. 'Digle is not content with the money he can rook from the living but he has been systematically presenting claims against the estates of the dead. The bills he produces are obviously forgeries and the signatures have been obtained by this request for a letter. According to his bank book—which I looked at—there's nothing wrong with him financially. The story of him losing hundreds and thousands of pounds is all nonsense, though I'm glad my sleuth put me on to that track, or I might not have pursued my investigations into his affairs. The man has nearly eighty thousand pounds in fluid cash.'

'What he seems to have done,' said Paul, when he had heard everything, 'is to have waited a reasonable time until the new estate was settled before presenting his bill for repayment. Most of the people to whom he presented his account preferred to pay up rather than allow the matter to go through the Court. I've never heard such a confoundedly mean trick in my life.'

Anthony nodded.

'This is the sort of job in which you hope I need your assistance, isn't it, Paul?' he asked.

'It is, rather.'

'Well, I may need it. Mr. Digle must be cleared out, lock, stock and barrel. I want every penny he possesses. I may be able to repay a few of the people he's fleeced.'

'That appeals to me,' remarked Paul. 'May I ask you how you intend to get it?'

'That will come,' said Anthony grimly. 'I'm going to study Mr. Digle, and if at the end of a day or two I haven't found a way of transferring his portable possessions to my pocket my name's Schmidt.'

. . . . .

Mr. Oliver Digle was a methodical man with a methodical mind. He was a pastmaster in the art of economical living, and it was his boast that he had never wasted a halfpenny. He was a fat and red-faced man, with faded blue eyes and thin, faded brown hair and he dressed in the manner of a churchwarden. Nobody could deny that he was a most sympathetic man, with a willing ear and a willing purse for the voluble and needy.

It is true that something more than volubility was required of the needy, as he asked for and usually obtained the highest references and the most tangible security for every penny he loaned. He had two passions: the one was for making money, and the other was for losing money. It was perfectly true that he had lost fairly heavily on racing, but even the great have their weaknesses, and did not Homer nod?

He was a secretive man, too, and banked with the most secretive bank in London—Pollack's Private Bank, which had enjoyed a reputation for discretion for over a century. There had been ugly stories told about him, and disconcerting inquiries made by the Metropolitan Police. Nevertheless, Mr. Digle pursued his unruffled career, paying little and taking back much.

He sat one afternoon in his office with the evening paper spread before him, deploring inwardly the tendency of owners to 'ready' their horses for Epsom, when there came a knock from the office of his one clerk—an elderly lady, who looked more antique by reason of the powder which adorned her face.

'There's a young man to see you, sir,' she said, dropping her voice.

'What sort of a young man?' asked Mr. Digle.

'I think he may be—a client. He looks very much upset,' said the lady clerk.

Mr. Digle scratched his chin and folded away his paper.

'Show him in,' he said, for he did not despise even the smallest client.

The man who entered was obviously worried. His mouth was downturned. The hour was 2.20—a circumstance to keep in mind.

'Well, sir,' said Mr. Digle, benevolently, 'and what can I do for you?'

The young man glanced at the lady in waiting, and at a nod from Mr. Digle she withdrew.

'I want to speak to you privately,' said the visitor in an agitated voice.

'Sit down, sit down,' said the benevolent Mr. Digle. 'Pull up your chair to the desk and say what you wish. Have a cigarette?'

The young man took a cigarette with shaking fingers and lips.

'Mr. Digle,' he began, 'what I have to say to you must be sacred.'

A melodramatic beginning and Mr. Digle. not unused to such happenings, nodded.

'I have heard many secrets here,' he said with truth; for in that very room he had interviewed and financed not a few of London's crooks. 'Now, my lad, you can say just what you like, and you may be sure that it will not be repeated.'

Still the young man hesitated.

'Suppose,' he said haltingly, 'suppose this is a matter which affects the police?'

Mr. Digle smiled.

'It doesn't matter; if it doesn't affect me,' he said good-humouredly. 'I don't care how much it affects the police. You can take me into your confidence and make me your father-confessor, and be sure that not a word you utter in this building will be repeated outside.'

The young man nodded.

'Thank you very much, Mr. Digle,' he said gratefully. 'I understood you were a gentleman one could trust.'

'I hope I am,' said Mr. Digle, curious to hear the other's story.

'First of all,' said the visitor, 'let me tell you that I have two thousand pounds' worth of Government Stock which I can convert tomorrow, and which I have here.' He put his hand in his pocket and produced an envelope.

Mr. Digle was surprised. He was not used to visitors who could produce two thousand pounds' worth of reliable security.

'I want a loan until tomorrow,' said the young man. 'I want exactly a thousand pounds and I am prepared to pay a good interest, and leave this security with you until the morning.'

'Well, there's no difficulty about that,' said Mr. Digle, looking up at the clock. 'The bank doesn't close till three o'clock, and when we've gone through this stock and found it in order, I shall be most happy to give you a cheque for a thousand at, say, ten per cent.'

He looked inquiringly at the other.

'I don't mind what the interest is,' said the young man impatiently. 'I must have the money almost immediately.'

He stopped again. There was no reason, apparently, why he should go on. He had produced all the security that was necessary to obtain the loan. But Mr. Digle sensed a mystery about it all, and was anxious to probe the matter to the bottom.

'Now you're with a friend,' he said emphatically, 'tell me all about it.'

'Well, I'll tell you, sir,' said the young man eagerly, 'because I feel that I ought to take your advice. I want the money to send my brother out of the country. He must leave this evening before they find out.'

'Oh,' said Mr. Digle, jovially, 'so your brother has been doing that which he shouldn't, eh?'

The young man nodded.

'He has been doing something which he should never have done,' he said gravely. 'He has committed what I believe to be the crime of the century. I can trust you, I know. I can see honesty in your face, and I feel that I have a friend in you, Mr. Digle.'

Mr. Digle, secretly amused, smiled.

' "The crime of the century" seems rather a tall order,' he said. 'What do you call the crime of the century?'

The other looked at him.

'What would you say if I told you that he has robbed a bank of two hundred thousand pounds?'

Mr. Digle raised his eyebrows.

'I should say that was very nearly the crime of the century,' he said.

'Oh, it's terrible, terrible!' moaned the young man. 'This may mean ruin to hundreds of poor people. And what makes it worse is that my brother knew that the bank was shaky and yet went on with his evil scheme.'

'Well, most of the banks can stand that loss,' said Mr. Digle. After all, it was not his affair. He was getting ten per cent for a day's loan, and that worked out at something like three thousand one hundred and fifty per annum. 'What bank is it?'

'Oh, it's a private bank,' said the visitor. 'It wouldn't matter if it was one of the big corporations.'

'A private bank,' said Mr. Digle slowly. 'What bank?'

'I don't want to tell you,' said the young man, shaking his head.

'Come along, tell me,' said Digle sharply. 'What bank is it that is shaky and that has been robbed of two hundred thousand pounds?'

'Pollack's Bank.'

The effect on Mr. Digle was electrical. He jumped to his feet, his rubicund face an ashen grey.

'Pollack's Bank?' he stammered. 'Do you mean to tell me that that's been robbed, and is shaky? Do they know?'

'No, no,' said the visitor, 'they don't know, but they'll find out by tomorrow, and then heaven knows what'll happen. Probably the bank will break. I'm almost inclined,' he said, 'to go to the bank and tell the manager, and let matters take their course.'

'You'll do nothing of the sort,' roared Mr. Digle.

He leaped up, picked up his hat and his brief-case, opened a drawer of his desk and took out a cheque-book.

'You stay here till I return,' he said. 'I'm just going—I'm just going to get your money!'

He tore down the stairs, and jumped into the first taxi that passed. At twelve minutes to three he passed through the ancient swing doors into that more ancient interior of one of the few private banks which had weathered the financial storms of a century. He made his way straight to the grey-haired cashier who greeted him with a nod.

'Will you kindly tell me my balance?' said Mr. Digle, with an anxious glance at the clock.

'Certainly,' said the courteous cashier, and left him. He came back in five minutes and passed a slip of paper under the rail.

'Seventy-nine thousand eight hundred and forty-two pounds,' read Mr. Digle. He opened the cheque-book and wrote. He passed the slip across the counter and the cashier read it without any evidence of surprise.

'I see you have drawn the whole of your balance, Mr. Digle,' he said. 'I suppose you know that this practically closes your account?'

Digle did not trust himself to speak, but nodded.

Once that cheque was honoured, and the money passed across to him, Pollack's Private Bank could go to the devil for all he cared.

The cashier went away, and was absent for some time. Digle paced the tessellated floor of the bank impatiently. Would the manager come and plead with him to keep the money in? Had the secret leaked out? Would there be any trouble about paying over the money? None of these things happened. The cashier came back with a case, counted out seventy-nine thick bundles of ten-pound notes as if they were seventy-nine pence, added a smaller bundle, ran his pen through Mr. Digle's signature, and went back to his business.

Digle put the money into his pocket with a trembling hand. It wanted two minutes to three. There was not time now to go to another bank, but he was capable of looking after his wealth.

As he came out through the swing door somebody touched him on the arm, and he looked round. The person who spoke to him was naturally mild-looking, but on this occasion he wore a severe and authoritative air.

'You're Digle, aren't you?' he said.

'My name is Digle,' said that gentleman with dignity.

'I'm Detective Rause, Criminal Investigation Department, Scotland Yard,' said the man, 'and I have a warrant for your arrest on a charge of forging the name of Edward Sinclair, and attempting to obtain the sum of one thousand pounds from his widow by means of a trick.'

Mr. Digle gasped.

'What do you mean?' he said, when he had recovered his self-possession. 'This is a disgraceful charge.'

'Are you going quietly?' asked the man.

'Certainly,' said Mr. Digle, and entered the waiting taxi.

The detective took his seat facing him.

'Put out your hands,' he said.

'I protest——' began Mr. Digle, but before he could speak the steel handcuffs were about his wrists.

'When we get to Scotland Yard,' said the detective, 'you can protest as much as you like. I'm only doing my duty, you understand.' He took a silver cigarette-case from his pocket, lit a cigarette, then offered the case to Mr. Digle, who at first refused, and then, with a laugh, selected an Egyptian cigarette with his manacled hand.

'I suppose it's all in your day's work,' he said good-humouredly, 'but I think you'll discover how bad a mistake you've made.'

The detective held a match to the cigarette, and Mr. Digle puffed steadily. It was at about the sixth draw that he noticed that the cigarette tasted queerly.

'What is the meaning of this?' he asked, and his voice was already very drowsy.

'You'll discover in time, Mr. Digle,' said the 'detective' cheerfully.

. . . . .

That evening somebody walking across Chislehurst Common heard a groan, and found a very well-dressed man with a dazed expression sitting behind a bush. There were handcuffs on his hands, but nothing in his pockets. They had seen to that—the distracted young man who had called at his office, the 'detective' who had arrested him, and the taxi-driver who had driven him to this deserted part of the common and who, behind his glasses and temporary moustache, was that same distracted young man who had asked his help; otherwise, Anthony, The Mixer.

5: Mr. Limmerburg's Waterloo

'Good,' said Anthony, 'I have been waiting for that.'

Paul picked up the journal which the other had dropped and raised his eyebrows.

'I did not know you were a student of the sporting press,' he observed. 'Is it a winner you have found?'

'It is not,' replied Anthony, 'and it is, if you will forgive the ambiguity of the answer. If you will look at the bottom of the third column you will see that Mr. Michael Limmerburg, the eminent bookmaker, has been called before the Stewards of the Jockey Club and severely cautioned as the result of the erratic running of one of his horses.'

'And what does that mean?' asked Paul.

'It means that if Mr. Michael Limmerburg comes again before the Stewards of the Jockey Club he will be warned off, and that is the last thing in the world that he wishes to happen. He has a wife on the edge of Maida Vale society; he has two boys at public schools; and he is well enough off to look forward to playing a part in local politics, and acquiring some day or another a knighthood for his services to whichever party he offers his dubious allegiance.'

'And who is Mr. Michael Limmerburg?' inquired Paul, interestedly. 'Of course, I know he owns horses, and that's not in his favour.'

'Michael Limmerburg,' explained Anthony, 'is the proprietor of Mackintosh & Grimstead, the biggest firm of bookmakers in England. He is also the proprietor of half a dozen other little firms bearing different names and, in addition, he is a gentleman who has acquired enormous sums of money by swindling the young and guileless.'

'What Sandy would call the mugs?' suggested Paul.

'Exactly. Vulgar, perhaps, but apt,' agreed Anthony. 'He has built up his business upon the activities of the rich and youthful who don't know one end of a horse from the other, but who can easily be persuaded that they're experts in the art of getting rich quick. They say he ruined young Stollson, although he was a compatriot of his, and young Stollson was only one of many.'

'What do you propose doing? Getting him warned off the Turf?'

'No,' said Anthony thoughtfully. 'I wouldn't do anything so cruel. But it does seem to me that he has got too much money, and I think the hour for which I have been waiting has struck.'

He placed his elbows on his knees and sat, with his knuckles to his teeth, frowning out the problem which the situation presented. Paul took up the cards and began to play patience, which he usually did whilst the other worked out his schemes.

'Paul,' said Anthony, suddenly, 'do you know a horse when you see one?'

'I rather flatter myself——' began Paul.

'Don't do that,' laughed Anthony, 'but just tell me if you know anything about racehorses.'

'I think I do,' said Paul, with a twinkle in his mild eye. 'I probably never mentioned the fact that my father had a racing stable.'

'All the better,' said Anthony. 'Now I'll tell you what I want you to do. I want you to go up and down the country, visiting as many trainers as you know, and finding out where there's a good first-class selling-plater that can be bought privately. I want this horse to be a little above selling-plate form, and I don't mind paying a fairly stiff price for him. You understand?'

Paul nodded.

'I think I know the type you want,' he said.

'He must be fit enough to enter in a race in about a month's time,' Anthony went on. 'Now keep in touch with me, and I think you'll see some fun.'

What The Mixer had said of Michael Limmerburg was little short of the truth. Mr. Limmerburg was what was known in racing circles as a 'twister'. He bet honestly enough and he was known as a man who had a very respectable balance indeed at his banker's.

He was a tall, fleshy, yet good-looking man, who invariably dressed in perfect taste. Quiet, even gravely spoken, he impressed the stranger to whom the name of 'bookmaker' was synonymous with flashy and extravagant attire as being something out of the ordinary. He attended the principal meetings, though he did not usually bet upon the course. He owned, as Anthony had said, not only the flourishing firm of Mackintosh & Grimstead, but a number of other small firms equally flourishing, all dealing with a credit business, and all making a very handsome profit. The multiplicity of his activities served him very well.

He was dining one evening at the Manchester Grand Hotel, and with him was Stinie Moss, who was not only a fervent admirer of Mr. Limmerburg's business methods, but contributed to no small extent in enhancing the capital of those businesses.

They were evidently waiting for a third party, for Mr. Limmerburg looked at his watch at intervals and made impatient noises. It was a little over three weeks after The Mixer had planned his raid, and from the placidity of Mr. Limmerburg's demeanour it was clear that that raid had not materialised. Save for his impatience and the unpunctuality of his guest, he was in excellent humour.

'What does Bill say?' he asked, after examining his watch for the fourth time.

'What about? About Billy Boy?'

Mr. Limmerburg nodded, and his satellite's broad face was all the broader for a smile.

'Billy Boy!' he said scornfully. 'Why, Billy Boy couldn't beat a donkey. I tell you that friend of yours is about the biggest mug I've ever seen.'

Mr. Limmerburg shook his head reproachfully.

'Never use that word, Stinie,' he protested. 'The gentlemen who patronise me aren't mugs. They're clever, they're as wide as Broad Street. And Mr. Cannes is wider.' And they both laughed together.

'What made him buy Billy Boy?' asked Mr. Moss curiously. 'He beat nothing in that selling race he won at Bath.'

'It was I who persuaded Mr. Cannes to buy Billy Boy,' said Mr. Limmerburg suavely.

'Where did he get his money from?' asked Stinie. 'It's a shame that men like that have money, while people like me are always broke.'

'He's got a rich papa in the Argentine,' explained Mr. Limmerburg, 'and I believe he's got pots of money. In fact, I know he has,' he corrected himself. 'When he opened an account with me I took up his bank reference and asked them if he was good, as he said he was, for fifty thousand, and the answer was very satisfactory.'

Stinie nodded.

'What made him buy that horse Billy Boy?' he asked again. 'It's not worth a penny. It was doped when it won.'

'Shut up,' said Mr. Limmerburg under his breath. 'Here is the lad.'

A young man came gaily across the floor, and greeted Mr. Limmerburg boisterously.

'You know my friend?' said that gentleman, indicating Stinie with a magnificent wave of his hand.

'Glad to meet you, old boy,' remarked Mr. Cannes. 'Any friend of the old Limburg is a friend of mine.'

Mr. Limmerburg produced the tolerant smile appropriate for the occasion.

'Have it your own way,' he said genially. 'Now what are you going to do about Billy Boy?'

'About Billy Boy?' echoed Mr. Cannes in surprise. 'Nothing, dear old boy. He's at the trainer's you recommended me and, according to the latest reports, he's doing very well indeed.'

'Hum,' said Limmerburg. Then, after a pause, 'Well, if you take my advice, and the horse is fit, I should gamble on him on Saturday.'

'On Saturday? Oh yes, he's in a selling race. But do you think he'll win?'

'Nothing is more certain. I think you've got the others stone cold.'

Mr. Cannes scratched his chin thoughtfully.

'I'm not so sure about that,' he said. 'I've been looking up the form of Year Book, and it's jolly good, you know.'

Mr. Limmerburg shook his head.

'Don't you worry about Year Book,' he said. 'Billy Boy will give him twenty lengths' start, and then beat him. You don't know what sort of a horse you've got, my dear Mr. Cannes.'

The young man beamed.

'I flatter myself I'm a pretty good judge of a horse,' he said, 'and when I bought Billy Boy last week, I said to myself—"That's a horse!"'

Limmerburg kept a straight face and agreed, and a few minutes later they were discussing the details of the coup which Mr. Cannes, in his innocence, intended to work on the long-suffering bookmaking fraternity.

'What you've got to avoid,' said Limmerburg, 'is going into the ring and letting them know that you're backing this horse.'

'But how can I avoid that?' asked Cannes.

'By wiring the money away to various bookmakers. I know half a dozen who will take five hundred pounds up to the time of the race, and if you be guided by me you'll write these people and ask them to let you open an account on the understanding that they accept wires up to, say, a monkey.'

'A monkey?' inquired the puzzled Mr. Cannes. 'Oh, you mean five hundred pounds.'

Mr. Limmerburg nodded.

'That's a great idea,' said the young man after a while. 'But suppose these beggars repudiate the bet?'

'How can they repudiate it if they agree to take it?' asked Limmerburg, patiently. 'Now we'll go into the writing-room, and I'll give you all their addresses. They're all reliable men and they'll pay out if they lose.'

'But what about Year Book?'

'Don't you worry about Year Book. I'll look after him.'

Mr. Cannes spent that evening addressing some eight firms of bookmakers, the names of which Limmerburg had obligingly supplied, as well he might, for he was the proprietor or part-proprietor of all of them—as any racing man could have told Mr. Cannes, had he asked for the information.

But Mr. Cannes asked for no information. That was his brightest and most engaging quality from Limmerburg's point of view. He never asked questions; he was, indeed, the most delightfully green young man that had ever crossed Mr. Limmerburg's path.

That night the great bookmaker had a consultation with his satellite.

'Year Book,' he said, 'has pretty good form. He is owned by Mr. Paul Robinson. Now who is Paul Robinson?'

Stinie chuckled.

'He's another like Cannes,' he said. 'He's got pots of money too; his father was in the car manufacturing business, by all accounts, and he's just started racing.'

Limmerburg pursed his lips.

'Can he be got at?' he asked.

'Easily,' said Stinie emphatically. 'He's staying in this hotel, and he hasn't any pals among the "heads". I'll have a talk with him if you like.'

Mr. Limmerburg shook his head.

'No, I think I'll do all that business, Stinie. I can trust myself and I can't exactly trust you.'

It was half past eleven at night when this conversation occurred, and inquiries from the hotel porter elicited the fact that Mr. Paul Robinson had gone to bed—or, at any rate, had retired to his suite. Limmerburg took a bold step. He went up to the suite occupied by this millionaire's son, knocked at the door and was invited to enter. He found Mr. Paul Robinson sitting in his pyjamas and dressing-gown, smoking his pipe and reading a novel.

'I'm very sorry to intrude upon you at this hour, Mr. Robinson,' said the newcomer. 'My name is Limmerburg. You've probably heard of me. I operate pretty largely.'

'Oh yes,' said Mr. Paul Robinson graciously. 'Won't you sit down, Mr. Limmerburg? What can I do for you?'

'Well, the fact is,' Limmerburg began, 'I've come on a very delicate mission. You have a horse running in Saturday's selling-plate?'

'Year Book,' nodded the other. 'Yes, he will about win.'

'Well, sir,' said Mr. Limmerburg solemnly, 'if he wins I can only tell you that one of the brightest young men amongst my acquaintances will be ruined.'

Paul Robinson opened his eyes in surprise.

'I don't understand you,' he said.

'I must explain myself,' went on Mr. Limmerburg, who was a fluent liar. 'There is a horse in the race, Billy Boy, owned by a Mr. Cannes, and—I hope that my confidence will be respected, sir?'

'Certainly,' said the other, putting down his book.

'My dear young friend, Mr. Cannes, has had very heavy losses,' Limmerburg continued, 'and he is going to gamble on

Billy Boy to get out of all his trouble on Saturday. The only thing that can beat him is your horse, Year Book.'

Mr. Paul Robinson cogitated for a moment.

'In that case, I needn't run my horse,' he said. 'He's in several sellers during the next few weeks and he's bound to win one of them.'

Mr. Limmerburg shook his head.

'No, sir, that wouldn't do. What I would like to suggest, if you won't take offence, is that you run Year Book, and——'

'And not win with him, eh?' said the other with a smile. 'Well, I dare say that could be done for a consideration.'

The last phrase took Mr. Limmerburg's breath away. He had hoped to play upon the sympathies of a wealthy and ingenuous young man. Mr. Robinson was not quite so young as he had expected, but his appearance and manner had been promising. He certainly did not anticipate that he would come up against such an absolute lack of scruple in one of so mild and moral an air. A broad smile dawned on his face.

'That can be arranged,' he said. 'I'll stand you a hundred pounds.'

'A hundred pounds isn't enough. Give me five hundred pounds down, and Year Book will be dead and buried on the day of the race, figuratively speaking,' he added.

There was a look of admiration in Mr. Limmerburg's eye as he took out his flat note-case and counted out fifty ten-pound notes.

'You're a bit hot,' he said.

'Perfectly true,' agreed Mr. Paul Robinson, calmly. 'Will you have a drink?'

Mr. Limmerburg graciously assented, and rejoined his anxious companion in the hall.

'It's all right, Stinie,' he said. 'He didn't want much working. I've straightened him out. His idea was not to run the horse, but that wouldn't have suited us at all. Year Book will start favourite and we can lay against it.'

'He won't be favourite very long if you start laying against him,' said Stinie, and he was a true prophet.

The day of the race was the busiest day of the week. The enclosures were crowded and Mr. Limmerburg, from his favourite position in the ring, observed the flow of easy money with approval.

In the interval between two races he saw the agitated Mr. Cannes returning from the telegraph office.

'It's all right,' said Mr. Cannes ecstatically. 'All those chaps you told me to write to have replied saying that they would take my bets up to five hundred pounds. I am having four thousand pounds on.'

'Good boy!' said Mr. Limmerburg, patting him on the back, 'and I hope you won't forget your old friend when you win.'

'Not at all,' said Mr. Cannes, shaking him warmly by the hand. 'You've done me a good turn. I suppose all these book-makers are reliable?'

'Absolutely,' said Mr. Limmerburg with truth. 'I'm going up in the stand to watch the race.'

'You don't think there's any chance of Year Book winning?'

'None whatever,' replied Mr. Limmerburg, and in proof of his faith he fielded so generously against what should have been the favourite and the horse which opened favourite that his fellow pencillers grew a little alarmed. Like a flash it ran through the enclosure and paddock that Year Book was 'no good'. From two to one, the price went out to four to one, nine to two, and when the tapes went up it was possible to back Year Book at five to one.

Curiously enough, for all his confidence, Billy Boy was at an even longer price. There were seven runners, and conspicuous from the very start was the red, white and black jacket of Year Book, who jumped off in front at flagfall and held that position till they came into the straight. Mr. Limmerburg, looking through his prismatic glasses, saw with some satisfaction that Billy Boy was occupying the position he anticipated, namely a bad last. He turned to Stinie.

'Year Book's going too well to please me,' he said.

'He'll come back in a minute,' said the optimistic Stinie. 'Harrogate will win.'

But Year Book did not 'come back'. At the distance there was no doubt of the issue. Year Book was going like a machine, with two lengths clear of his field, and he increased that distance, passing the post a winner by four lengths.

Mr. Limmerburg said unkind things about the amiable Mr. Robinson.

'He's twisted us,' he said. 'Still, it doesn't matter. We more than get out on Billy Boy. Here comes the mug.'

'The mug' was Mr. Cannes, and he was pushing his way through the press of people.

'He looks cheerful over it,' said Mr. Limmerburg. 'We ought to get a little more out of this cove. Hullo, Mr. Cannes! Bad luck!'

'Awfully bad luck,' said Mr. Cannes briskly. 'You're referring to Billy Boy, I suppose?'

'Of course I'm referring to Billy Boy. I expected him to win.'

'I didn't,' said Mr. Cannes surprisingly.

'You didn't?' Limmerburg was staggered.

'Not a bit,' said the cheerful young man. 'I thought he'd finish last, didn't you?'

A dreadful thought dawned upon Mr. Limmerburg.

'What did you back?' he asked in hollow tones.

'Oh, I backed Year Book. I've got four thousand pounds on him,' said Mr. Cannes with a little grin, but looking the other steadily in the eye. 'And it's all on with reliable firms, Mr. Limmerburg—firms in which I believe you have an interest.'

Limmerburg's face was purple.

'Do you expect to be paid?' he asked.

'I do indeed,' said the other confidently. 'I expect to be paid because I am willing to take odds that you will not go before the Stewards again—not for a year or two, at any rate.'

Mr. Limmerburg said nothing, but swallowed largely.

Later he unburdened himself to his sympathetic ally.

'Stinie,' he moaned, 'I've been had, and I've got to pay. Those two young gentlemen—(He did not say 'gentlemen')—worked the rig together. One got five hundred ready, and the other looks like getting twenty thousand pounds.'

'Why pay?' asked Stinie.

'Don't be a fool,' said Limmerburg. 'Do you think I want to face Tattersall's committee? Me with two boys at school, and the missus getting the O.B.E. next week? By Heaven!' he said with a sudden fury, 'I'd like to know who those fellows were.'

But he never knew—at least, not for a long time, for The Mixer hid his own and his secretary's identity remarkably well.

6: A Close Call—and its Sequel

Miss Millicent K. Yonker was a reputedly wealthy American lady, who had rented No. 496 Fortman Square from the Earl of Bradsham. She paid a fabulous rent and, in proof of her great wealth, had a fleet of cars, a box at the opera and all the other distinguished etceteras of a society lady. But to her intimates Miss Yonker was better known as Milwaukee Meg. She was a slight, pretty woman with pleasing eyes, though perhaps a thought too light to satisfy the connoisseur, regular features and a shock of dull-gold hair.

She was writing in her drawing-room, a wonderful apartment containing some priceless tapestries, when a young man was ushered into her presence. He took careful note of the priceless pearls about her throat, the great diamond rings which glittered upon her fingers and approved the grace of her carriage as she rose from the desk and came across the room to him, holding his card in her hand.

'Mr. Anthony Smith,' she read. '*Daily Megaphone*. You are a reporter?'

She spoke with the slightest American accent, and Anthony bowed.

'You wish to interview me about the charity matinée I am organising?' she asked.

'I really wished to interview you about Mr. Seton Kerriman,' said Anthony quietly, his eyes never leaving her face.

If he expected her to change colour, or show some sign of embarrassment or terror, he was to be disappointed. She merely raised her beautifully-arched eyebrows.

'Mr. Seton Kerriman?' she repeated. 'The name seems familiar.'

'He was the gentleman who shot himself in the High Cross Hotel yesterday evening,' explained Anthony.

'How dreadful!' said the girl with a slight shiver. 'But why should you come to interview me about him? I don't know him.'

'I think you do,' said Anthony. 'May I sit down?'

She nodded.

'What makes you think so?' she demanded.

'Because I know that he dined with you three nights ago. I know also that you were at the theatre together a week ago, and that he came to London from Leicester to pay you five thousand pounds in banknotes as the price of your silence.'

Again the eyebrows went up.

'My silence? This sounds dreadfully romantic,' she said, a hint of sarcasm in her voice. 'My silence about what, Mr.—er—Smith?'

'You discovered through your agents,' Anthony went on steadily, 'that this unfortunate young man had served a term of imprisonment in South Africa. That was before he inherited his uncle's money. As a price for your silence for the past three years he has been paying five thousand pounds every Midsummer Day, and his suicide is due to the fact that you increased your demands and asked for twenty-five thousand pounds cash within a week.'

She showed no indignation. She merely looked at him with a smile.

'Very clever indeed,' she remarked. 'Now how did you find all that out?'

'That is beside the point,' replied Anthony.

'Now I'll tell you something,' said the girl, and the touch of pink in her cheeks was the only evidence of her emotion. 'There s in London a crook who is going about swindling the swindlers. He is known as The Mixer. I dare say you've heard of him.'

'I've heard,' Anthony acknowledged quietly.

She fingered the pearls at her neck and she did not look at Anthony as she spoke.

'I believe he has a policy which may be roughly described as obbing the robbers. It is therefore only natural that he should extend his operations to—blackmailing the supposed blacknailers.'

She looked up quickly and caught his steady gaze.

'Well?' she challenged.

He smiled.

'I want twenty thousand pounds from you,' he said.

She nodded.

'I thought so.' And then, with a laugh, she walked back to her bureau. 'My dear, good man,' she told him over her houlder, 'if I were the kind of person that you thought I was, loesn't it strike you that I should have all sorts of assistants on hand to deal with people like you? If I'm so clever as to make all this money that you think I make out of the gullible and nervous public, do you suppose that I shall have a fit the first ime that I am confronted by a bluff like you?'

It was Anthony who laughed.

'On the contrary,' he said, 'I give you credit for taking reasonable precautions. Behind that door'—he pointed to a door half hidden by a brocade curtain—'is young Van Deahy, who I understand is one of your private assassins. In the room immediately above this, and probably glaring down on me with 'fierce and vengeful eyes", is Mr. Thomas Sethern, also in your ay.'

'Wonderful!' she said admiringly. 'But then I ought to have nown, if all the stories about you were true and not apocryphal, that you would have reconnoitred the position fairly well.'

She took from the desk a small silver cigarette box, chose a cigarette herself and then offered him one.

'Why don't you join us?' she asked. 'This Claude Duval business of yours is a great waste of money and a great waste of time.'

'Thank you, no.' He waved the cigarette aside. 'And that refusal applies alike to your doped cigarettes and to your kind invitation. The point is, what are you going to do about this large sum of money which I have demanded from you?'

'I can tell you that right away,' she replied. 'You are not going to get it.'

There was a faint tap—it sounded to Anthony as though at the door he had indicated—and the woman suddenly hesitated.

'I will consult my friend,' she said. 'As you suggest, there is someone in the next room who is rather interested in this matter.'

Anthony bowed and the girl, without another word, left the room. She was gone five minutes and came back apparently converted to Anthony's point of view.

'My confederate agrees with you,' she informed him. 'He thinks the sum is rather a large one, but what guarantee shall we have that you will leave us in peace?'

'I'm afraid I can't give you any guarantee,' Anthony smiled pleasantly, 'and it is my duty to warn you to get out of Britain as quickly as you possibly can. You are paying this blood money as the price of your freedom.'

She nodded slowly.

'Well, you must return at eight o'clock tonight. Naturally, we haven't that much money in the house. We're afraid of burglars.' She held out her hand. 'Till eight o'clock,' she said.

Anthony went away from the house a little puzzled, a little uneasy. He discussed the matter with Paul when he reached the hotel where they were staying.

'It's too easy,' he said. 'She's got something up her sleeve.'

'If you don't mind my saying so,' remarked Paul, 'you don't appear to have conducted this matter with your usual artistry. You discover a blackmailer, and instead of devising one of those pretty little plans which you better than any other man can invent, you go slap-dash at her, which seems to me to err on the side of simplicity.'

Anthony shook his head.

'You can only deal with that kind of woman by the direct

method,' he replied. 'Don't you see how perfect her organisation is? She spotted me at once. She has an intelligence bureau second to none, and in addition she has that native cunning which every great criminal possesses; and her identification of me was probably due to the latter more than to any exact information she may have had about me.'

He walked up and down the room, his hands clasped behind him, for some time.

'I've bitten off more than I can chew,' he said. 'Milwaukee Meg doesn't confine herself to blackmail and she's probably behind the Selzer gang.'

'What makes you think that?' asked Paul in surprise. 'I thought the Selzers were high-class forgers, who worked on their lonesome. Besides, she wouldn't be so cheerful if she associated with the Selzer crowd, would she? The police are after them. You gave that as a reason for not attacking the Selzers direct.'

Anthony nodded.

'That is true. And listen, Paul, that's going to be my rule. I'm never going after a thief whom the police are after, or I shall find myself bagged with the fish. No, it's too easy,' he went on; and then, after a moment's though, 'Get ready to clear tonight. Tell Sandy to have the big Wolseley ready at the corner of Fortman Square and you stand by, Paul, to pick me up if there's any trouble. I'd better take a gun, although somehow I don't think I shall need it.'

The Mixer was admitted to the house in Fortman Square that night and apparently, from his cheerful demeanour and the confidence in his smile, he anticipated no difficulties.

The girl was waiting for him in the drawing-room. She was lying on a settee, but rose at his entrance.

'Well,' she greeted him, and looked at the table. Following the direction of her gaze, Anthony saw three orderly heaps of banknotes. 'There they are,' she said, and added with a reproachful smile, 'robber!'

Anthony looked at the notes.

'I suppose they're all right?' he said, and tested one.

'What did you expect?' asked the girl coolly.

'I expected some of the excellent artistic handiwork of your friends the Selzers,' returned Anthony.

She laughed.

'I'll put them together for you when you've counted them.'

'Don't worry,' he said.

But she took the notes from his hand and dropped them into a big envelope, licking down the flap.

Anthony was reaching out his hand for the package when a shrill voice behind him cried:

'Hands up!'

He wheeled round in a flash, and moved so quickly that the girl did not at first observe the revolver in his hand.

The room was empty, but in the corner where the voice had come from was a parrot.

The girl's laughter made him feel foolish for a moment.

'You're not scared of a parrot, are you?' she demanded scornfully.

'That was no parrot's voice,' replied Anthony.

He took the envelope from her hand and stuffed it in his inside pocket.

'Poor Polly,' laughed the girl, 'she frightened a great Mixer, did she? You can put your revolver away,' she added.

'Thanks very much,' he returned politely. 'I prefer to keep it handy.'

It was not until the front door closed behind him that he slipped the gun into his pocket. He came down the stairs into the street, and as he did so two men crossed the road, and he caught a glimpse of one of them, and it was a uniformed policeman.

So it was a different kind of trap from the one he expected. He saw the flicker of a torch on the garden side of the square, and that flicker was Paul's danger signal. The first man who crossed the road reached out his hand to catch him, but Anthony dodged under his arm. The policeman was more difficult, but The Mixer slipped him also, and raced to the corner of the square, where he knew the car was waiting.

He heard the whistle blowing and as he turned the corner he ran full pelt into the arms of another policeman. He thrust the officer backwards, bolted across the road as the car was moving. Paul held the door open as he jumped in. Sandy was at the wheel. They dodged through the streets into Oxford Street through Soho Square and into Charing Cross Road.

'Sharply to the left,' said Anthony. 'It will take some time to get a divisional call through, and with any kind of luck we ought to reach open country before the stations warn the men on duty in the streets.'

'Did you get the money?' asked Paul.

'It's here,' replied The Mixer.

He took the envelope from his pocket and showed it to them

then tried to double it as he transferred it to an inner pocket, but it refused to be doubled and he ripped off the cover.

By the light of a flashlight he looked at its contents, and whistled.

. . . . .

Two nights later, Miss Millicent K. Yonker dined with her friend and confederate, Van Deahy, and Mr. Van Deahy's saturnine face was gloomy.

'I'll tell you what, Meg,' he said. 'You've missed!'

'What do you mean?' she asked.

'I mean to say,' he explained, 'that you had a chance of putting one over on The Mixer—is that what he calls himself?'

She nodded.

'And a chance of putting the police off the scent about the Selzers. Now take my tip, get Adolph Selzer out of the country, and cut out that line of business altogether.'

'Selzer's gone,' she said shortly, 'and, as you suggest, I am cutting it out. But I thought I had The Mixer,' she went on a little wistfully, 'and really our plan deserved to succeed. When you shouted "Hands up" from behind the curtain I changed the envelope quickly enough, and he put it in his pocket, without realising that he was carrying enough forged banknotes to get him ten years, even if I hadn't included one of the plates which Selzer had engraved. I can't understand why the police didn't get him. They're fools, anyway. Did you phone them in time?'

Mr. Van Deahy nodded.

'Luck was with the boy. He got away all right. Now I warn you, Meg, to watch out for that fellow, because he is going to get you.'

She laughed and looked at the jewelled watch on her wrist.

'We shall be late for the first act if we don't hurry,' she reminded him, taking up a beautiful bag from the chair at her side.

'Where did you get that?' he asked. 'Good Lord, that's a beauty.'

'Sent to me today by an unknown admirer,' she said carelessly. 'It must have cost a couple of hundred. Look at the diamond clasp.'

She opened the bag and displayed the rich interior.

'And look at the size of the mirror,' she said. 'It's rather heavy, but I couldn't resist the temptation of bringing it out. I'll change it later for a lighter one.'

Deahy paid the bill, and they entered the car which was waiting for them. As they had anticipated, the play had started, and the vestibule was empty, save for three men who, on Miss Yonker's appearance, moved forward, and formed a little semicircle about her. Miss Millicent K. Yonker was not conscious of this fact for a moment, and was walking to the door leading to the stalls when one of the men laid his hand on her arm.

'Excuse me, miss.' he said. 'I am Inspector Colforth, of Scotland Yard, and I have information that you are connected with the Selzer brothers, one of whom was taken into custody at Dover today.'

The girl was not dismayed, nor did a muscle of her face move.

'Your information is altogether absurd,' she told him haughtily.

'My further information,' calmly went on the officer, 'is that you are in the habit of carrying forged notes about in the lining of your bag, and that you have a plate from which forged notes are printed skilfully disguised as a mirror.'

They took the bag from her unresisting hand, and later at Scotland Yard, when they had stripped the silk from the back of the mirror they discovered the plate. The notes were easier to find, for they were sewn into the bag.

Milwaukee Meg took her sentence cheerfully, and the only comment she made before she left the dock was one which puzzled most of the people in court.

'When I come out I'll settle with The Mixer,' she said.

'Au revoir, dear girl,' responded Anthony, who was sitting in a back seat of the public gallery, but he said it to himself.

7: How a Famous Master Criminal was Trapped

'The residence of Julius Heimer, 940 Parkside, Wimbledon, was entered last night, and jewels, valued at £4,000, were removed. The police have reason to believe that the burglar is a man known in criminal circles as "The Dandelion". This is the seventh jewel robbery in the past two months which is attributed to this pest of society, and it reflects very little credit on Scotland Yard that he has not been discovered by now. The man's method is identical in each case. He makes his entrance to the house when the family is at dinner, etcetera, etcetera, etcetera.'

'And what is the etcetera about?' asked Paul.

'Nothing much,' replied Anthony. 'What do you think about it?'

'What do I think of The Dandelion? I think he is a fairly clever gentleman,' said Paul. 'The only thing I do not admire about him is his penchant for whacking over the head any unfortunate person who happens to surprise him.'

'He's clever, but a bit of a brute,' mused Anthony. 'Which means that he lacks something in mentality. And by the way, this is not his seventh but his ninth robbery during the past two months, and in each case I have traced the bait——'

'The bait?' exclaimed Paul, in surprise. 'Is that what you have been looking at those musty files for?'

Anthony nodded. He had spent three days engrossed in a perusal of the press, and the journals, neatly folded and tied in bundles, stood in the corner of the room.

'There are several curious facts,' he went on, 'and not the least is that before every robbery you will discover some reference in the columns of one or the other newspapers to the house and to the wealth and possessions of the victims. For example, there was an article in the *Daily Megaphone* last week on the collection of emeralds Mr. Heimer possesses.'

'And what is your idea?' asked Paul curiously.

'I have several. One is that the robber is a highly developed psychologist, who has made a study of human vanity, and has reached the conclusion which I reached some years ago—that the man who boasts of his wealth is careless of his wealth. You never read about the Rothschilds and Vanderbilts that they keep their money and their property lying loose about the house. And by the same token, it is easier to get gold out of the sea than out of their strong rooms. There is a certain type of man, however, who cannot refrain from telling everybody all about it. And particularly is this the case with a man who possesses something unique in the way of jewellery, who as a rule concentrates all his care upon that particular article of value and is immensely careless about other portable property.

'Going through the accounts in the newspapers, I find that in no case has The Dandelion taken the particular article which has been written about. He has contented himself with the loose trifles which he found lying about. It is much easier to pinch the watch and chain of the gentleman in charge of the jewel-house than it is to get away with the crown and sceptre. Naturally the guardian's mind is on the Koh-i-noor, and he doesn't notice the light-fingered hook who relieves him of his twenty-five-pound Albert.'

Anthony sat for a while, drumming his fingers on the table, deep in thought.

'The most important of my theories I will tell you later. I've a good mind to have a cut at The Dandelion,' he said. 'I think I could loot him. It would mean spending a little money, but it would be worth the experiment. Pass me over the paper. You have an eye for the advertisement column; see if you can find me a furnished house in, let us say, the Ascot district—something about forty guineas a week. I am going to be Andreas Machilatos, a wealthy Greek gentleman of eccentric habits. Sandy, of course, will come with me, but you, Paul, will hold a roving commission on this occasion, and be unattached to the establishment, which means——'

'That I'm to stay in a poky little hotel and discuss racing through the Ascot week with all sorts of undesirable personages,' murmured Paul, forlornly.

'The only satisfaction you can get out of that,' rejoined The Mixer, 'is that if they knew your association with me they would regard you as infinitely more undesirable than you regard them.'

That day's newspapers contained three likely advertisements. There was a house at Bagshot, another house near Goodwood, and to the agent for the first of these Anthony sent a telegram. Late that evening, when he met his secretary at dinner:

'I say, that agent person is rather a hustler,' he said.

'Which agent person?'

'The one I sent a telegram to about the house at Bagshot. He invites me to see it tomorrow, and promises to call on me after breakfast. It seems simpler than I thought and, by the way, my advertisement was unnecessary.'

'What do you mean?' asked Paul.

'I'll tell you one of these days,' was the cryptic reply.

Anthony was seated at a solitary breakfast the next morning when the agent arrived. The card came up and he read:

'Mr. Rolandt Robyns.'

The gentleman who followed the card was immaculately dressed, affable—indeed, voluble.

'This house, sir,' he said, 'is a bargain—it really is. And I think it will suit you down to the ground. You're an invalid, aren't you, sir?'

'I am rather,' Anthony admitted, sadly.

Between the receipt of Mr. Robyns' card and the arrival of that gentleman he had slipped into his dressing-gown, and was sitting, a forlorn figure, by the fireplace when the visitor was introduced.

'Well,' said Mr. Robyns, 'under those circumstances this is the best place you could take. The air is lovely, and the rent is low.'

The figure he named might indeed have surprised The Mixer, who expected to pay anything up to fifty guineas a week but for a theory he had formed.

'If it is all you describe,' he said, 'I will certainly take the place, and I will send my man down today to view.'

'I'll take him down myself,' volunteered Mr. Robyns. 'If he meets me at Waterloo Station at eleven o'clock——'

Anthony nodded. When the man had departed he rang for Sandy:

'Remember I'm an invalid,' he warned, 'so you are a kind of valet-nurse. You'll find the elegant Mr. Robyns waiting on the platform for you. I don't think you can mistake him. He wears a gardenia in his coat, and wears the newest bowler I have ever seen.'

'Hope he don't ask me too many questions about your complaints,' remarked Sandy, who secretly expected to have an appalling day.

As a matter of fact, he found the elegant Mr. Robyns a most talkative and pleasant companion. Mr. Robyns had a great admiration for aristocracy, and reeled forth a list of his acquaintances in the peerage.

'Your gentleman seems to be pretty well off,' he said, and Sandy thought he would be doing no harm if he emphasised the extraordinary wealth of his employer.

'I thought so,' said the elegant Mr. Robyns, and added to his category of acquaintances a further list of millionaires.

'You can move in almost at once,' reported Sandy that night. 'It's really a lovely house, and this dope with the gardenia is quite right that it's a bargain.'

A fortnight after this conversation an advertisement appeared in all the London newspapers. It ran:

'Lost between Waterloo and Ascot Station, a small box containing twenty pearls. A reward of £500 will be paid to any person who returns the same to Andreas Machilatos, Holly Heath Lodge, Ascot.'

There were several people who were interested in this advertisement, not the least of whom were the local and Metropolitan Constabulary. They made inquiries at Holly Heath Lodge, and discovered that Mr. Machilatos suffered from chronic asthma, and could not be seen.

His Scots valet-nurse, however, explained that although the loss was not a very material one to Mr. Machilatos, that gentleman was naturally anxious to secure the return of his lost gems. No blame attached to the railway, and information had not been given to the police because Mr. Machilatos did not wish to give trouble.

Then came the inevitable reporter, and him the gentle invalid himself, in broken English, stuffed with the elements of a 'good story'.

'I think he'll bite,' said The Mixer, sitting up in his dressing-room and reading this account the following morning. 'The more so as jewel stories have been rather rare in the papers lately.'

'What are you going to do with The Dandelion when you get him?' asked Sandy.

Anthony smiled grimly.

'He's going to lead me to his illicit hoard and split fifty-fifty,' said he.

'And if he doesn't lead you to his what's-it hoard?' inquired Sandy.

'Don't worry,' said The Mixer. 'He'll lead.'

Two days passed, and three, and four, and still there was no sign of The Dandelion's arrival. The pantry windows had been left invitingly open. Anthony had himself wheeled on to the lawn that all the world might see how helpless an invalid he was, but no game crept into the trap.

A week passed, and Anthony grew a little irritable.

'I'm rather tired of playing the invalid gentleman,' he complained to Paul, who had taken rooms in the village and was an occasional midnight visitor. 'I'll give him another couple of days, and if he doesn't turn up I'll recover my health and strength and write off this little adventure to profit and loss. Anyway,' he added, 'I've fooled the whole thing, because I ought not to have advertised for the house until I had announced the jewel loss.'

'I'm afraid I don't understand,' said Paul.

'The tactics were all wrong,' said Anthony, shaking his head. 'I realise it now.'

That night he went up to his room early, leaving Sandy on watch near the conservatory door, which had been left ajar. At eleven o'clock he went downstairs to the conservatory.

'I'll relieve you till one,' he offered, but Sandy shook his head.

'No, thank you,' he replied. 'I'm horribly wakeful. Besides Paul is hanging about, and he may want to come in before daybreak.'

'Well, I think I'll doze in my chair,' said Anthony. 'You might wake me as soon as it begins to get daylight, and then we can go to bed like respectable people.'

He went back to his room and sat in an armchair with a book in his hand. He did not remember even feeling sleepy, but he must have dozed off almost at once. He came back to consciousness with a sensation of cold. It was a curious cold. Before his eyes opened he located it at his chin. He opened his eyes quickly, and saw the cause. A man was standing before him, the lower half of his face hidden behind a red handkerchief, and in his hand was a long-barrelled revolver, the muzzle of which he had rested lightly on the sleeper's chin.

'Don't make a fuss,' said the visitor. 'Not unless you're anxious to end your days in suffering.'

'What do you want?' asked Anthony, rapidly recovering his senses.

'You can cough up some of that jewellery you have about your person,' said the visitor.

Anthony's eyes went from the burglar to the door, and The Dandelion must have guessed his thoughts, for he laughed.

'I've settled with your pal,' he said. 'Waiting for me in the conservatory, wasn't he? Well, I came in through the front door.'

'Exactly what do you mean by my pal?' asked The Mixer, temporising to gain time.

'I mean your valet. Look here, guv'nor, you must have a lot of jewels in this house if you have to put on a special guard against burglars.'

'Diamonds and emeralds and ropes of pearls,' said Anthony coolly. 'Would you like to see the treasure house?'

'I don't want any funny talk from you,' retorted the stranger sharply. 'You get comic with me and you'll know all about it. Get up!'

Anthony obeyed.

'Before we go any farther,' he remarked, 'I'm most interested to know what you did to my man?'

'Oh, him!' said the other contemptuously, 'I just coshed him.'

'Oh, you did, did you?' said Anthony softly. 'Well, that makes all the difference. I was going to let you off lightly.'

'I tell you, don't you try any funny tricks on me,' said the man threateningly; 'and don't raise your voice. At the first sign of anyone coming into this room I'll put you out.'

'Lead the way,' said The Mixer.

'You go first,' said the man.

Anthony walked nonchalantly forward, the muzzle of the man's gun in the small of his back. They were near the door when he whipped round, threw off the revolver with his right hand, and grinned into the other's face.

'Let go!' cried the man. 'Let go, hang you——'

He had got so far when Anthony's fist caught him under the jaw, and he fell to the floor like a log. Anthony's first act was to stoop and pull the mask from the man's face. As he had expected, it was the elegant Mr. Robyns.

He took one glance at the man, and saw that he was unlikely to recover for a second or two, then raced down the stairs. A movement in the conservatory and a muttered curse told him that Sandy had recovered consciousness, and he assisted his unfortunate ally to the dining-room. Sandy was no pleasant sight, for his face was streaming with blood.

'I didn't feel the blow,' he said. 'The beggar must have come in behind me.'

'I ought to have known that he would come in at the door,' said Anthony. 'I messed this job. Do you feel well enough to come upstairs and assist at a little cross-examination?'

'If it's a cross-examination of the man who biffed me, I'm as fit as a fiddle!' said Sandy.

Mr. Robyns was sitting up with a dazed look in his eye when the two returned.

'Get into that chair,' said Anthony sternly, 'and answer the questions I'm going to put to you.'

'Are you going to send for the slops?' asked Mr. Robyns, rubbing his jaw ruefully.

'There'll be no slops yet awhile,' said The Mixer, 'but you're going to share your swag with me, my dear old Dandelion, or you're going through it.'

'How did you know it was me?' asked the man in surprise.

'I knew it all along,' said Anthony. 'I've been reading the papers, and the papers have told me something. Then I've made a few private inquiries, and they told me a lot. All these houses which you have been burgling were furnished houses which were let by an obliging agent at a nominal figure. It was a clever idea, my friend, to go round hiring up the best houses.'

'It cost me nearly eight thousand pounds,' said the prisoner with a touch of pride.

'Took them for a year, I suppose, and then sub-let them?' said Anthony, not without admiration.

Mr. Robyns nodded.

'Sometimes in one name, sometimes in another,' he said. 'I only took houses where the owners or agents would allow me to sub-let them. It took me three thousand pounds to hire that house on Wimbledon Parkside, but I knew that Heimer was after that kind of house, and I just got in ahead of him and sub-let it to him in the name of Jones. That's my game—to find someone who has a bit of money and persuade them to take a house in the country. It's easier than you think.'

He shot a suspicious glance at Anthony.

'What does this mean about sharing the swag?' he asked. 'You ain't a policeman, are you?'

'Do not libel the police,' said The Mixer severely. 'Now I'm going to put it to you straight, Robyns, or Dandelion, or Jones, or whatever your name is. Somewhere in this little town you've got a nice store, and in one of your banking accounts you have a pretty large balance. You're going to sign a cheque to-night for twenty thousand pounds, payable to bearer.'

'Why twenty thousand?' asked the other with a look of surprise.

'That's my rough estimate of half the amount you've pinched in the past twelve months,' said Anthony. 'I think possibly I'm letting you off very lightly.'

'Suppose I don't agree?'

Anthony smiled. He was toying with a life-preserver, which he had taken from his pocket, and when Mr. Robyns' apprehensive eye fell on that instrument he shifted uneasily.

'If you don't,' said The Mixer, 'you'll be picked up on the Ascot Road tomorrow by a regular and incorruptible policeman. I shall leave behind with you evidence of your identification, together with a record of your various crimes.'

Mr. Robyns drew a long breath.

'Well, anyway,' he said, with some satisfaction, 'I can't give you a cheque, because I haven't a cheque-book.'

'But I have,' said Anthony, walking to his desk and opening a drawer. 'I've a cheque here on every branch of every bank in

London. The collection has been a labour of love. Choose your form, make out the cheque, and be good and you will be happy; be bad, and my friend here, who is feeling very sore with you literally and figuratively, may do you a very serious injury.'

Mr. Robyns chose a form, signed a cheque, and handed it with a scowl to The Mixer.

Anthony read it.

'Payable to bearer,' he nodded approvingly. 'You can go up to the attic. You know the house. I gather you know all the houses you let, or you wouldn't find your way into them so jolly easily. Sandy, lock the door on him, and beat his head off if he gives you any trouble. You're going to stay there until this cheque is cashed, and if you make a fuss, you'll wish you hadn't!'

Mr. Robyns walked to the door, followed by the vengeful Sandy, gripping a life-preserver in a most suggestive fashion.

'Oh, by the way,' said Anthony, and Mr. Robyns came back, 'before you go, you might tell me where you buy your hats—I rather admired your bowler.'

8: *Mr. Sparkes, the Detective*

'Do you remember Miss Millicent K. Yonker?' asked The Mixer of Paul, who nodded instantly.

It was a gorgeous summer's day and they were sprawling in a punt which was moored in a backwater, under the leafy shades of a tree.

'The blackmailing lady?' said Paul. 'Yes, I remember her. What's happened?'

'She's out,' replied Anthony.

Paul struggled to a sitting posture.

'But she got years and years,' he protested.

'Perfectly true, but there was a flaw in the indictment, and as the lady was an American citizen the Embassy got busy, and although the flaw was a very little one, international courtesy demanded the setting at liberty of this elegant creature. There was a paragraph in the paper about it this morning.'

'Humph,' said Paul apprehensively. 'I'm afraid that's going to give you a little trouble.'

Anthony inclined his head.

'She's one of the few people who've seen The Mixer and identified him,' he declared, and, if you remember, her last words as she left the dock were most uncomplimentary to me. She has a pretty large organisation, by the way, and they'll be coming after me just as soon as Mill gets busy.'

'Why on earth don't they deport these criminals?' demanded Paul, with a virtuous indignation that drew a roar of laughter from The Mixer. 'Do you know where she is?'

Anthony drew a telegram from his pocket and read:

'Highbury Manor House, Wilcombe-on-Sea. She is living under the name of Miss Morrison.'

'Your intelligence department seems to be busy,' observed Paul.

'My intelligence department is myself,' returned Anthony. 'I trailed her ladyship to Wilcombe-on-Sea and sent the telegram to myself, being well aware that all the time I was writing out the form at the Post Office I was being watched by one of Madam's agents. My object was twofold,' he explained. 'In the first place it gave Miss Morrison the impression that I was being well served in the matter of intelligence; and, in the second place, I particularly wish her to know that I am aware of her whereabouts. In a couple of days' time, Paul, you're going down to Wilcombe-on-Sea, and you're going to hang about in the quiet, ostentatious manner of the private detective, so that Miss Morrison and her friends will receive the impression that her house is being watched. Whilst I do not suppose that you will get any useful information, you will lay the foundations for rather an interesting experience. Particularly do I want you to look out for Miss Stillington.'

'Who the devil is Miss Stillington?' inquired Paul.

'Miss Stillington is an unfortunate young lady who has accepted the post of companion to Milwaukee Meg, and is not aware of her employer's identity.'

Paul shifted round in the punt to take a more comfortable position, and relit his pipe.

'And what's the idea? Do you think that Milwaukee Meg has her loot at Highbury Manor House?'

Anthony put on a sage air.

'I'm certain,' he said. 'She has got young Van Deahy there, and I should imagine there are reasons why that fellow should lie pretty low.'

'Why doesn't she get out of the country?—she's got all the money she wants,' exclaimed Paul.

'Because she's laying for me,' said Anthony, quietly. 'You need have no doubt about that. She's going to put one over on The Mixer if she dies in the attempt.'

'I'd really rather she died!' declared Paul mildly. 'And when do I go to this place?'

'The day after tomorrow. You'll go down by the night train. And don't forget that she has a young army of spies at Wilcombe-on-Sea. Probably your telegrams and letters will not be free from interference.'

'Then why——'

'Wait and see,' said The Mixer, with a wink. 'I have an idea I shall win out.'

Wilcombe-on-Sea was not the spot which a lady of fashion would have chosen for retirement, but it suited Miss Millicent K. Yonker, alias Morrison, alias Milwaukee Meg, because it was remote from the busy centres of recreation and was a place to which the tripper did not come. A straggling, untidy and ugly town led to a hideous front of stucco villas; and the only good-looking residence on what was humorously described as the Marine Parade was a large old-fashioned house which had existed before the jerry-builders had fixed upon Wilcombe as the site of their speculative enterprise.

A few days after this conversation between The Mixer and his secretary had taken place, Miss Morrison was walking in her big garden, a dainty figure of a woman, whom none could associate with the prisoners' dock at the Old Bailey or the bleak cells of Aylesbury Gaol.

With her was a girl perhaps six years younger, a girl whose deep-set grey eyes and delicate features gave her an attraction which was absent from the pretty but expressionless face of Miss Morrison.

The lady from Milwaukee was talking, and talking somewhat impatiently.

'My dear Miss Stillington,' she said, 'I think you are absurdly prudish. I'm sure Mr. Van Deahy doesn't mean to be offensive. I've known him for years, and he's one of my oldest friends.'

Jane Stillington made no reply, and Miss Morrison went on:

'He likes you very much. Surely there's no harm in that? Most young girls like to be liked.'

'I like to be liked too,' said Jane Stillington with a smile, 'but I certainly do not like being made love to by a man whom I never knew until a week ago, and for whom I have no very generous feeling.'

The other laughed.

'You've got to get used to the ways of the world, my dear,' she said, laying a hand patronisingly on the girl's shoulder. 'You're not in your little village now, but in the great big world.' She made a grimace. 'At least, we're a part of it.'

She saw a young man walking through the trees at the far end of the lawn and, dismissing the girl, walked towards him.

'Van,' she greeted him, 'you've got to be careful with this little girl. Make love to her as much as you like when we've finished our business. But just now we can't afford to divert our attention from our main scheme.'

Van Deahy nodded.

'I'm terribly struck by that girl,' he remarked carelessly, and Miss Morrison's lip curled.

'You're always terribly struck by somebody, but leave her alone for the present. Perhaps later I can induce her to go to South America, and then——'

'When are we going?' asked Van Deahy.

'As soon as we are through with The Mixer,' said the girl with a frown. 'I've told you I'm going to settle that young man, and settle him for good.'

'Have you seen his watcher this morning? He's out there.' Van Deahy jerked his head towards the garden wall. 'He's sending messages in plain through to a telegraphic address in London, and evidently one which has been recently registered, for it doesn't appear in the Directory.'

'They are code messages, of course,' said Miss Morrison, biting her lip thoughtfully.

'Whatever is he after, that boy? What does he expect?' asked Van Deahy irritably.

'He expects trouble.' The girl was unconsciously repeating The Mixer's words. 'He thinks that if he keeps close to us the trouble will be minimised. I suppose our people haven't located him yet?'

Van Deahy shook his head.

'No,' he said. 'I've got three of our best men working in London, and we're trying to find out the address to which these code messages are going.'

The girl shrugged her shoulders.

'Even if you do, you'll probably find that it's an accommodation address.'

'I don't agree with you,' said Van Deahy. 'At any rate, we can only watch and pray.'

'And in the meantime,' added the girl, 'you will leave Miss Stillington alone.'

Van Deahy agreed, though with no good grace. So matters went on for a week, Milwaukee Meg maturing her plans, the silent watcher keeping vigil; and at the end of that week Van Deahy came to the girl's study in a state of some excitement.

'We've had a rare bit of luck,' he said.

'What's that?' asked the girl.

'We've found a letter from this man, who signs himself Paul. He's staying in Seaview Road, but until now none of our people have been able to get hold of anything but the telegrams which have gone through the office. Here is the letter.'

He laid it on the table, and Milwaukee Meg took it up.

'Addressed to the Poste Restante for Mr. Smith,' she said. 'How did you manage to get it?'

'We've been watching the watcher,' chuckled Van Deahy, 'and one of our men saw that he bought a large quantity of light blue stationery. We have therefore been looking for the light blue envelopes as they passed through the post, and this is the first one we've struck.'

With the aid of a thin knife and a teacupful of boiling water she opened the flap and took out the letter, which was short.

Dear Mr. Smith,

This job is very monotonous, and I do not think that any useful purpose can be served by my staying any longer. I see nothing of her ladyship, and it is really very wearisome.

There was a postscript hastily written, which said:

I have just had your letter saying that you are sending a man from Quilter's Detective Agency to take over my work. I think you are wise. I don't think he'll find much more than I shall, and anyway, he can report direct to you, not by telegram, but by periodical journeys to London when he can come straight to the flat and tell you all that has happened. I will get a room for Mr. Sparkes—is that the name of the gentleman? I cannot quite decipher your writing—and I dare say he will enjoy this salubrious spot more than I shall.

The girl read the letter again, and her eyes narrowed.

'I think we may get our friend,' she said. 'Sooner or later

these clever people always make a mistake, and if this Smith, or whatever his name may be, has not made a mistake this time, I am very wrong.'

The next day a new face appeared upon the promenade, and the girl, watching the watcher from an upper window, laughed softly. She sent Van Deahy out to report, and he brought back news which pleased her.

'His name is Sparkes, and he's a private detective.'

'What sort of a man?'

'Oh, a fuddled, foolish man of middle-age, partial to drink and quite content to sit on the front from now till doomsday as long as he gets enough money to buy beer. If you go walking you can't miss him. He's got shaggy eyebrows, a ruddy nose, and straggling whiskers.'

She followed her companion's advice, and found that Van Deahy had described the detective faithfully. He sat twiddling his thumbs and sucking at a short briar pipe, his weary eyes fixed upon the sea, and he did not even trouble to look up as she passed.

'Now I think we can have The Mixer,' she said on her return.

'I don't exactly see,' began Van Deahy.

'You'll see soon enough,' replied the girl. 'This man has got what I am anxious to get—the address at which The Mixer can be found.'

That afternoon they sent their emissaries forth, and Mr. Sparkes found life was very interesting. There were all sorts of nice people who stopped and spoke to him and discussed the weather and the Government. There was one at least who invited him to refreshment and, albeit reluctantly, Mr. Sparkes refused.

'I'm very sorry, guv'nor, and nothing would please me better than to have a drink with you,' he said, 'but I've got a job here, and I might lose it if I went away.'

The polite man who had issued the invitation scoffed at the idea, and after a little persuasion Mr. Sparkes adjourned with his new-found friend into the nearest bar.

'Do you know the people who live in that old house opposite where you were sitting?' asked the spy, innocently.

'I do not,' said Mr. Sparkes, a professional reticence apparently aroused.

'They're very nice people—old friends of mine. Of course, they've got a lot of enemies,' said the other, 'and I hope you're not one of them.'

'I do my duty as per instructions,' said Mr. Sparkes, cryptically.

'Now I'm going to put all my cards on the table,' said the spy, who also was acting on instructions. 'You're down here watching that house, and the lady who lives there is annoyed.'

Sparkes closed his lips and said nothing.

'I don't know what you get from your employers, but maybe I could put a hundred pounds in your way and nobody would be any the wiser.'

'A hundred pounds?' inquired Mr. Sparkes, interested. 'Of course, I've got my duty to do——'

'This wouldn't be contrary to any orders you have received,' persisted the other eagerly. 'Now take my tip, Mr. Sparkes, come up and see my friend tonight, after it's dark and there's nobody around.'

Sparkes scratched his chin, fingered the wispy hair on his cheeks, rubbed his red nose, and finally said:

'Well, if it wouldn't be against orders and against my duty——'

'Let's say half past ten, when it's quite dark enough. What do you say?'

Mr. Sparkes nodded.

He was instructed to walk through the lodge gates, up to the house and to knock at the front door and his companion promised to be there to show him in.

Exactly to the hour and the minute Mr. Sparkes shuffled through the gates and up the shrub-bordered avenue that led to the front of the house. He was half-way up when somebody stepped from the darkness and laid her hand on his arm. He turned round in surprise, and in the faint light saw the face of a young girl.

'I don't think you ought to go to the house,' she said. 'I heard them talking. Won't you please tell me what is so dreadfully mysterious about these people?'

'Nothing mysterious, miss,' said Sparkes, genuinely taken aback.

The girl seemed distressed, and her hand still detained him.

'I heard them talking,' she explained. 'I know you're watching the house. Why? They said you were coming up, and—and—please tell me what it's all about!'

'Lord bless you, miss,' said Mr. Sparkes cheerfully, 'don't you worry. And at the same time, miss,' he added, lowering his voice, 'take my tip and get out of this place as soon as you can.'

He watched her step back into the shadows, and then went on

his way to the door, which was opened instantly to his knock. His companion of the morning led the way to a large, old-fashioned drawing-room, and there he found an engaging Miss Morrison and a most polite young Van Deahy. There was a table covered with a white cloth, and on that were many bottles with familiar gold labels.

The preliminaries were few. Miss Morrison invited Sparkes to take a seat by her and went straight to the heart of the business.

'I am willing to give you a hundred pounds a week for two weeks, and a bonus of another hundred pounds if you do as I ask you.'

'Excuse me, miss,' said Sparkes, 'but you won't be wanting me to do anything against me duty?'

She stopped him with an impatient gesture.

'I'm not paying you a hundred pounds a week for the pleasure of your conversation. Now, first of all, will you serve me or will you not?'

Sparkes thought for a moment.

'Yes, miss, I will,' he agreed.

'Good!' said the girl. 'You're more sensible than I thought. Now, won't you tell me where you send your telegrams to?'

'I don't send telegrams, miss,' said the man. 'I report every few days.'

'To where?' she asked eagerly.

Sparkes hesitated.

'Give him the money,' commanded Miss Morrison.

Van Deahy took a flat case from his pocket and extracted ten ten-pound notes, laying them before the detective. He folded them and put them in his pocket.

'Number six hundred and four Cathedral Buildings, Westminster,' he observed.

'Good!' cried the girl, exultantly. 'That's where he lives?'

'Yes, miss. He's got a big flat—eight rooms, and two of them never opened, from what I've heard.'

'That's where the loot is,' exclaimed Van Deahy.

The girl paced the apartment in thought, then came back to the table.

'Let us all have some champagne. I'm sure you'd like to drink champagne, Mr. Sparkes?'

'Rather, miss,' said the other with alacrity, and watched the foaming liquid poured into the shallow glasses with eyes alight.

'Now, miss, before we drink,' he said, 'there's one thing I want to tell you.' He lowered his voice. 'This young gentleman is well off.' He looked round the apartment. 'There ain't nobody listening behind that door, is there?'

'No,' replied Van Deahy in surprise.

'I wish you'd look, sir. I'm as nervous as a cat.'

Van Deahy walked across to the door and threw it open, and with his satellite, who accompanied him, walked into the next room and switched on the light.

'You see, you have nothing to fear. Now, what is it?'

'Well, miss,' said the detective, taking up his glass, 'he's leaving the country, this young gentleman, in two or three weeks' time.'

'He's leaving the country, is he?' repeated the girl quickly. 'That's valuable news. Where is he going?'

'To Spain, from what I can understand.'

'Is he? Well, here's your health, Mr. Sparkes.'

'Good health to all!' said Mr. Van Deahy, and raised his glass from one to the other.

'That's a drop of good stuff,' observed Mr. Sparkes, wiping his mouth.

They stood staring at him, their empty glasses in their hands. Van Deahy was the first to collapse, and the man with him went down almost immediately. Mr. Sparkes caught the girl in his arms as she swayed forward and lowered her to the floor.

He took the little bottle of chloral hydrate, concealed in the palm of his hand, corked it and replaced it in his pocket—for he had poured the contents into their champagne when their attention was diverted to the door. Then he went out of the room, locking it behind him, and went softly upstairs, where for ten minutes he was busy. He passed through the hall and out of the front door, none challenging him, raced down the drive, and leapt into the car which was waiting.

'All right?' inquired the driver, anxiously.

'All right, Paul,' returned Mr. Sparkes. 'It was the only way I could ever have got into that house, but I think I have taken most of her portable property. Home, James.'

'James' grinned in the darkness, and the car moved forward.

9: The Naval Coup

'There's one thing that worries me,' said Anthony, just as the train from Torquay was running into Paddington.

'I hate the thought that anything worries you,' said Paul, solicitously. 'It's nothing serious, I hope?'

'I was thinking about Milwaukee Meg.'

'Why, she's all right, isn't she?'

'Oh, the dope worked off, and the lady is in the best of health, though somewhat penniless.'

It was less than a week since he had held up Milwaukee Meg in her country house, but it was not remorse which was troubling him.

'Do you remember, Paul, that I told you Milwaukee Meg had a companion? . . . I saw her just for the space of a few minutes——'

'But that was sufficient?' inquired Paul, sympathetically.

'What do you mean?' demanded Anthony, a little haughtily.

'Nothing at all,' declared Paul, blandly.

'The girl tried to help me,' explained Anthony, 'and ran some risk in doing so. When I sent you down to make inquiries at Wilcombe-on-Sea I expected to hear that she'd gone, and to my surprise I learned that she was still in the house. Now that's not natural, because she was suspicious of these people, and anxious to get away, and my last word to her was to advise her to clear out as soon as possible. I would have told her more, only I was afraid she had been sent down by Meg to test me out.'

'She's still there?' inquired Paul, thoughtfully. 'That's curious.'

'Yes. The man I sent down to nose around told me that "the other young lady" had found the insensible bodies of the unhappy victims.'

The Mixer was brooding and he said no more until he was at home in the furnished house at Brixton which he had taken months before, and which he was now using for the first time.

'I'll swear she isn't one of the gang. Somehow I hate to feel that I am leaving her behind.'

'Then we're going?' asked Paul, and the other nodded.

'A few months ago,' he explained, 'I bought an ex-Navy boat, and I've had it provisioned at Torquay against a possible emergency. I've enough petrol on board to take us to the Azores if necessary, though I don't think we need go further than Bilbao.

A voyage would do us a lot of good and I may find it extremely healthy in other ways.

'I've got everything on board,' he continued, 'including naval uniforms, which may come in handy; and, I have passports for Spain, in case of necessity.'

Paul sighed. He knew The Mixer had recently come under the notice of the police, and there was a possibility of trouble. He had made many enemies, and been identified twice; and it would be remarkable if his foes did not cook up some case against him. But if he had enemies, he also had friends. His generosity had provided both Paul and Sandy with sufficient funds to maintain them comfortably whilst they looked for a more orthodox employer, but neither of them for a moment considered the possibility of leaving him. Valet, secretary-companion, assistants, confederates—whatever they were in fact, in feeling they were simply his faithful followers. Paul had trailed down to Torquay that morning, not knowing why, content to await developments. The Mixer had been absent for two hours, apparently making a last examination of the *Flying James*, by which whimsical name he had called his acquisition.

'I've plenty of money to be going on with,' said Anthony. 'We've nothing to worry about, all in American notes in a safe deposit.' He stopped with a frown. 'I put the last in yesterday,' he said slowly, 'which was infernally foolish of me.'

'Why?'

'I haven't been to the safe deposit since I became acquainted with Milwaukee Meg, and I have been so used to going there without any fear of shadowing that it never struck me that she might have somebody on my tail.'

Then he laughed.

'I give her too much credit, yet I don't think I can give her too much, for she is as deep as the pit, and as wide as Broad Street.'

'She'll have to be clever to get round the safe deposit people,' said Paul. 'They won't let you inside unless you're identified.'

'Dinner,' announced Sandy, who, at this period, was cook-general of the establishment.

'Thank you,' returned Anthony, absently, as he rose.

He said little during the meal. He carried in his mind's eye the picture of a frail, delicate face and the big, pleading eyes, which had looked up to him in the darkness on that memorable night when he had bearded the lioness of Milwaukee in her den.

What he had not told Paul was that he had sent a note by a trusty agent, in the hope that it might get into the hands of the girl, offering her a safe asylum and promising to find her work; he in his turn did not know that the note had fallen into the hands of the woman who had good reason for hating him.

He came down to breakfast the next morning with a sense of approaching disaster. His secretary noted his gloomy mien and the unusual curtness of his replies. When Sandy brought in the breakfast he carried a newspaper under his arm.

'I say,' he said, 'that's a bit thick.'

'What's a bit thick?' asked Anthony, quickly. He was ready for any development.

'Why, here's an advertisement in the newspaper to say you're dead.'

'Let me see it,' said Anthony. He took the paper from the man's hand and read in the obituary column:

> 'SMITH.—Anthony Smith, suddenly, after a brief illness, at 409 Balham Road, Brixton, aged 24, Commonwealth papers please copy.'

He put down the paper with a frown.

'That's rather weird,' he declared. 'I wonder what the idea is'

'Why not go and see the editor of the paper?' suggested Paul. 'I understand he's a very nice man.'

'Yes, we'll go as soon as we've had breakfast. He may be able to tell us something.'

'Anything I can do?' asked Sandy, who liked to be where there was a chance of excitement, despite such unpleasant results as the crack on the head he had received from The Dandelion.

'Not this time, thank you, Sandy. If there's any excitement in this business it's not of my planning.'

Paul drove him to the editorial offices, and waited in the car whilst he went to interview the person responsible for the insertion of the obituary notice. No explanation was forthcoming, as the advertisement had come in in the ordinary way. As he came back to the street, two workmen, who were arguing violently as they walked towards him, brought their disagreement to a climax. Suddenly one of them struck out at the other and missed him. In attempting to escape, he fell backwards on to Anthony.

'Beg pardon, guv'nor,' he cried. 'You saw that fellow try to hit me.'

Anthony pushed him back.

'It's a pity he didn't kill you before you put your big foot on my toe,' he said, and the quarrelling two passed on.

'Are we returning to Brixton?' asked Paul, and Anthony nodded.

'We might as well, though our days there are short,' he said.

'Why?'

'Because the lady has already located us. I don't like this at all.'

'Do you think it was done for a joke, or by way of warning?' asked Paul, but The Mixer shook his head.

'She doesn't do that sort of stuff. There's a real good reason for every step she takes.'

Just as they were passing through the maze of traffic at the Elephant and Castle, Anthony put his hand in his pocket and uttered an exclamation.

'My keys have gone,' he said. Then, with an oath: 'What a fool I am! That quarrel was got up for my benefit!'

'What, you don't mean——!'

'Back to the safe deposit,' he cried. 'They've got the key of the safe deposit.'

The car swung round and went back by way of Westminster Bridge at full speed. As they reached the corner of the street in which the big safe deposit was situated they saw a car disappear round the other corner.

The doorkeeper, who knew The Mixer, looked aghast when he saw the young man's face.

'Why—why, sir,' he stammered; 'I thought——'

'You thought I was dead? I want to see the secretary, quickly!'

He was ushered immediately into the secretary's office, and that gentleman showed as much alarm and concern as his subordinate.

'Why, Mr. Smith,' he exclaimed blankly. 'I thought——'

'I know you thought I was dead. What's happened?'

'Why, not less than five minutes ago the lawyer in control of your estate came here with all the necessary papers and your key and cleared the safe.'

'I see,' muttered Anthony between his teeth.

'Was it a case of theft, sir?'

'Yes, it was a case of theft, but you needn't worry the police about it. I'll do my own police work.'

He went out and rejoined his secretary.

'It's gone,' he said. 'Every bit.'

'Milwaukee Meg?'

He nodded.

'The whole thing was beautifully timed, as she always times her coups. The dud lawyer was waiting with the papers; the advertisement was in the newspapers, and had evidently been brought to the attention of the secretary—I didn't trouble to ask him, but I bet I'm right. Along comes the man with the key; in go the administrators of my estate—beautifully done, I repeat, and beautifully timed. But now, Milwaukee Meg, there is going to be trouble.'

He did not go to Brixton, but to the little office which he rented in the City, and telegrams went out in all directions. A telephone call put through to the seaside residence of Milwaukee Meg disclosed the fact that she had left there two days before for an unknown destination. Where that destination was he was to learn the following morning, when he received a letter postmarked Southampton, and written on the notehead of the ss. *Obo.*

Dear Mr. Smith [ran the letter],

We are going to South America. As we are fitted with radio you will have no difficulty in procuring our arrest, if you dare inform the police of your loss and the methods by which we secured your money. We are taking with us that charming young lady who seems to have attracted your attention when you were at Wilcombe-on-Sea. The touching letter you wrote her is in my possession—or rather, in the possession of Mr. Van Deahy, who is fascinated to an extraordinary degree by the youth and beauty of your protégée. Some day, perhaps, we may meet in one of the South American States, and I will be able to tell you personally how simple a matter it was to lift your very magnificent savings.

Yours truly,
Milwaukee Meg.

He read this letter twice, then passed it to Paul.

'What now?' queried Paul, looking up from it.

'Wait,' said Anthony, and summoned Sandy.

'I want you to take the car and go down to the South American Line and discover what cabins are booked by Meg and her party, and bring me back a plan of the ship. If she's got Jane Stillington with her she must still be calling herself Morrison.'

When Sandy disappeared The Mixer took down a *Lloyd's Register* from the shelf and turned its pages.

'The *Obo* has a speed of twelve knots,' he observed. 'She

sailed from Southampton at three o'clock yesterday afternoon. Notice the beautiful timing. It is now nine o'clock, and there is a train for Torquay which leaves Paddington at eleven-thirty. That's the Riviera Express. I'm not worrying.'

'What are you going to do?' asked Paul.

'We're going to Bilbao. But before we reach Bilbao there's going to be something doing.'

'What about money?' inquired Paul. 'As the lady has appropriated yours, hadn't I better——'

'Not quite all. I've got about a thousand pounds in the bank, luckily, and I intend to have some more before that's done. I'll make out a cheque for it now, payable to bearer, and you can take it straight along there now.'

Sandy was back in half an hour with all particulars.

'Garage the car, Sandy, and meet me at Paddington in time to catch the eleven-thirty.'

Paul returned with the money, and they made their way to the station. Anthony scarcely spoke during their journey to the West of England. He spent most of the time examining the plan of the steamship *Obo* and working out calculations in his note-book.

They reached Torquay at seven that night, taking a car over from Newton Abbot to save precious minutes, but it was nearly nine o'clock before they found the shipmaster in charge of the boat and got her ready for sea.

The Mixer took his place at the engine, and the big launch went chuck-a-chucking into the night. Once well clear of the shore he grew more communicative.

'Those naval uniforms are going to come in very handy,' he said. 'I reckon we shall pick up the *Obo* at daylight. Make yourself as smart as you can, Paul. You're my second officer. Sandy is chief engineer. Get the signal locker unfastened—is the radio working, Sandy?'

'Yes, working well,' answered Sandy, as he sipped the cup of cocoa which he had made in his tiny engine-room.

'We'll make for a point south of the Eddystone Lighthouse,' announced Anthony, 'and hang about till day. If my calculations are right we ought to see three ships coming down channel—the *Arizona*, bound for New York, a tramp steamer, the *Carpeto*, and the *Obo*. I've made a careful study of Lloyd's list, and they're the only three ships which are passing on this particular course.'

At two o'clock in the morning they picked up the great bulk of the *Arizona*, and in the stillness of the night the throb of her engines came to them like the beating of a muffled drum. At three, when the sky was growing grey, the *Carpeto* wallowed past, although the sea was calm, and half an hour later The Mixer, looking through his glasses, saw the smoke of the *Obo*.

'Switch her off, Sandy. Keep her on a parallel course, and we won't lose sight of her until this evening, when she ought to be somewhere west of Land's End.'

They had no difficulty in following a parallel course, and in the afternoon, when the sea was clear of ships, save for the little *Obo*, which was one of the smallest of the packets in the South American service, Anthony put his wheel over, increased his speed, and stood in to the ship, his radio working.

Presently the radio of the *Obo* answered, and Anthony sent the message:

'Heave to. I am coming aboard.'

He was resplendent in naval uniform, and the White Ensign flew from the one tiny mast.

Obediently the skipper of the *Obo* stopped his engines, and ten minutes later the little motor-boat ran alongside and Anthony went nimbly up the monkey ladder and saluted the Captain smartly.

'You've got some people here I want to interview,' he said authoritatively.

'Passengers?' asked the Captain.

'Yes, sir,' said Anthony, his eyes ranging the curious group for some sign of Milwaukee Meg.

'The only passengers we're carrying,' explained the Captain, 'are two ladies and a gentleman who came on board at the last minute. We don't run passengers with the *Obo*, although we have a licence. We're chock full of cargo, and haven't any room. But this gentleman's a friend of the owner, or has some influence with the company and we had to clear out three staterooms for them at the last moment. What is he wanted for?'

'Espionage,' said Anthony, glibly.

'Well, they're down in the saloon having tea now—at least, all except the young lady, who is an invalid.'

'The pale young lady?' asked Anthony, quickly.

'Yes, sir. She's in her cabin. I'll show you the way.'

He walked quickly through the alleyway, followed by The Mixer, and came at last to a suite on the upper deck. The first door was locked.

'That's the young lady's room,' said the Captain. 'I believe she's a little bit——' He tapped his forehead significantly.

'I understand,' said Anthony. 'But she's the person I want.'

He put his shoulder to the door and burst in the lock. A girl who was lying on a bunk sprang to her feet with a startled face.

'Just take charge of that lady for one moment, Captain. I want to search the cabins of the other people.'

His search was thorough and complete. Beneath the bunk, evidently occupied by Milwaukee Meg, was a steel box, and this he opened with a key of peculiar design, and took out a flat leather case, which he pressed lovingly. He slipped it into his pocket and came back to the Captain.

'Let one of your men see that lady on to my ship,' he said, and the Captain smiled at the description of the motor-boat which was rolling by the steamer's high side.

'Now I'll see the other passengers.'

They indicated a companionway, and down this he went, and came face to face with Milwaukee Meg and her companion as they were leaving the saloon.

The girl's face paled, not so much at the sight of the revolver in The Mixer's hand as at his bulging pocket.

'I want you,' announced Anthony, 'and I've come a darned long way to see you.'

'This man is a swindler!' screamed the girl. 'He's The Mixer. Don't let him take me! Don't let him take me!'

Anthony had no intention of taking her, but this fact he did not reveal.

'Have you a warrant?' asked the troubled Captain.

'I have no warrant,' said Anthony. 'It was left behind at Devonport.'

The Captain shook his head.

'You cannot take her without a warrant,' he said.

'He has something of mine in his pocket!' cried the girl. 'Don't let him leave the ship with that.'

The old Captain scratched his head.

'I don't know what to do,' he said. 'The best thing I can do is to radio for instructions.'

'The best thing you can do,' advised Anthony, boldly, 'is to put back to Plymouth,' knowing that that was the last course in the world the Captain would willingly take. 'Here is my card.'

He handed his pasteboard to the Captain, who took it reluctantly, and then, before any of them realised what was happening, he was up the companionway, and was racing along the deck, and had dropped on to the rolling deck of his little boat.

'Cast off!' he said.

The girl was sitting in the shelter of the tiny cabin as he gave the command.

'Hi! Come back!'

It was the Captain calling from above, and beside him was Milwaukee Meg, addressing him furiously, her gestures more eloquent than words.

Sandy started the engine, and the two vessels drifted apart; and Paul, with a radio receiver at his ears, grinned joyously.

'He's calling Plymouth,' he said.

'Jam his radio,' directed Anthony, and put the nose of his boat due south.

10: A Strange Film Adventure

Bilbao on a hot day is very hot indeed, but the lady who sat under a red-striped awning on the broad stone balcony of Bilbao's best hotel did not notice the heat. She was young and pretty, though her beauty was somewhat marred by the perpetual frown upon her face, and she was attired after the Spanish fashion in black. On the hotel register she was described as Madame Gilot, of Paris, but the police of half the world knew her as Milwaukee Meg, and the man who had just joined her as Van Deahy—the name he most frequently used.

The girl looked round as he flung himself into a chair beside her.

'Well?' she asked.

'No news,' growled her companion. 'These Spanish detectives will discover nothing.'

She shook her head.

'I don't agree with you. Gonsalez was the cleverest detective in Spain until he went crooked and was kicked out of the force.'

'The Mixer is too smart for us.'

'Rubbish!' exclaimed the girl sharply. 'He is no smarter than the police. We've got the better of them for years—I'm not going to knuckle under to an amateur. Do you realise that this fellow has got the bulk of my fortune?'

The man laughed softly.

'Let me remind you, my dear Meg,' he said, 'that we have still a very comfortable fortune—quite sufficient to live on for the rest of our lives. I was with you in your desire for revenge, up to a point, but I think that for you to come to Spain on the track of The Mixer, having in your possession considerably over sixty thousand pounds, is an act little short of madness.'

'You're afraid of him,' she scoffed.

'I am,' he admitted. 'I am afraid of his ingenuity and genius. Isn't there reason? Look at the matter as I do. Here is a young Britisher, a brilliantly clever man, who decides in cold blood to rob the robbers. If his activities were generally known he'd have the sympathies of the public behind him. As it is, the people he fleeces dare not bleat for fear of bringing down the police upon themselves. You and I have cleared up pretty well.' he went on, puffing thoughtfully at his cigar, 'and, in addition to the money which you have so foolishly brought to Spain, we have very considerable investments in South American banks. Therefore I say, my dear Meg, let us cut our losses and clear out. That was the view I expressed to you on our way back to Devonport when the British destroyer came to our aid.'

The woman rose abruptly.

'And that is the advice I reject,' she stormed. If you've got cold feet, why, that's your business. I'm going out after the loot right here in Spain, and when I've got that loot, and not before, I will throw in my hand, and retire to South America.'

Van Deahy shrugged, and was about to say something when one of the hotel servants came deferentially through the french windows, and said something in Spanish to his companion.

'Show him in,' the girl replied in the same language. Then turning to her confederate—'It's Gonsalez,' she explained. A few seconds later a stout little man with a heavy black moustache and an unshaven chin followed the servant through the doors on to the balcony.

'Well?' asked the girl.

Señor Gonsalez did not immediately reply. He bowed ceremoniously to the girl and to Van Deahy before he seated himself; then, after mopping his brow, produced a voluminous package of papers, which he consulted from time to time.

'Señorita,' he reported, 'I have been very successful in tracing the caballero. He arrived here sixteen days ago in a small motor launch, with two others. He was accompanied by a young lady, a very beautiful young lady. They stayed at the Hotel of the Four Nations, and the lady went back to England by the first boat.'

Milwaukee Meg nodded.

'They sent her to a place of safety, eh?' she remarked grimly. 'Well, I think they were wise. You've lost your girl, Van.'

Van Deahy laughed.

'When I lost my money I lost most of the things that were worth living for,' he replied dryly.

'Well,' continued Meg, addressing Gonsalez, 'what happened then?'

'Afterwards,' replied the detective, again reading his notes, 'the three caballeros lived for a little time at the hotel, all together, as friends, and then took their departure by the Madrid mail. They arrived in Madrid a week ago, and stayed at the Hotel de la Paix on the Puerta del Sol.

'They are there now?' asked the girl quickly, but the detective shook his head.

'No, señorita, they are not there now,' he replied triumphantly. 'Gonsalez has traced them back to Burgos, where they are living in a small villa which they have rented from the Marquis d'Algeciras. Apparently only one is there, an English noble gentleman with two servants, but the two servants are the señors who were staying at the Hotel of the Four Nations.'

'How long are they likely to remain there?' The detective shrugged his shoulders.

'He has taken the villa for three months, though why anybody should take a villa, or even build a villa in Burgos is beyond my comprehension, señorita, because it is the most diabolical type——'

The girl interrupted him with a gesture.

'Put your men on to watch the place. Inform me when he leaves,' she commanded, 'and hold yourself ready to act as I shall direct.'

She took a bundle of Spanish notes from her pocket, and handed them to the detective, who received them with a flourish.

'At your disposition, señorita,' he said, conventionally.

A fortnight later Anthony and Paul sat in the secluded orangery of the Burgos villa. The day was stiflingly hot, despite the thunderstorm which had passed that morning, but the garden was shady, and whatever breezes there were came to them from the eastern hills.

'I have often heard the expression "a castle in Spain",' observed Paul, lazily reaching for a cigarette, 'but I never realised how sultry such a place could be.'

Anthony did not reply. His eyes were fixed far away, and he was biting his lips like a man who was solving a problem.

'That's the third time I've spoken to him,' soliloquised Paul, aloud. 'If he doesn't feel like answering, or is too hot to talk, it would be a great help if he'd make a significant gesture. Spain is a land of significant gestures, and we've been here long enough to acquire the habit.'

'I beg your pardon,' apologised Anthony, waking up. 'I didn't hear you speak.'

Paul laughed.

'She's been back in England over a week now,' he remarked, soothingly. 'You ought to be getting a letter soon.'

Anthony went red.

'What on earth are you talking about?' he demanded angrily.

'Sorry,' murmured Paul. 'I thought I was talking about what you were thinking about.'

'Don't be a fool,' growled Anthony.

Paul hastened to change the subject.

'May I ask,' he inquired, 'where we go from here?'

'Anywhere,' said Anthony indifferently. 'I thought of taking a trip to Australia. We could work our way down through Spain, and pick up the mail boat at Gibraltar.'

'And be picked up on the mail boat at Gibraltar?' exclaimed Paul. 'It's a hot place is Spain, but personally, if I may say so, I'd prefer to put in another ten years here.'

'Perhaps you're right. It would be risky,' assented The Mixer.

'What about your old friend Milwaukee Meg,' asked Paul, suddenly, 'has she arrived in South America yet?'

'Milwaukee Meg!' repeated Anthony slowly. 'Milwaukee Meg has not even left England—at least, the last time I heard of her she was in Devonport.'

'You don't say! Did she go back to England?'

Anthony nodded.

'When I'd relieved her of her ill-gotten gains, the Captain of the ship radiod to Devonport, and a destroyer came out. Milwaukee Meg decided to return in that destroyer.'

'She was taking a risk,' said Paul.

'Milwaukee Meg would risk a lot,' rejoined Anthony, 'for the sake of getting even with me, and I don't mind telling you it is any odds that her ladyship is somewhere in Spain looking for me with a gun. And talking of guns,' he continued, putting his hand in his hip-pocket and taking out a letter, 'reminds me that I have had a letter from the big gun from whom I hired this villa.'

'The Marquis d'Algeciras?'

'The same gentleman,' said Anthony. 'It appears that this villa of his has a history. It was originally built by the Cid. And now a Spanish film company, the Hispano, has applied to the Marquis for permission to film an historical scene with his château in the background. He has written to me a letter full of apologies asking whether I would allow myself to be inconvenienced.'

'I always thought you would appear in films sooner or later,' murmured Paul.

'I shan't be asked to appear in films. They are bringing their own actors, and this is not a comedy, anyway.'

'You do yourself an injustice,' rejoined Paul, politely. 'When are they coming?'

'In two or three days' time. I've sent a telegram to the Marquis to say that I haven't the slightest objection. And in the meantime the director of the film company, anticipating my agreement, has sent me a florid letter of thanks telling me that he will be here at nine o'clock in the morning with a choice assortment of men in armour, brigands, knights and distressed females.'

'Which sounds very interesting,' announced Paul.

The Wednesday morning brought the troupe, under the charge of a tall, voluble Spaniard, who spent a quarter of an hour apologising for the liberty which the company intended taking.

Anthony listened, amused and amiable.

'We have one favour to ask Your Excellency,' went on the director; 'it is that you yourself will be good enough to keep away from the house, also all your servants, who are in modern garments. The appearance of anyone in twentieth-century clothes would, as Your Excellency knows, detract from the beauty of the film.'

'That I see,' conceded Anthony. 'Exactly what is going to happen?'

The tall man explained that the story was of a beautiful señorita who was imprisoned in the house, and who begged the help of a passing knight from an upper window. The beautiful señorita was apparently to be a nun of the period.

'She'll be veiled, then?' asked Anthony quickly.

'Certainly, señor,' replied the other. 'The nuns of the period were closely veiled.'

'And the knight? What of the knight?' continued Anthony, who was now thoroughly interested. 'Will his face be seen?'

The other shook his head with a smile.

'No, señor, the knight will have his visor lowered.'

'Oh yes,' said Anthony, softly, 'will you tell me the names of the excellent actor and actress who will play these parts?'

But here the director could not assist him. They were great

actors who had been specially engaged for the parts, and he understood that they were French. In fact, the idea of the film had come from France, and the director had only to gather together the subsidiary actors and work according to the scenario provided by his French employers. He expected the leading actor and actress at any moment, he said, glancing at his florid watch. They were staying at a small inn about twenty miles away, and were arriving by car.

Afterwards they were leaving directly for France. This the director knew because he had seen their luggage on the roof of the big car that had brought them to the village.

'I see,' said Anthony, and went in search of his secretary.

'Tell Sandy to pack up our things in as small a compass as possible,' he directed in a low voice. 'Shift them to the little wood, which is three or four miles on the northern road. If you see a car approaching, keep out of sight.'

'What's the matter?'

'I'll tell you all about it later. I'm going to give you the joke of your life. Wait for me in the wood, both of you.'

'If there's any trouble coming along——' began Paul, but Anthony stopped him.

'Do as you're told, like a good boy, and that's all the help I require.'

It was not until eleven o'clock that morning that the big car, after bowling down the road in a cloud of dust, came to a purring halt before the great gate which led to the villa's garden. From this car emerged two strange figures—one a man dressed in silvery armour, the other a veiled, slim figure. They were greeted effusively by the director and his little bunch of mediæval-looking actors.

'Everything is in readiness,' he said. 'The señor who occupies this house has given us full permission to do as we please. Let me show you the way into the house, señorita.'

The veiled figure murmured its thanks, and followed the tall director down the path, through the great doors of the villa, into the cool flagged hall.

Here Anthony was waiting, a nonchalant figure in white. He offered his hand to the nun, and murmured a few commonplaces in French. The girl shrank back for a second before taking the hand that was offered to her, and the director led the way up the stairs to Anthony's bedroom—for such it was—from whence she was to be rescued.

Anthony strolled out into the garden and watched the play for a few minutes before walking away. The tall director grew apoplectic in the course of the rehearsal that followed, only the knight in armour being exempt from his frantic directions.

'You will stand here, Pizario.'

'But——'

'You will register on your face a look of villainy—fool, that is not villainy, that is stupidity! You, Gomez, will walk across the courtyard like a soldier, glancing up to the window where the señorita is imprisoned. Now, monsieur'—he turned to the man in armour—'you will come forward, keeping within range of the camera, and when I say "Right" you will draw your sword and attack these men. Then the lady will let down a ladder, up which you will climb.'

Van Deahy, perspiring behind the closed visor of his helmet, cursed the director and his artistic sense, and looked up through the bars of his helmet to the room where Milwaukee Meg was, as he knew, making her inspection of The Mixer's treasure house.

He had to give her time. There might be cases to open and indeed there was a case by the side of the bed and Milwaukee Meg was at that moment manipulating keys very deftly and cleverly—but for all he knew there might be a dozen and one handicaps, and it was Van Deahy's business to delay the taking of the scene until Milwaukee Meg was ready.

Presently she appeared at the window and gave a signal. So she had been successful. His heart leapt joyfully at the thought. He had been against this expedition, and had opposed it, but now he forgot all his objections in the sense of achievement.

The girl at the window held clutched against her breast a stout package wrapped in black paper and there was exultation in her voice when she cried:

'Got it!'

To the confoundment of the film director, she did not drop a rope ladder over the sill, but disappeared, and came down a few moments later through the door.

'Got it!' she cried again, and then in Spanish: 'The picture-taking is postponed, señor.'

'But—but—but——' wailed the director. 'I have all the people here.'

'It is postponed,' she said firmly. 'Come.'

She gripped the mailed arm and walked rapidly back towards the car, but the gate which had been open was now closed and locked, and through the steel bars she witnessed a sight more remarkable than any she had expected to see that day.

The chauffeur of her car was gone—he had been sent to the kitchen by the obliging gentleman who now sat in his place.

Anthony turned to the 'nun' with a grin.

'My trick, Meg,' he smiled. 'I see you've got your bags packed, and I guess the rest of your loot is on board this car somewhere. You hired this company from France—a clever idea!'

The girl tore the veil from her flaming face and her eyes were hard with hate.

'That's a fair exchange, Mr. Mixer,' she cried, and held up the packet in her hand.

'Old newspapers, my darling,' said Anthony. 'I planted them for you the moment I'd tumbled to your trick. So long!'

As the car moved forward the girl pulled a gun from her blouse and fired twice. Before a third shot could be fired Anthony and the car had disappeared round the wall, and she saw him speeding up the north road, towards the wood now shimmering in the heat haze where his two companions were waiting for him.

A week was to pass before she heard from The Mixer again. The letter that came to her was addressed to Milwaukee Meg, and she found it stuck in the letter rack of her Bilbao hotel.

Dearest Meg [the letter ran].

I have left Spain, and business having lately been so prosperous, I intend to take a holiday. I should feel tremendously guilty if I thought I had taken your every penny, but I have an idea that you have still enough money to live on, so that my conscience is not pricking so vigorously as it might otherwise do. If you wish to keep what you have, don't follow me. It may interest you to know that I am devoting half of the treasure you so kindly had waiting for me in the car to an excellent charity.

Yours sincerely,

The Mixer.

11: The Girl from Gibraltar

Baltimore Jones had cleaned up the Levant. From Piraeus to Alexandria, from Tripoli to Messina, sad men had heard the ruffle of his cards and had watched him, ever smiling, rake in piastres and drachmas, liras, pounds sterling and dollars, and had heard his pleasant voice in a regretful—'Sorry, gen'lmen—the luck of the game. We can't *all* win.' Which was true. For only Baltimore Jones could win as the game was played and the cards were stacked. With a nice tight roll in his hip pocket and three ostentatious cigars erupting from the left top pocket of his waistcoat, B.J.—as they called him admiringly in transatlantic circles—came to Gibraltar for a final séance or, failing that, for recreation and amusement.

Of business there was none. He met recreation sitting on a dark seat on the Alamida crying softly into a threadbare handkerchief, for the band had finished the evening performance and had gone home, and the spectators, civil and military, had gone home too, and only Agatha McCall (who was known also as 'Bessie') was left to sob out her young heart in the dark.

Baltimore heard and, being a man of gallantry, had endeavoured to appease. The soft voice that could beguile real money from the net purse of a Greek currant merchant had no difficulty in creating an atmosphere of disinterested sympathy with Bessie McCall, and he heard the story of the stony-faced wife of Colonel Sipp and the browbeaten governess.

He walked home with her and caught a glimpse of her face under a street light. And he saw that it was good. Thereafter he met her when the band played on the Alamida and saw her to her fortress home. He did this for a week and then grew tired. For she had declined his invitation to go over to Algeciras —which is in Spain and thirty minutes away by boat—to see the bullfight and stay the week-end. She had declined because she did not think it was 'right'. Baltimore Jones summoned the full battery of his arts and opened a steady and accurate fire, beginning with his famous 'There are only two people in the world, you and me, and the rest don't count,' and ending with a dissertation on the artificiality of the marriage bond. But the defence won. She stuck to that word 'right' and some of the gravest philosophy that had ever been let loose on the Alamida fell bent and shattered before that concrete word.

Then, after a particularly bad day with the stony-faced wife of the Colonel (women are responsible for about ninety per cent of women's misery), Baltimore Jones suggested that she should run away. He would escort her by the overland route via Cordova and Paris. And he spoke eloquently of her home, of her people who would be waiting with open arms to welcome her. She was enchanted. And all might have gone well with

Baltimore Jones and his scheme but for the proximity of a young man who had nothing and nobody to do.

After a long holiday The Mixer had ventured to test the forgetfulness of those whose vigilance had made it advisable for him to leave this part of the world some time ago.

He had gone to Gibraltar, and his secretary sat in the beautiful garden of the Hotel Reina Cristina at Algeciras, overlooking the Bay of Gibraltar. The Bay was vivid green and reflected the grey mass of the famous rock; and its harsh lines softened by distance presented a memorable picture. It was the hour after sunset and a girdle of light at the rock's base showed the line of the Waterport. The fragrance of innumerable flowers hung in the still evening air, and no sound broke the silence but the clatter of a mule laden with cork-slats on its way to the quay. Yet despite the glory of the scene, Paul looked bored.

He looked up with interest as Sandy approached.

'Boat's in,' said Sandy. 'It's the last boat from the Rock, and Anthony's pretty certain to be in it. Anything special on?' he queried.

'I don't know, Sandy,' returned Paul. 'He's been investigating the affairs of Mr. Baltimore Jones, with particular reference to Miss Agatha McCall.'

'The governess?'

'The governess,' repeated Paul, soberly.

'That don't tell me much,' remarked Sandy, as he passed on.

A few minutes later Paul rose to meet a boisterous young man who raced along the gravel path of the garden.

'What's the hurry?' smiled Paul.

'Sheer exuberance of spirits,' replied The Mixer. 'I've had a happy, happy day in Gibraltar.'

'And a happy night too.'

'Not so happy,' said Anthony, shaking his head. 'Baltimore Jones is a very difficult man. At any rate, I know all about it. I sat on the seat behind them on the Alamida last night, and I heard the sad story of Bessie's life.'

'I thought it was Agatha.'

'She calls herself Bessie, or rather Baltimore Jones calls her Bessie,' said Anthony. 'She has an aunt in Stirling, her only relation in the world, except three cousins, who left home at a very early age and are working in London somewhere. Her aunt's name is Maggie. Bessie went to school is Glasgow and once spent a fortnight at Blackpool. And that's the extent of my information concerning the family tree of the McCalls. About Baltimore Jones I can tell you a whole lot.'

'Is he the crook?' asked Paul, interestedly.

'He certainly is a crook,' grinned Anthony, 'and his bedroom is filled with strange and wonderful apparatus for prying loose the hard-earned money of the rich. Seven and twenty packs of cards, all beautifully arranged, and of a size easily palmed. I took the liberty of bringing five of them away. If he misses 'em it can't be helped, but it's doubtful that he will, for he left in a hurry today.'

'Is he here?' asked Paul.

'Staying at the Continental. Came over by the same boat as me. He has booked two sleepers for Madrid, and he's escorting Bessie McCall to her native home.'

'Oh yes,' said Paul, politely. 'That means she doesn't get beyond Madrid. They're leaving by the morning train, I presume?'

Anthony nodded.

'The young lady comes away in the early morning. She's allowed out for half an hour to take a constitutional, and she's going to take the boat instead.'

'With Baltimore Jones waiting to receive her. Just so.'

'It's fate,' said The Mixer. 'I've been trying for a week to decide whether to go back to London or not, and now it's decided for me: for back to London we go.'

'Pack,' said Paul, laconically, as he rose, and they went back to the hotel.

The early morning boat brought a pretty fresh-complexioned girl, and she was met on the landing-stage by Mr. Baltimore Jones, a tall, good-looking young man. The girl was nervous, yet there was a radiance in her face which the adventure could not fail to create.

'I'm so scared,' she said. 'I thought I saw the Colonel's wife on the quay, but thank heaven it wasn't!'

'Your troubles are all over now, dear,' said Baltimore Jones tenderly. 'In a few days you'll be in London and on your way to the north.'

'We go right through, don't we, to Paris?' asked the girl anxiously.

'We may have to wait a few hours at Madrid,' said Baltimore Jones, 'but that needn't worry you.'

The girl heaved a sigh of relief and then, before she could say anything more, three men, talking together, and linked arm in arm, walked towards her and her escort. They were passing her when one stopped.

'Why, if it isn't Bessie McCall!' he said.

'Not Cousin Bessie?' said another.

'Cousin Bessie it is,' said Sandy, with great confidence. He felt that, being really a Scot, he could with ease play the unusually large part assigned to him in this particular exploit. 'How do you do? Don't you remember me? You remember Sandy McCall?'

'I don't remember you at all,' said the girl with a smile. 'But you're surely not my cousin?'

'We're all your cousins,' they said in chorus. 'Fancy meeting Bessie here!'

The girl was overjoyed, though she did not recognise one of them. Mr. Baltimore Jones was not overjoyed. If looks could have destroyed, Bessie McCall would have been without cousins.

'I can't recall your faces a bit. I only remember you when I was very small,' said Bessie.

'I know where that was; that was in Stirling,' said Anthony. 'I remember you quite well. I never forget a face if I've seen it once. When did you last see her, Sandy?'

'The last time I saw her,' said Sandy, shaking his head, 'she was very small too. Then I went up to see her in Glasgow, but she was on her holiday in Blackpool. That's how many years ago?'

'About four,' said the girl obligingly. 'Well, isn't that extraordinary? Do you know Mr. Jones?'

They bowed to Mr. Jones, and Mr. Jones bowed to them. They hoped he was well. Mr. Jones said he hoped they were well, but he did not mean it.

'Well, Bessie, we'd better be getting along,' he said.

'Where are you off to?' asked Anthony.

'We're going to Madrid,' said the girl. 'Mr. Jones is very kindly seeing me through to London.'

'By this train?' asked Anthony in surprise. 'Well, isn't that extraordinary? *We're* going by this train.'

The girl was delighted.

'Isn't that fine?' she asked, her eyes dancing.

Mr. Jones looked fiercer than ever, and said it was fine. He walked a little ahead of the others, the girl at his side.

'Do you know these fellows?' he asked.

'Know them?' she said. 'No, I don't know them, but they're my cousins.'

'How do you know they're your cousins?' he demanded.

'How absurd you are!' she laughed. 'Why, of course they're my cousins. They know all about their mother, Aunt Maggie, and they know Stirling, and they know I was on my holiday in Blackpool.'

Mr. Jones was silent. He escorted her to the sleeping-car, and the others got in the same car. Happily, there was no great run on the sleepers, and Anthony had procured two compartments.

'I'll come along and see where you are, Bessie,' he said.

'It's all right. I'm looking after the young lady,' said Baltimore Jones.

'And very kind of you, I'm sure,' said Anthony, but he pushed past the fuming Mr. Jones and came to where the girl was gazing ecstatically upon the well-appointed sleeping quarters.

'Wonderful!' said Anthony, admiringly. 'And you've got this compartment all to yourself?'

'I think so,' said the girl. 'I don't know how these things are arranged. Mr. Jones did everything.'

Jones was at his elbow, when Anthony turned.

'She's got that compartment all to herself, hasn't she?'

'I suppose so,' said the other ungraciously.

'Unless, of course, there's a lady travelling who wants to share it,' said Anthony. 'How long will you be in Madrid, Bessie?'

'Oh, we're going straight through,' answered the girl.

'But you can't go straight through,' said Anthony, gently. 'There's no connection till the next day. You'll have to spend the night in Madrid. Didn't Mr. Jones tell you?'

She looked from one to the other in dismay.

'I thought you said we went straight through, Mr. Jones?'

'I don't know the time-table as well as this gentleman,' he returned. 'Perhaps he's right.'

'Fine,' said Anthony, enthusiastically. 'Then you can stay at the Hotel de la Paix. We're staying there.'

'I've booked rooms at the Paris,' said Baltimore Jones loudly.

'Then you must come over and see us,' said Anthony. 'We shall be delighted, shan't we, Bessie? And by the way, if you haven't booked your berth, you can sleep in my compartment, Mr. Jones.'

Mr. Jones reluctantly and ungraciously accepted the invitation.

He was more gracious later in the evening, when Anthony told him he had been buying mules in Morocco for the Italian Government and that he had cleaned up a very large sum of money with which he was returning to London to have a good time. Anthony further explained that he did not believe in bank drafts, but preferred to carry his cash with him; and later he let drop a hint that he thought of going to Monte Carlo to have a little flutter. Whereupon the business instincts of Mr. Baltimore Jones stood up on tiptoe and asserted themselves.

That morning, as they were leaving the Sud Station, Mr. Baltimore Jones carelessly suggested that he would come round and see them after dinner.

'What about a little game of poker?' he said. 'I don't know much about the game myself,' he added modestly, 'and I suppose you people will relieve me of all my loose cash, but I rather like you boys, and I'll take a risk.'

It was Sandy who looked dubious.

'I don't mind playing,' he said, 'if you'll tell me which is best, two pairs or a full house.'

Mr. Jones went to the Hotel de Paris, feeling that perhaps his journey was not altogether wasted. That night he arrived and found the four installed in a private sitting-room at the Hotel de la Paix.

'Oh, here you are,' he said, gaily. 'And how is my little friend?' He shook hands warmly with the girl.

'Your little friend is just going to bed,' said Anthony. 'She's had a very trying day and a very trying night, and as we leave early in the morning I have advised her to sleep.'

'And good advice too,' said Baltimore Jones, heartily, though he had looked forward to skinning his victims in her presence.

It was Sandy who brought up the subject of poker.

'I was wondering whether you would play,' said Baltimore Jones, 'and I took the liberty of bringing a pack of cards, knowing how difficult cards are to get—I mean the British and American packs of cards.'

'That was the thing that was worrying us,' said Anthony, as he prepared the table. 'You don't mind playing four-handed? It makes a very cut-throat game.'

'I don't mind playing two-handed,' replied Baltimore Jones, good-humouredly. 'Now what's the limit?'

'Limit?' said Anthony. 'I don't know the word!'

'Do you play without limit?' The eyes of Baltimore Jones narrowed.

'Absolutely,' said Anthony. 'That's my game. I don't suppose I shall lose more than a fiver, because I'm a very cautious player.'

'I can see I'm going to lose my money,' laughed Baltimore Jones as he shuffled and cut the cards. 'Your deal, Mr.——'

'Call me Anthony,' said The Mixer. 'It sounds more friendly.

For half an hour the game fluctuated. Nobody lost very much, and nobody won very much.

'We are getting slow,' said Baltimore Jones, whose turn it was to deal. 'Hand me the cards.'

Nobody saw him make the change, substituting the pack which he had palmed in his right hand for the pack they handed to him.

'Wait a minute,' said Anthony. 'That's a curious deck of cards. Isn't there an ink mark on the top?'

'Look at it for yourself,' said Baltimore Jones, good-naturedly. For a moment he thought he had been detected in the act of making the change, and he was relieved to discover that it was an imaginary inkspot which had attracted the other's eye.

Anthony handed back the cards.

'Sorry,' he said, and the man began to deal.

He glanced at his cards. He had four aces. He knew it was either four aces, a straight flush, or something equally high, because it was the way his cards had been set.

'I've a very good hand,' said Anthony, 'and I'm going to bet.'

He pulled a roll of notes from his pocket, and Baltimore Jones's eyes glistened.

'Since you show me your money,' said Paul, 'let me show you mine,' and he brought a wad down on the table with a crash.

'Being a Scotsman,' said Sandy, 'and Scotsmen being proverbially cautious, I'll not risk more of my siller than three hundred pounds on this call.'

It was Sandy's call.

'I'll see that,' said Baltimore Jones.

'I'll raise it three hundred,' said Anthony.

'And three hundred,' said the laconic Paul.

Cards had been drawn and discarded, and Mr. Baltimore Jones sat in the placid, purring mood of a tiger into whose paws, from heaven, have fallen three nice fat calves.

The betting had risen to three thousand pounds when Mr. Baltimore Jones, suspicious of being frozen out, saw the other hands. All the players save Anthony had expressed their willingness to 'see'. It was rather fortunate for Mr. Jones that he did not go any farther, because Anthony was for doubling when it came to his turn.

'I've four aces,' said Mr. Baltimore Jones, and laid them down.

'I've a small straight flush,' said Sandy, and laid down the three, four, five, six and seven of clubs.

Mr. Baltimore Jones went pale. He stared at the cards incredulously, then turned them over and examined them one by one. Very reluctantly did he count out the money and pass it across to Sandy.

'Right!' said Paul, and shuffled and dealt rapidly.

Baltimore Jones looked at his hand and took heart. He had a straight flush to the king—as he was entitled to have for, taking advantage of a discussion between Anthony and Paul, he had substituted the gathered pack for another, and mistakes could not happen twice in one evening.

Again the betting began, this time cautiously; and it was Baltimore Jones who 'raised and 'raised', until it was six thousand five hundred pounds to 'look'.

'I'll see you,' said Anthony.

'I'll see you,' said Paul.

Sandy looked at his cards for a moment, then threw them into the discard.

'Gentlemen, you pay,' said Baltimore Jones in his regretful voice. 'The fortunes of war, gentlemen. The cards run this way sometimes, and we can't all win.'

'What have you got?' asked Anthony.

'I've a straight flush, king high.'

'Sorry,' said Anthony coolly. 'I've a straight flush, ace high.' He laid it down.

The hand of Baltimore Jones moved instinctively towards the pile of notes he had already staked, but Anthony's hand was like lightning. He counted the money dexterously.

'I want another two thousand from you, Mr. Jones.'

'I'll give you a cheque in the morning,' said Jones. 'I haven't got any more ready cash with me.'

'I promised my maiden aunt upon her death-bed,' said Anthony sorrowfully, 'that I would never take a cheque for poker losses, and I'm sure you'll dig up another wad if you look for one.'

With a curse Mr. Jones put his hand in his hip-pocket and took out a thick packet of notes.

He was both pained and bewildered, for such a thing had never happened to him in all his career. He was too skilled a man to make the mistake of setting the cards so that his opponent would get a higher hand than he.

'I'll have another flutter,' he said, and again the cards were dealt, this time by Sandy. And again Mr. Baltimore Jones, with lightning rapidity, had substituted a different pack from the one which had been gathered up from the table.

He looked at his first card. It should be either the ace of diamonds or the king of clubs, if the third combination was at work. It was the ace of diamonds, and he sat back happy. Ace, king, queen, knave, ten of diamonds he had—an unbeatable hand. He laid his cards face downward on the table, and the betting began. It went higher and higher, till Mr. Baltimore Jones knew that he had touched his bottom pound. 'I can't bet any more,' said Anthony. 'I'll see you.'

Paul had already thrown in his cards at two thousand pounds, and Sandy had not played from the beginning.

'I don't think you'll beat this,' chuckled Baltimore Jones, as he saw all his lost money coming back. 'A straight flush, ace high.'

'That beats me,' said Anthony. 'Let's have a look at it.'

'You unbelieving person,' smiled Baltimore Jones, and turned the cards face upwards.

There was certainly a straight flush from the ace, but in some mysterious fashion a sixth card had got into his hand.

'Sorry,' said Anthony. 'Six cards—one too many. My stake, I think.'

With a howl Baltimore Jones snatched up his money.

'Put that down,' said Anthony.

Sandy was already at the door, and the gun in Anthony's hand was eloquent.

From the moment he left that room until the train drew out of the Nord station of Paris on its way to Calais they did not see Baltimore Jones again. Curiously enough, Miss Bessie McCall, who in Paris had acquired some wonderful gifts from the three young men, was speaking of Baltimore Jones when Paul came hurrying along the corridor.

'Wasn't it bad luck that he was taken ill in Madrid?' she said, and then Anthony caught the eye of his secretary and went outside.

'Friend Jones is in the last compartment of this coach,' he said, 'and he has with him two of the nicest-looking lads that ever escaped the guillotine. There's going to be trouble.'

Anthony thought.

'Yes, of course,' he said. 'There's a long tunnel between Boulogne and Calais. That's where it will happen. We can sit quiet till then.'

His surmise proved correct. It was not until the train had plunged into the long tunnel behind Cap Gris Nez that things began to move. Suddenly all the lights in the coach went out.

'Put the girl in the corner,' said Anthony in a low voice, and Paul guided her to a place of safety, and to her amazement began piling the seat cushions round her.

The attack began with extraordinary suddenness. A light suddenly flashed in Anthony's face, he heard the whizz of something falling, and ducked. A loaded cane struck one of the cushions with a crash and ripped it open. Before it could be raised, Anthony had low-tackled his assailant and flung him through the open door into the corridor. Again the light flashed, and Anthony saw the gleam of a knife. Paul saw it too, and, gripping the hand that held it, twisted it with a sharp jerk. There was a scream of pain in the darkness, and then Paul followed up the attack with a well-directed kick at random. It landed on something soft.

'Your torch, Sandy,' said Anthony.

Sandy obeyed the summons, and a circle of light fell on the corridor and upon two figures, lying one on top of the other.

'Bring them in,' said Anthony. 'Quickly!'

Under the light of the torch they conducted a swift search of the unconscious men. Then, taking the lamp from Sandy's hand, Anthony raced along the corridor to the end compartment.

Mr. Baltimore Jones was not a fighting man, and not even the pleasure of avenging himself upon the three who had fleeced him had induced him to leave the security of his compartment. He was waiting for the return of his hirelings when Anthony came in and flung the light on his face.

'Who's that?' he asked.

'Why, it's Baltimore Jones!' said Anthony, as if in surprise. 'Don't get up to welcome me, unless you want a shot through your stomach.'

'Robbing me, eh?' said Baltimore Jones, indignantly, as the other's deft fingers went through his pockets.

'Thank you, I've got what I want,' said Anthony. 'You'll find your two private assassins by the side of the line—that is, if the train still slows down on coming out of the tunnel as it used to do.'

At that moment the train was slowing down and he raced back along the corridor in the dark and jerked to their feet the two men who had now recovered and were expressing violent dislike for their enemies in a language which happily Miss McCall could not understand. In two seconds Anthony ran them out on to the little platform at the end of the coach.

'Messieurs,' he said, 'you can either drop off the train or be kicked off the train.'

'You've broken my arm,' growled the man whom Paul had ju-jutsued.

'It isn't broken,' said Anthony. 'Do you jump off, or are you kicked?'

'We jump,' they said together, and as the train emerged from the tunnel at a slow speed they followed the words by the action, and Anthony went back to his compartment with a broad grin.

On the boat he had a little talk with the girl. It was a fatherly talk and a fraternal talk, and it dealt with the inadvisability of trusting strange protectors on the Continent of Europe.

'Oh, by the way,' he said, taking something from his pocket, 'Mr. Baltimore Jones asked you to accept this as a little souvenir of his acquaintance. I forgot to give it to you before.'

'Why, it's a gold watch!' she said.

Anthony nodded.

'Put it in your bag and give it to your young man when you find one,' he said with a smile. 'And remember, trust nobody.'

'I trusted you,' smiled the girl.

'Oh yes, but we're honest,' said Anthony, virtuously, and went back to his secretary and told him what he had done.

'I suppose Baltimore Jones isn't on this boat by any chance?' asked Paul.

Anthony shook his head.

'I don't think so,' he said, 'unless he could get on board without a passport and without tickets, and those I chucked into the sea as we were leaving Calais.'

'Pardon me,' said Paul, as an afterthought. 'Did you tell Miss McCall we were honest?'

'I did,' said Anthony, calmly. 'Honesty is a relative term.'

'And how would you explain the relationship?' asked Paul curiously.

'We are cousins to honesty,' said Anthony, glibly. 'Cousins once removed, and when we have seen that girl safely through London I'll be twice removed, for I intend to embark upon a career compared with which my old exploits will be as exciting as a game of push-ball between two infant schools.'

12: A Gambling Raid

The Mixer and his secretary walked slowly along the Brighton front, their hands in their pockets, apparently enjoying the beauty of the morning, for neither of them spoke. But their silence is explained by the rule which Anthony had made and to which they faithfully adhered that they would not speak together in public.

Anthony had a theory which he had often put into these words:

'You may disguise your face and your figure, but you cannot disguise your voice. People may pass you without noticing your appearance but they cannot pass you without hearing your voice, and it is easier to recognise a voice than a face.'

It was not until they had trudged back to their big, airy, and sunny room for breakfast that Anthony spoke.

'I tell you what, Paul,' he said, unfolding his table napkin; 'this town is too full of the idle rich to please me. It gives me a pain to see that fat woman in the mink coat.'

'It must have cost three thousand guineas at least,' said Paul, sadly. 'It seems an awful extravagance, because it only makes her look fatter.'

'I thought that too,' said Anthony, shaking his head, 'but suppose we'd gone up to her and taken it from her, what could we do with a mink coat?'

'You can do with a new rug,' replied Paul, thoughtfully, and the picture of himself covering his draughty knees with a three thousand-guinea rug was too much for Anthony, who exploded into a fit of laughter.

'Did you notice anybody on the promenade?' asked Paul, presently.

'I noticed Mr. Groggenheimer with a four-hundred-pound pearl in his tie, and that insufferable Stork, wearing a fur-lined coat which you would no doubt suggest I should use as a hearth-rug. And Mr. Kandeman——'

'Kandeman?' repeated Paul. 'I don't think I've ever heard of anyone called Kandeman.'

Anthony chuckled.

'I thought that would get you,' he said. 'Really, Paul, you're a million years out of date. You're like last year's ready reckoner. You're——'

'Perhaps you will tell me who Mr. Kandeman is?' interrupted Paul mildly, unmoved by the aspersions.

Anthony did not reply immediately, and Paul refrained from pressing his question until the meal was finished and cleared away.

'Mr. Kandeman,' explained Anthony, 'is an immensely wealthy and an immensely smug gentleman who is the leader of the anti-gambling association, the anti-smoking corporation, and the anti-booze bureau. I haven't got their names quite correct, but I imagine I am conveying to you the high moral condition of Mr. Kandeman's mind.'

'What does he do for a living besides anti——? It sounds rather like poker to me,' said Paul.

'He does nothing for a living,' explained Anthony, 'except draw dividends. He is the head of the biggest provision store in Britain—in other words he is the boss of a multiple shop system which sells you sugar as a favour. He lives at 903 Princes Gardens, London. He is a bachelor, a bore, and in many ways a bonehead. He loathes pleasure of all kinds unless it is his kind of pleasure. I am lunching with him today,' he added unexpectedly.

Paul raised his eyebrows.

'Are you going to get reformed?' he asked incredulously. 'I don't suggest there is any room for improvement——'

'I'm going to get reformed,' said Anthony complacently.

He had a peculiar habit of wandering alone in the most unlikely places. Meetings of any kind had a special attraction for him. Any advertised public function was sure of a patron in The Mixer, whether it was a baby show or a meeting of advanced anarchists. On the previous night there had been a meeting called by the Brighton Brotherhood to protest against the proposal that games should be allowed in the park on Sunday, and Anthony had been a joyful participant in that orgy of prohibition. And here he had met Mr. Kandeman, a thin, hectic gentleman, and had even risen and addressed the meeting—for Anthony was an accomplished speaker. He had been warmly congratulated by Mr. Kandeman, and had hinted that there was a secret sorrow in his life and that he needed but to meet a man with a large, broad knowledge of the world to whom he could divulge the misery which was gnawing at his heart. Mr. Kandeman had bitten hard upon the bait and had invited Anthony to a *tête-à-tête* luncheon. For there never was a hard and narrow-minded bigot in all the world and in all time who did not believe that he was a broad-minded man of the world endowed with a superabundant quantity of human sympathy.

'No,' said Anthony, thoughtfully, in answer to a query which Paul put, 'I don't think there is any money in it unless I can induce the old devil to bet.'

'To bet?' said Paul in astonishment. 'You don't imagine that a man of that character will bet?'

'You never know,' was the cryptic reply.

Anthony went out to lunch wearing the most sober of his suits and a black tie as though he were in mourning for his past iniquity. Mr. Kandeman awaited him in the hall of the largest and most expensive hotel in Brighton, and rubbed his hands as he saw the penitent figure enter.

'Ah, here you are, Mr. Jackson,' he said. 'I'm glad to see that you are punctual. The young men of today do not seem to take any heed of time. Why, I was kept waiting last Wednesday for fully five minutes by a young—er—I mean a young person.'

'That is a thing which I cannot understand,' said Anthony. 'My dear Uncle John impressed upon me the necessity for punctuality. Would that I had followed his other excellent precepts!' He sighed and shook his head, and Mr. Kandeman looked at him with the interest which a naturalist bestows upon a new specimen of bug.

'It is never too late to mend, as I told you last night, Mr. Jackson,' he said, as he bustled along the corridor, leading the way to the dining-room. 'I've got a table in a secluded corner, for I feel that you wouldn't wish to tell me your sad story unless you were sure that there would be no eavesdropping.'

When they were seated at the table and a modest meal was placed before them, Mr. Kandeman poured out a glass of water and placed it on the right of Anthony's plate.

'I myself take a little Rhine wine, though I hate the stuff, but my doctor ordered it—doctor's orders, my dear sir, doctor's orders!'

For a man who was drinking an abominable beverage he made a brave show, for he smacked his lips with every evidence of enjoyment.

'Terrible stuff!' he said, shaking his head. 'Terrible stuff! Water is the thing, my boy, pure water. Lions drink it, ha, ha! Lions drink it!'

Anthony thought that asses drank it too, but said nothing.

'Now, Mr. Jackson,' said Kandeman, when they had reached the dessert. 'You told me last night that you had something preying on your mind which I, as an earnest Christian'—he lifted his eyes to the painted cupids on the ceiling—'might help you to forget.'

Anthony played with his fork with a distraction and an embarrassment which would not have been out of place in a young girl who was listening to her first proposal.

'It's perfectly true, sir.' he said at last, in a melancholy tone. 'There's something which is on my mind, and since listening to your denunciation of Sunday games and gambling, my remorse has become a little more poignant.'

'Please go on,' said Mr. Kandeman, obviously enjoying himself.

'Oh, if only I had listened to my Uncle John,' moaned Anthony. 'Oh, if I had never become a professional gambler.'

'A professional gambler?'

Mr. Kandeman looked at him with a new interest and a new respect. It was the interest with which the temperance reformer regards the unquenchable drunkard or with which the bacteriologist views a new and deadly microbe.

'Yes, sir,' said Anthony. 'I am a professional gambler, a crook, a robber of foolish men, a racecourse tout and what-not.'

He did not explain what a what-not was, but Mr. Kandeman thought he knew.

'A week ago,' said Anthony, gloomily, 'I gloried in my practice. A week ago I was satisfied that by next Wednesday I would be a rich man. But what are riches?'

'Ah!' said Mr. Kandeman, sympathetically. 'What are they indeed?'

'I could almost wish that Greylegs would not win,' said Anthony, still moody and despondent, 'but for the fact that if it lost the bookmakers would be enriched, and they as a class should be suppressed.'

'I quite agree with you,' said Mr. Kandeman. 'What is this—er—Greylegs?'

'It's a horse,' said Anthony, 'and, of course, it will win the Jesland Handicap. There's no doubt about that, and there's still less doubt that I shall win twenty thousand pounds. But what does that mean? It means that I shall make money by gambling. And whilst the foolish public are falling over one another to back Pinkie, a few sinister men like myself are laughing up our sleeves because we have arranged for the race to be won by Greylegs. It's abominable!'

'Terrible!' said Mr. Kandeman, but without much warmth.

'Of course,' said Anthony, brightening up, 'I could always give away the money for a good cause.'

'That's a splendid idea,' said Mr. Kandeman eagerly. 'It would be rather—er—poetic justice to take this money and put it into a—er—reserve for a good purpose. But, of course, the horse may not win, and then, my young friend, you lose money.'

'I can afford that,' said Anthony, with a shrug of his shoulders, 'but have no fear! The horse Greylegs has been tried and is a certainty.'

'I do not understand the terminology of horse-racing' said the smug, Mr. Kandeman, 'and perhaps you will explain what you mean by "tried and is a certainty".'

So Anthony explained at length, and Mr. Kandeman became more and more interested. Anthony said that the only chance of the horse not winning was if he should drop dead in the race, and to meet even that remote contingency the horse had been heavily insured.

Anthony returned home after a luncheon which had dragged on till three o'clock, until Mr. Kandeman and he were the only occupants of the dining-room, and without a word he laid before the astounded Paul a cheque for two thousand pounds.

'It's incredible!' gasped Paul. 'Kandeman isn't a fool.'

'Kandeman is clever,' agreed Anthony, 'he's clever and business-like. They are the people who are easiest to rob. It isn't the fool who gets bitten, it's the wise one. Get a man outside of his own business and he's usually a mug.'

'What vulgarity!' murmured Paul.

'It's vulgar, but it's true,' said Anthony, seriously. 'The so-called business man is a man who knows all about his own business, and if anybody can interest him in something outside his own particular line—why, he's lost to the world. I have always found,' he went on, thoughtfully, 'that reformers are the most credulous of people. The easiest man to interest in a new whisky company is a temperance reformer, because he kids himself that millions are made out of drink, and that if he was some controlling influence he can restrict the output. Of course, he never wants to restrict the output, because that means restricting dividends. Who do the three-card tricksters find the easiest to take in? Why, the good card-players of course, because they think they're so clever that they can't be deceived. A man who never touches cards never loses money by the three-card trick.'

'But you actually persuaded him to back Greylegs?'

Anthony nodded.

'Of course, he explained it all to his own satisfaction, that he was going to use the money to fight the gambling influence, and after he had pocketed the winnings he said he would make a public announcement telling the world that he was fighting the gamblers with money he had won from them!'

'And perhaps he wouldn't!' said Paul, dryly.

'And perhaps he wouldn't,' agreed Anthony.

He took up the cheque and looked at it thoughtfully.

'It is incredible,' he said, after a moment's thought, 'but I suppose there is a streak of cupidity in all of us—even the best of us.'

He folded the cheque and put it in his pocket.

'However,' he said with a smile, 'that isn't the best joke. I've agreed to give a private session in Mr. Kandeman's house in Princes Gardens.'

'A private session! What does that mean?' asked Paul.

'I'm a professional gambler,' said the solemn Anthony. 'I'm going to show Mr. Kandeman just how the poor public are robbed. He and a select few of his friends are going to witness a demonstration which has never been given before, namely, the method by which the croupier at Monte Carlo throws the ball on any number he wishes.'

'Nonsense!' exclaimed Paul. 'Why, you're too wise to believe that kind of talk. It can't be done. It's been tested again and again by the cleverest of croupiers——'

Anthony was laughing, silently and joyously.

'We know that, but he doesn't know it. The anti-gamblers believe that anything can be done. If I told him that the money won by people at Monte Carlo was systematically stolen from them as they passed the attendant at the door he would believe it, and so would all his kind.'

That night he had an interview with Mr. Kandeman.

'I have fixed the demonstration, sir,' he said, 'and I think all the appliances can be secured in London. The only thing——' He hesitated. 'I hardly like to say this . . .'

'Say on, my lad,' said Mr. Kandeman, in a kindly and almost friendly voice.

'Well, it's this, sir. I'm naturally not proud of my past, and I am most anxious that your staff should not know that I am a gambler and that none of your people in your house should be aware of what is going on. Naturally, if it comes out, and the other gamblers learn that I've betrayed them, I shall have a very bad time.'

Mr. Kandeman dropped his hand on the other's shoulder and favoured him with a benevolent smile.

'You need have no fear,' he said. 'As a matter of fact, I keep very few servants, and those are old and trusty. In addition to that, we have meetings that one might, I suppose, describe as the cabinet meetings of our Purity League, which are secret, and to which admission is never granted to outsiders. These meetings,' he went on, impressively, 'are held in my drawing-room, which is on the second floor of my house. You may think it strange that I should have a drawing-room on the second floor,' he went on, 'but the truth is I do not encourage entertainment and I like a drawing-room for my own use, where I can be relieved of all sorts of hangers-on who come in on the off-chance of getting a cheap cup of tea.'

'I understand perfectly,' said Anthony. 'You miserable old devil!'

He said the last four words to himself.

'I can arrange that your implements can be brought into the house at a time when only my butler—an earnest abstainer who has been with me for twelve years—is present. You may bring all your instruments by night through the garage entrance, and nobody will be any the wiser. I quite understand your desire to avoid publicity,' he added.

Anthony looked gratefully at him, or at least he hoped the inane smile he gave carried some hint of gratitude.

'How many people will you invite to the demonstration?' he asked.

'Let me see,' said Mr. Kandeman. 'I shall ask Mr. and Mrs. Dawby, who are members of the anti-racecourse club—you will like Mrs. Dawby; she is a charming woman and breeds most beautiful Pekinese dogs. And I shall ask Sir John Smather, who sometimes addresses us, and——'

He enumerated a dozen other people, and Anthony listened with unholy joy in his heart.

'They had better bring a little money with them,' he said, considering deeply. 'I wish them to sit around the table, so that they will see what the ordinary gambler sees, and after I have manipulated the ball I will invite them to come behind and watch my methods.'

'They will be delighted,' said Mr. Kandeman with truth.

Two days later a taxi drove through the gateway into Mr. Kandeman's garage in Princes Gardens, and Anthony emerged and, with the assistance of an aged butler, conveyed many mysterious articles to Mr. Kandeman's drawing-room under Mr. Kandeman's own eyes. And Mr. Kandeman had not been idle. He had gone secretly to some of his most rabid friends and had whispered in their ears the story of this extraordinary demonstration, and they who were specialists in sin and were rather hazy as to what form the sin took, were eager to witness the manipulations of one who had 'come into the light', as Mr. Kandeman so poetically described the conversion of Anthony.

On the evening, half an hour before they assembled, Anthony put the finishing touch to the table. It was a long table which he had covered with green baize, and on that green baize he had marked out, scientifically and accurately, the squares and oblongs which constitute the tom-tiddler's ground of the Riviera.

In the centre of the table stood a large roulette wheel which he had purchased at considerable expense. He had placed the table under a chandelier which he had artistically draped and lowered, so that it bore some resemblance to the covered lights above the tables familiar to frequenters of 'The Rooms'.

'A wonderful fellow,' Mr. Kandeman was explaining downstairs, 'and I consider myself very blessed and fortunate that, owing to my exertions and advice, he has quitted his terrible career of crime.'

'Is he old or young?' asked Sir John Smather.

'Quite young, quite young,' said Mr. Kandeman.

'I always wanted to see how gambling was conducted,' said a stout lady with a red nose. 'I think it's a very fascinating experiment, Mr. Kandeman.'

Mr. Kandeman beamed.

'I am not taking a great deal of credit to myself,' he said, 'because the young man suggested the demonstration.'

One of the company—and a sour-looking company, and a bald-looking company and a wizened, round-shouldered company it was—looked at his watch.

'Half past nine,' he said.

'That's so. Half past nine,' agreed Mr. Kandeman, 'and it is that now. Will you follow me?'

He led the way upstairs to a broad landing. He opened one of the two doors leading to the drawing-room and ushered his company in. Anthony, in evening dress, was standing behind the table, a picturesque figure.

'Will you seat yourselves at the table, ladies and gentlemen?' he said. 'Will you come here, Mr. Kandeman? I want you to sit in the croupier's place and take this rake. Whilst I am making a few preparations I want you to spin the wheel, and any lady or gentleman present to bet, in imagination, upon certain numbers. I want you all to put your money in front of you, just as though you were gamblers at Monte Carlo.'

The company was only too pleased to oblige. It felt so delightfully wicked and so absurdly ridiculous, that even the most sour had a self-conscious smile.

'Now you spin the wheel. It is done thus,' said Anthony. 'Not too fast, please. Now throw the ball in the opposite direction to that in which the wheel is revolving. Excellently done, sir, excellently done.'

Mr. Kandeman was delighted with his dexterity, and again the wheel spun and again the ball click-clattered into its little compartment.

'Zero has won, which means that the table has lost,' said Anthony. 'Now, will you please continue, Mr. Kandeman, whilst I make my preparations.'

With a little bow, he withdrew from the room by a door leading to the staff entrance.

'Upon my word,' said Mr. Kandeman, jovially, 'I feel like a Monte Carlo person already.'

He spun the wheel and flicked the ball, and he did it many times. And suddenly the main door of the drawing-room burst open and an inspector of police, followed by three uniformed men, came in at a run.

Mr. Kandeman stared aghast. He recognised the inspector.

'Why, why, Mr. Wilson,' he stammered. 'What is the meaning of this outrage?'

The inspector shook his head.

'I'm surprised at you, Mr. Kandeman. You know what efforts we are making to cut down these unlicensed gambling houses, and here you are running a little game of your own. This will look bad in the papers.'

'Do you mean to say that I am gambling?' screamed Mr. Kandeman. 'Where is Mr. Jackson?'

But Mr. Jackson had disappeared.

'I can explain in a moment,' said Mr. Kandeman. 'These ladies and gentlemen are friends of mine.'

'I know all about it,' said the inspector, 'and you can do all your explaining to the magistrate.'

The explanation apparently was a very feeble one, for Mr. Kandeman, despite his excellent record, was fined one hundred pounds at Bow Street on the following morning, and the newspapers were filled with stories of the paraphernalia which was taken from his beautiful and virtuous drawing-room.

'In accordance with information,' said the inspector, giving evidence, 'conveyed in a letter from a well-wisher of the police who signed himself Jackson, we raided number 903 Princes Gardens and there found the prisoners round a roulette board.

There was a considerable amount of money on the table, and the prisoner, Mr. Kandeman, was spinning the wheel.'

. . . . .

'Another gambling raid,' said The Mixer, as he read the story in the evening paper.

'As you engineered it, I wonder you don't join the police,' observed Paul.

'That's not a bad idea,' said Anthony, and for the rest of the morning he was very quiet.

13: The Gossamer Stockings

Brighton became a little too hot to hold Anthony, and he journeyed to London and took accommodation in Westminster. Mr. Kandeman, shining light of the anti-gambling corps, had discovered that, in addition to his other misfortune, he had trusted that irrepressible young man with two thousand pounds to back a horse called Greylegs, which had been dead for some years.

Mr. Kandeman could explain, though he did not attempt to explain to the police, that he had parted with two thousand pounds in order that he might accumulate a large sum which he intended devoting to the cause of purity. He did not make that explanation. When he stopped his cheque and found that it had been specially cleared, he lodged a complaint with the local police that a man had by a trick succeeded in getting two thousand pounds out of him, and he trusted to his hitherto unblemished character to refute any story of gambling which Anthony might bring forward.

It is true that, to his astonishment and indignation, he had been fined a hundred pounds, but that fine was now the subject of an appeal before the Supreme Court, and he hoped to clear himself of this slur upon his name. In the meantime he was most anxious that he should recover a very large sum of money which now reposed in one of Anthony's innumerable banking accounts.

The police had no difficulty in associating this fraud with The Mixer, because The Mixer had operated from Brighton before. It is perfectly true that the police were not completely unsympathetic to this young man who lived to rob the robbers, but sympathy and duty do not always go hand in hand, and there was a hue and cry which compelled The Mixer to seek sanctuary in the Metropolis.

So there arrived in this furnished flat a very studious-looking young man who wore glasses and who was accompanied by a yet more studious-looking young man, and a third young man, also wearing glasses, but not so studious-looking—though Sandy was doing his best.

The apartments were situated in a small block of flats, and Anthony established their identity and hinted at their profession when he confided to the hall porter that he expected a visit from his uncle, and would the hall porter very kindly tell this visiting relative that his industrious nephew was to be found at the Middlesex Hospital.

'Medical student,' said the porter to himself, and resolved at the earliest opportunity to obtain free medical advice in the matter of bunions.

'I think, Paul, I'd better lie low for a month or two,' said Anthony, 'in fact until after the arrival of the Rajah of Tikiligi, who is coming to this country in a few weeks' time to buy expensive jewellery.'

'I wonder where you learned that,' said Paul, admiringly. He was a painstaking reader of the London and provincial press, and items such as the arrival of wealthy rajahs seldom escaped his notice.

'Oh, I just picked it up,' said Anthony carelessly, and changed the subject by suggesting a game of cards.

Their apartment was on the second floor and, situated as it was, within a stone's throw of St. James's Park, it had many advantages. The flat, which was the property of an engineer who was in India—it had been let to them by the agent—was well furnished and tastefully decorated.

Anthony went to bed that night and slept from the moment his head touched the pillow, the sleep of the complacently just. He was awakened by a cry, a shrill piercing cry, and he sat up in bed listening. Some time passed before the cry was repeated, and then he heard a faint scream followed by a thud and looked up at the ceiling. Whatever was happening was in the flat above him. The door of his bedroom opened and Paul came in in his pyjamas.

'Did you hear that?' he asked. 'I'm afraid there's trouble upstairs.'

'I just heard it,' said Anthony. 'It sounds like a free fight.'

There was a murmur of angry sounds, and Anthony got out of bed and took from a drawer a small brown box wrapped about with a long flex. He unwound the flex and applied two small receivers to his ears. He fixed a second length of wire to a plug in the box. At the end was a third receiver, and mounting nimbly to the top of a chest of drawers he applied the receiver to the ceiling and listened. He was using a small microphone which he had found very useful on occasions. Presently he said in a low voice:

'Dress yourself and get out,' and Paul, at first startled, knew that he was repeating what he heard through the instrument.

'I can't go out at this time of night,' he went on—'that's the woman talking, Paul.'

'Dress yourself.'

He stiffened suddenly, and a curious look came into his face.

'I think he hit her,' he said, and looked at Paul.

Paul was visibly perturbed.

'I suppose we can't interfere between a man and wife?' he asked.

There was a cry, more piercing than that which had awakened Anthony from his beauty sleep, and a still heavier thud.

'Man and wife, or no man and wife,' said he as he dropped down to the floor, 'I'm going to see what the row is about and explain to the gentleman that ladies must not be hit.'

He got into his overcoat and slippers, took his torch and went up the dark stairs. He was half-way up when he heard a door slam and a sob, and flashing his light upwards, he saw a woman in a nightdress and dressing-gown leaning against the wall and sobbing. She looked round with an exclamation of fear as Anthony appeared.

'Can I be of any help?' he asked.

She shook her head. He reached out his hand to press the bell by the side of the door, but she stopped him.

'Please don't,' she begged. 'It's no use, and he won't come. He'll think I rang. If he did come he would say horrible things.'

'But you can't stay here all night,' said Anthony, gently. 'Will you come down to our flat? I'm afraid we have no women there.'

She looked back at the door, and then:

'I suppose I'd better,' she said, listlessly. 'I've either to accept your offer or go out into the street. He won't open the door to night. He kept me outside the door the whole night three weeks ago.'

'Is the gentleman your husband?' asked Anthony, and the girl hesitated.

'Yes,' she said, defiantly, he thought and he very wisely forbore to press the question. He got her back to the sitting-room of his flat, and went hurriedly to apprise Paul of the unexpected visitation.

'Come and help to entertain her, Paul. What's the time?'

'Half past two,' answered Paul. 'What are you going to do with her?'

Anthony shook his head.

When he returned to the sitting-room, leaving Paul to dress himself, he found the girl sitting by the table, her head on her arm, sobbing painfully. It was some time before he could calm her. She was pretty, in spite of her swollen eyes and the red weal across her face. Presently she grew calmer and could talk quietly of her plans.

'My people live in the country,' she said. 'Perhaps you could get me some clothes in the morning, and if you can lend me some money——'

'Why surely,' said Anthony, heartily. 'I'll do all I can for you. You won't go back to your—your husband?'

'Never again,' she said, bitterly. 'Oh, what a fool I've been, what a fool!' Her lip quivered, and she calmed herself with an effort. 'If he'd been a decent man it wouldn't have been so bad, but he's a crook, and I've known he was a crook all the time. Wait and you'll see.'

Anthony's eyes narrowed.

'A crook, is he? What kind of a crook?'

She seemed to realise that she was saying too much, and yet there was such a lot that she wanted to say.

'I can't tell you. I'm not going to betray him, brute as he is. But he'll not get away with his gossamer stockings!'

Anthony's interest was piqued.

'Gossamer stockings?' he said, carelessly. 'Oh yes, you mean——' He paused encouragingly, but she closed her lips the tighter and not another word did she say.

In the morning he was relieved of the embarrassment of procuring her a wardrobe. Apparently the man went out early to his work and she was able to slip up unobserved and open the door with a key which was in her dressing-gown pocket.

'After my previous experience,' she said, 'I had the key sewn into my pocket, and I'd have gone in last night, only he bolted the door.'

He only saw her again for a few minutes and then, with the money which he was able to lend her, she went on her journey and passed out of his life.

He went out to get information about the tenant upstairs. He came back with surprisingly little.

'John Bidder, of the firm of Bidder and Bidder,' he said. 'He has two rooms in Long Acre, is a regular advertiser in the daily and cheap weekly publications and usually sells bargains.'

'Bargains, for instance, like——' queried Paul.

'Job lots that he has bought from the Government, which he sells at a small price and what is evidently a very small profit. They know nothing about him except that he has no debts, pays his way, and his advertisements are accepted without question by all the best newspapers.'

'Well, there's nothing crooked in that,' said Paul, a little disappointed.

'What did she mean by gossamer stockings?' asked Anthony, pacing up and down. 'Don't you see anything peculiar about that reference, Paul?'

Paul shook his head.

'No, I can't see anything peculiar about gossamer stockings,' he remarked, 'except that they sound like things which most women would like.'

Anthony bit his lip thoughtfully.

'Curious,' he said.

He took the trouble to lie in wait for Mr. John Bidder that night, to give him what Sandy called the 'once over'. Mr. Bidder was a tall, lithe, dark young man, rather flashily dressed. He wore diamond rings on his well-manicured hands and a bowler reposed at a rakish angle on his small curly head.

He brushed past The Mixer, favouring that gentleman with an insolent stare, and walked up the stairs, leaving behind him the fragrance of the expensive cigar he was smoking.

The Mixer had little to do in these days, whilst he was lying low. He welcomed the interlude represented by Mr. Bidder with something like enthusiasm. He went out to make further investigations into this thriving firm. His method was a simple one. He made acquaintance with Mr. Bidder's clerk, a pimply youth of nineteen, who proved easier than he had expected.

Over a cup of tea in a nearby café, Mr. Willie Grames, for such was his name, discussed his employer with the greatest frankness.

'You wouldn't think he was a philanthropist to look at him,' he said, shaking his head in wonder, and employing exactly the same formula that he had used on previous occasions when discussing the eccentricities of Mr. Bidder—'but that's what he is. A regular philanthropist!'

'The name of Bidder is unfamiliar to me,' said Anthony, and Mr. Willie Grames guffawed.

'I should say it was,' he said, sarcastically, 'and it was unfamiliar to him until he used it. Here'—he leaned forward and lowered his voice confidentially—'my own opinion is that his name isn't Bidder at all; in fact I know it isn't,' he acknowledged, in an outburst of candour. 'I saw a letter addressed to him once. He left it behind him when he took some things out of his pocket. It didn't say Bidder on the envelope, it said Leggenstein.'

Anthony thought that this young man was unusually communicative, but his next words explained the reason.

'I'm leaving at the end of the week,' he said. 'Bidder or Leggenstein, or whatever his darned name is, he's too much of a handful for me.'

'Have you got the push?' asked Anthony.

'Me the push?' said the other indignantly. 'The man isn't living that would give me the push. No, I resigned.'

'When you say he's a philanthropist, what do you mean?'

'I mean this,' said Mr. Willie Grames, impressively. 'We've been in business eighteen months and I've been with him all the time. We've had a turnover of thousands and thousands of pounds, but he hasn't made enough profit out of the goods he sold to keep a cat alive! And mind you, that's not like him,' he went on earnestly. 'He's a mean devil and he's fond of money. Why, we bought a load of gloves, leather and fur-lined, that had been ordered for the Air Force. We got them at eighteenpence a pair, and it was almost certain we could have sold them for twenty-five shillings. What did he do? He spent a lot of money in advertising them at half a crown a pair! He barely made enough profit to pay for the advertisements, let alone the rent of the office.

'How many did he sell?'

'About five thousand,' said the other gloomily. 'Yes, he's worked up a name for bargains and straight dealing. Pays all his advertisement bills on the nail and has got a good reputation with the newspapers. I reckon that in eighteen months' trading he's about two thousand pounds out of pocket. How's that for philanthropy?'

Anthony thought for a while, and then asked:

'When you sold your gloves, how many applications did you receive?'

'About twenty thousand,' said the other. 'It took me a week to return the money to the people who couldn't be supplied. You must have seen his advertisements. Bidder's Bargains, they're called. He's sold all sorts of things, but the gloves were the big line we tackled. Of course, we don't do our business in the office. We just receive letters there. He's got a warehouse in the suburbs, and I'm told he's got another in Manchester.'

He rattled on about Mr. Bidder and his peculiarities, and The Mixer listened, sorting out the essential facts which were important to him.

'And I have come to the conclusion,' he told Paul when he returned home that evening, 'that we shall not see developments until Mr. Willie Grames is out of the way. The youth is perfectly emphatic on the point that he resigned, but I'd like to bet money that he was fired.'

Anthony's prophecy was justified. On the following Monday week Paul came into his bedroom before he was dressed, with a newspaper in his hand.

'Here are your gossamer stockings!' he said.

Anthony took the newspaper from the other's hand. He could not miss Mr. Bidder's advertisement because it occupied the whole of the page. It was a startling advertisement, one which caught the eye and arrested the attention. It was headed, 'Bidder's Biggest Bargain!'

And 'Bidder's Biggest Bargain' was in the loveliest of gossamer fine stockings. 'In all shades and all sizes.' Mr. Bidder announced to the world that he had by a fortunate stroke of luck purchased these so cheaply that he could offer them at the amazing price of five pairs for ten shillings! The lady who was ultra wealthy could purchase twelve pairs for a pound. There were pictures of these wonderful stockings, descriptions of them in flowery language, a drawing showing a beautiful lady displaying some eighteen inches of 'Bidder's Biggest Bargain', and the advertisement concluded with the significant tag 'If you look rich and feel rich, you are rich!'

There were ten thousand pairs and only ten thousand pairs, said the advertisement. You could not buy single pairs. You must spend ten shillings, and the ten-shilling note must be pinned to the coupon on the bottom right-hand corner of the page.

Anthony read the advertisement through very carefully.

'Is any other paper carrying this besides the *Megaphone*?' he asked.

A brief search disclosed the fact that all the papers had it.

'Now,' said Anthony, after a calculation, 'that means that he must have spent at least seven thousand pounds to sell fifteen hundred pounds' worth of stockings.'

Paul, conning the advertisement, read aloud:

'This offer is intended, as Bidder and Bidder frankly admit, to advertise their business. Look out for our March bargains, which will transcend all others.'

'It is computed,' observed Anthony, 'that a sucker is born into the world every minute—and by sucker I use the abominable American slang word for "mug", "can", or "credulous imbecile". Our friend stipulates that no cheques shall be sent, which means that he has three days to work his nefarious will upon the unsuspecting public. Paul, make tender inquiries of the hall porter and discover whether Mr. Bidder or Leggenstein is preparing to take a holiday abroad.'

Inquiries produced satisfactory results. The hall porter told Paul with some concern that Mr. Bidder's health had broken down under the heavy stress of handling the ten-shilling notes donated by unsuspecting ladies with an eye to a bargain.

'As soon as he gets these gossamer stockings off—you've seen his advertisement, sir——?'

Paul nodded.

'Well, as soon as he gets them posted, he's going away to Paris, he told me.'

Paul went back with the information.

Mr. Bidder's intention had not been accurately represented. Long before the stockings were dispatched, in fact, on the third night following the appearance of his advertisement, he returned to his flat early in the afternoon and packed a suit-case. He was humming a little stave, indicative of his lightness of heart and cheerful optimism.

His passport and railway tickets reposed on his desk, and a thick wad of never-to-be-settled accounts was stacked neatly on his mantelpiece. Mr. Bidder was a methodical man.

There was no knock at his door to arouse his attention or suspicion, and the first intimation he had that all was not well was when he heard a gentle cough behind him, and turned to see a man in a long coat, his face concealed by a black mask, standing behind him, and the first word of the intruder was by way of apology.

'Forgive the melodramatic concealment of my countenance,'

he said. 'I hate masking, but the temptation to use a lady's stocking with a couple of holes cut out for eyes proved too great.'

'Who the devil are you?' asked Mr. Bidder, turning very pale.

'I am Henry J. Nemesis,' said the other easily, 'and if you let your hands stray to your hip pocket I shall drill a hole in your liver. For,' he went on—Anthony could be very loquacious in such moments as these—'I have disregarded the police instructions that firearms should be registered, and you will suffer the ignominy of being shot dead with an illegal gun, thus adding insult to injury.'

'Scoot!' said Mr. Bidder, harshly. 'There's no sense in coming here. This isn't my flat. It's one I hired furnished.'

'I know all about that,' said the visitor. 'I want your brief-case, with all those nice new ten-pound banknotes that you got from your bank this afternoon, having exchanged for these the mouldy Bradburys which you have been taking from envelopes for the past three days.'

'I'll see you——' began Mr. Bidder, pardonably exasperated.

'You'll not see me at all,' said the inexorable mask, 'unless there is any truth in the spiritualists' theory. By the way, do you believe that you can photograph fairies?'

'Look here,' said Bidder, white and desperate. 'Fair play! Now, I don't want any trouble with you or with the police, and I'll give you a thousand pounds to clear out.'

'You'll give me as many thousand pounds as you have in your case,' said Anthony, coolly, 'and if you show fight, I'll not only take the money, but I'll burn your passport,' he added significantly, and Mr. Bidder collapsed into a chair.

It was nearly five minutes before he was thoroughly convinced that The Mixer meant business and they were five minutes of pleading, threatenings, outburts of rage and the shedding of not a few tears, for Mr. Bidder was a representative of an emotional race.

'I'll fix you for this,' he sobbed, as with shaking hands he picked up his brief-case and flung it on the table.

'The words sound familiar to me,' said Anthony, taking up the case and examining the contents in a leisurely manner. 'Eight thousand pounds!' He whistled. 'Sixteen thousand mugs!' He looked sharply at Mr. Bidder and shook his head. 'I think not. That is too modest an estimate, remembering that a sucker is born every minute, and that the papers in which you advertise enjoy enormous circulations. You've got another lot somewhere—ante-up!'

Shaking in every limb, and keeping his eye upon his passport and his book of tickets, Leggenstein meekly produced a second large package, and Anthony counted the notes.

'That's nearer the mark,' he said 'I suppose you've got an odd thousand or two in your shoes.'

The start which Bidder gave seemed to suggest there was some truth in this chance shot.

'I'll leave you that, anyway,' said Anthony. I'm no hog. I presume that you have let the newspapers in for your advertisements, and that you've been preparing for eighteen months for this little coup, establishing your good name, integrity and general character in preparation for the day when you would spring your stockings upon the women of Britain.'

Mr. Bidder found his voice.

'Are you a split?' he asked, hoarsely.

'Do splits go round wearing stockings over their heads and carrying deadly weapons in their hands?' replied Anthony, reproachfully. 'Have a bit of sense, Leggenstein. You know the police; you've been in gaol for a similar fraud to the one you are now trying to work. Take your bag, and go in peace, and remember I can watch you over the banisters as far as the hall.'

The man got as far as the door, then turned, his face distorted with rage.

'I'll have you for this, one of these days,' he almost wailed. 'If I am a hook, what are you? If I'm robbing the public, ain't you robbing them too?'

'No, sir, I am not,' returned Anthony, with some dignity. 'I am reading a useful moral lesson in economics to extravagant womanhood. It is a crime to waste your money on gossamer stockings—and now get! You have ten minutes to clear away from this building, and if you don't like my methods, you can complain to the police. I'd like to bet that the police are looking for your stockings already.'

Mr. Bidder left hurriedly.

14: The Case of Donna de Milo

The Mixer's business system was simplicity itself. It was summarised in his own words, 'Never to be where you are wanted.'

In his search for easy harvests, he flitted from town to town, but there were long periods of time when no victims came his way. Not that there was any shortage of evildoers who had accumulated fortunes, but because they were somewhat difficult to reach. There were also periods when, as in that following his raid upon the virtuous Mr. Kandeman, he considered it wise to abstain from any notable adventure.

He had told Paul that he intended to remain quiet until the arrival in the country of the Rajah of Tikiligi, but his negotiations with Mr. Bidder, and the interest of the police in Mr. Bidder's late habitation, convinced him that it would be wise to remove himself to another neighbourhood.

He accordingly rented a modest house in a part of London where neither his own nor Mr. Bidder's iniquities were likely to bring the inquiring police and it was here that, returning one morning at one o'clock, he awakened the amiable Paul, and dragged him blinking but uncomplaining to the dining-room.

'What's the trouble?' asked Paul.

'Sorry to disturb you, but I can't wait till morning.' He put his head out of the door and shouted: 'Sandy! Let's have some cocoa—must get the taste of perfumed cigarettes out of my mouth,' he said, as he came back into the room. 'Thank goodness Sandy doesn't keep such early hours.'

'What have you been doing?' asked Paul. 'Visiting the haunts of the idle rich?'

'You've got it first time,' replied Anthony, removing his black bow tie, and his dinner jacket. 'Pass my dressing-gown, and one of your cheap cigarettes. Yes, I've been to Magson's.'

'The night club,' exclaimed Paul in surprise. 'Are you a member?'

Anthony chuckled.

'That most exclusive of clubs has an entrance fee which precludes the possibility of any honest young man being a member,' he said.

Magson's was, as he had declared, the most exclusive, as well as one of the newest, night clubs in London. Its membership was limited and unless you could pay an entrance fee of a hundred guineas and a yearly subscription of a further hundred it was impossible to get your name upon the books. Even then one had to be proposed by a member, and the members of Magson's were not in Anthony's set.

'I went in as the friend of a gilded youth whom I met at Domingo's—Mr. Job Tillmitt,' explained Anthony. 'I won't tell you how I came to scrape an acquaintance with him, because it would make a very long story. The young gentleman was, however, in that state of mind when he welcomed any kind of companion.

'Broke?' asked Paul.

'In love,' replied Anthony, softly, 'and heart-broken. When I tell you that the lady of his choice is Miss Donna de Milo, you will understand how expensive sorrow may be. And I was glad to go,' he went on, 'because it gave me not only an opportunity of breaking into the halls of gilded extravagance——'

'Isn't it rather an early hour of the morning for moralising?' murmured Paul, plaintively.

'Perhaps you're right,' agreed Anthony. 'I'll continue. Well, I was very pleased to go to this club, the more so as I had an opportunity of meeting Miss Donna de Milo, who is as far removed from the ordinary brand of gold-digger as a Rolls-Royce car from an aged bone-shaker. In fact, she is the last thing in gold-diggers,' he went on enthusiastically. 'She has a wonderful house in Kensington, a gorgeous estate in Somerset, and a dear little villa on the Riviera. Incidentally, she has yards and yards of pearls, shovelsful of diamonds, and a banking account which would make many a so-called millionaire envious.'

'Are you joking?' demanded Paul.

'I am speaking the truth. As you have never heard of Donna de Milo——'

'I have heard of her,' nodded Paul; 'but I never regarded her as legitimate prey. As a matter of fact'—he hesitated—'I don't think this is quite in your line, is it? She isn't a woman like Milwaukee Meg, and any other woman——'

'If she isn't Milwaukee Meg, she isn't far removed, except that she takes less risks,' declared Anthony. 'You don't know the kind of woman she is. She's broken more young men, she's bled and fleeced more anguished parents, than any of her type in any age. What's more,' he continued, slowly, 'I'm afraid she's going to get the hundred thousand pounds that I made by the sale of my silver mines in Cobalt.'

Paul stared at him, and then laughed.

'I see what you mean. You have been talking to the lady?'

'I've had a very long talk with her—a very languishing talk, I might add,' said Anthony. 'To tell you the truth, I never expected that tonight's adventure would be at all profitable. Donna de Milo is a proposition which makes life not only interesting, but fascinating. I got you up to tell you that I'm leaving here tomorrow to take my place in society. I was nosing round a house agent's yesterday, and I found a very fine Piccadilly flat to let. The rent is sixty pounds a week furnished, and if that flat isn't already taken we shall be sleeping under its painted ceilings tomorrow night.'

He looked at Sandy, who had entered with a steaming jug of cocoa.

'You'll be my valet, then, Sandy,' he said. 'You, Paul, had better be my chauffeur. I must have a car and, as you know, I'm particular about my chauffeur.'

'Quite so' answered Paul.

• • • • •

Miss Donna de Milo descended from her Rolls at half past one on the following day, and the porter of the Park Hotel ushered her up the broad steps into the beautiful marble vestibule. A dozen pairs of eyes watched her as she came in, for she was known wherever society congregated. And there were not a few there who, being aware of her reputation, looked round for Donna's new victim. They found him in a good-looking young man, who came forward with every sign of eagerness to greet her.

'This is awfully good of you, Miss de Milo; I didn't expect you would keep the engagement,' he said as he took her hand in his and gazed rapturously into her china blue eyes.

'I never break an engagement,' she smiled, 'but I was wondering whether you would remember.'

He gazed at her reproachfully.

'As if I could forget,' he murmured.

As they walked side by side towards the dining-room, Anthony, who had never seen Donna de Milo by daylight, could not but admire the perfect contour of face, the purity of her skin, and the innate daintiness and femininity of her appearance.

She stripped her gloves slowly, her smiling eyes fixed on his.

'Do you often go to the club?' she asked.

Anthony shook his head.

'Not very often,' he said, simply. 'The majority of these places rather frighten me; you see I am a simple miner from the back blocks.'

'You look rather young for a miner,' she laughed. 'What are you doing in London, anyway?'

'I've come over to find some investments for my money,' he replied. 'I like London tremendously, but there are times when the call of Ontario almost makes me pack my grip and take the next boat back.'

'You ought to be able to do a lot with a hundred thousand

pounds,' she said, thoughtfully. 'I have a good many friends in commerce, and perhaps I could help you to find the right kind of investment.'

So that was it, thought Anthony. He wondered what line she would take. He was to be lured into a fake company, and he did not doubt that somewhere in the background she had willing helpers.

It was difficult to believe, looking at her innocent face, that she was the woman who had driven Neilson Grey to suicide and brought ruin to young Lord Feltan. Such was the illusion of her innocence that he felt himself weakening on his plan, and it needed her ill-timed reference to his fortune to bring him down to earth again.

'Of course, I know very little about business myself, but these friends of mine are very clever,' she prattled on. 'And I remember one of them telling me there was a wonderful company being floated called the Bencombe China Clay Company, which would make a fortune for anybody who put money into it. Perhaps,' she said with a little smile, 'it is as well you met me before some of these terrible people who lie in wait for rich young men met you.'

'It is certainly well for me,' he said, politely.

She made no further reference to his money, and he left her at the door of her Kensington house. He was to meet her again on the morrow, and there were several morrows. One day he took her to tea at a fashionable tea-shop in St. James's Street, once to dinner and a theatre, but the patient Paul groaned when he learned that The Mixer had taken a box at the Albert Hall for the New Year's Eve ball

'What are you going as?' he asked.

'I am going as a very commonplace clown, and at my suggestion the beautiful lady will appear as the Queen of Sheba.'

Paul's eyes narrowed anxiously.

'With all her movable properties?' he queried.

'Exactly. They say she wears a hundred thousand pounds' worth of pearls, and I am to be her good cavalier, and honest to goodness, Paul, I don't like it.'

'I think I suggested it was not your game in the beginning,' Paul reminded him. 'After all, man is woman's natural enemy, and when women turn round and get a little of their own back I think they should be allowed to get away with it.'

'I thoroughly appreciate your point of view,' answered Anthony, 'but I've got to go through with it.'

'Why? I know she's taken the stuff from the callow youth of

Britain, and that she has unloaded the ill-gotten gains of their fat papas, but that rather makes her more admirable to me.'

'More—rubbish!' retorted Anthony, irritably.

He liked the idea less because he had no definite plan in his mind. Had Miss de Milo been a man it would have been easy. Besides, he had discovered, to his amazement, that the fascination of the girl was growing on him. He cursed his own folly, and told himself that her charm was part of her stock-in-trade, but that did not help very much.

He met her on the afternoon of the day he was taking her to the fancy dress ball, and they had tea together in the lounge of the Circus Hotel. He found himself looking forward to the meeting, and grew alarmed. For as her power of enchantment increased, so did the chance of his coup diminish.

The meeting for tea was to prove an eventful one, though to the excitement of the afternoon Miss Donna de Milo contributed nothing.

He had paid the waiter, and they were moving slowly through the crowded room on their way to the door, when instinctively Anthony turned round to meet the gaze of a man who sat by himself in a far corner of the tea-room. Anthony had known that somebody was staring at him; that uncanny warning which comes to highly sensitive people had drawn his eyes in the direction of this stranger.

He looked round for a second, then looked away, and though the girl's eyes were upon him, she saw no change of colour, did not witness so much as a start of surprise. He said good-bye to her and returned to his Piccadilly flat by a circuitous route.

Sandy knew, as he came in, that something unusual had happened.

'Anything wrong?' he asked.

'I saw a man in the Circus tea-rooms,' said Anthony. 'Guess who he was.'

Sandy shook his head.

'It was Baltimore Jones. You remember the fellow we skinned in Madrid?'

Sandy shaped his lips in a whistle.

'Did he recognise you?' he asked, and Anthony nodded.

'I'm pretty sure he did. Baltimore is not a careless looker. I think he'd been watching me a long time before I realised. Is Paul in?'

'Yes, he's waiting for instructions for this evening.'

'Would you send him up to me, please.'

Entering in his uniform as chauffeur, Paul was quickly informed of the encounter with Baltimore Jones.

'It's hardly likely he'll make the kind of trouble most to be feared,' he said.

'I'm not so sure of that,' returned Anthony. 'Baltimore Jones struck me as the type of guy who would be most likely to go to the police.'

There was a silence.

'Anyway,' remarked Paul, 'he can't know that you're on the eve of a coup. Did he follow you here?'

'No, I went by taxi to Marble Arch tube, and we had a pretty clear road; then I doubled back to Chancery Lane and took another taxi there. But we must be prepared to flit tonight.'

'And what is the plan?'

'You hang on—keep your car next to the gate in the park, that's about a hundred and fifty yards from the main entrance of the Albert Hall. Have the engine running from ten o'clock onwards.'

'And what is the plan of operation?' asked Paul again.

Anthony was unaccountably irritated.

'I have no plan, I tell you,' he snapped. 'I'm going to do what I think best.'

Never had he undertaken a job that caused him such deep qualms as the contemplated robbery of Donna de Milo.

He went into the hall wearing the grotesque costume of a clown, his face whitened with paint but, in spite of his festive attire, he carried a heart of lead.

He arrived about half past nine. The floor was already crowded. Glancing round the tiers of boxes, he noticed Donna sitting demurely alone, and made his way up the stairway to the corridor. He knocked at the door of the box, and she called, 'Come in.'

He stood for a moment looking at her. She was amazingly beautiful that night. Row after row of pearls graced her beautiful neck and shoulders, her corsage sparkled with diamonds, while the flashing green fire of a large emerald, which she wore in her silk turban, looked to Anthony, in his disordered condition of nerves, like a great malignant eye.

'Come in,' she said, softly, 'and sit down. No, not over there; over at the back of the box.'

At her tone all Anthony's senses were alert. He knew without understanding, that there was danger, and if he sank into the seat she indicated with an appearance of unconcern, it was only because he was exercising remarkable self-control.

The place she had indicated was out of sight of the vast crowd below and he realised that he could not be seen from the other boxes.

Only for a second did his eyes rest upon the fortune she wore in jewellery, but something told him they would never be his and he had, too, so great a sense of revulsion at the deed he had contemplated that he could not have taken so much as a single pearl, even if he had the opportunity.

'That's better, Mr. Mixer,' she went on.

Despite his self-control, Anthony jumped.

'You're a nice boy,' she said, looking at him strangely, 'and I like you. You certainly fooled me with your story of a hundred thousand pounds.'

'I'm afraid I don't understand you,' began Anthony.

She shook her head.

'Don't let us pretend. This situation is too horribly dangerous for you.'

'For me?'

'There are four detectives in this hall looking for you,' she explained.

For a few minutes there was silence.

'Incidentally,' she continued, 'they are also looking for me.'

'For you!' he exclaimed.

'You can hardly call it looking, of course,' she said. 'They know where I am. Mr. Mixer—I don't know your other name—I dare say you think hardly of me, for I have spent a great deal of my life in relieving foolish men of their superfluous cash, but all the talk about my having driven men to suicide is twaddle. And, Mr. Mixer, one young gentleman has squealed. I suppose you know what "squealed" means?'

Anthony nodded.

'I think they know you are coming to me, and that is why they are waiting. There's a gentleman watching this box at this particular moment, but he isn't quite sure that you're here. Now take my advice and get out.'

'But what about you?'

She shrugged her white shoulders, and then suddenly looking down on the floor of the hall, she lowered her voice.

'Just lift your head; do you see that gentleman in scarlet with the black mask—he has taken his mask off now?'

Anthony looked cautiously and recognised the young man whose acquaintance he had made at Domingo's.

'That is mine enemy,' she said gloomily. 'And he is making

his way to this box to offer me some very unpleasant alternative to prison life.'

'I see,' remarked Anthony, softly. 'He is just about my height.'

He looked round the box. There was a screen leaning against the wall, evidently designed to keep out the draught from the box's occupants.

'This will do splendidly,' he said. 'The next box is empty, isn't it? And that door leads to it?'

'Yes,' she assented.

He turned the handle—the door was unlocked—and stepped into the empty box. Two curtains hung at each end. He drew one half across the box opening.

'Splendid,' he told her, when he came back. 'Do you know who has this next box? I've taken the liberty of bolting the door leading into the corridor.'

Donna mentioned the name of a famous actress.

Anthony grinned.

'She won't be here till midnight,' he said.

At that moment someone knocked, and a masked young man in the scarlet garb of Mephistopheles appeared in the doorway. He did not see Anthony behind the screen, nor was he aware of his presence until he felt the prod of a gun barrel against his spine.

'Get into the next box and keep quiet,' said Anthony. 'I want your beautiful clothes.'

Half an hour later a Queen of Sheba and a masked Mephistopheles strolled out of the entrance of the Albert Hall and the watching detectives looked at each other. They had orders not to make the arrest until Mephistopheles gave the word. That word was never spoken, for whilst they were still waiting, a bound and gagged young man, scantily attired, was struggling to free himself in the curtained box.

In a few minutes Anthony and his companion were in the car and speeding towards South Kensington.

'Now, Miss de Milo,' said Anthony as the car stopped at her door, 'you've got about ten minutes to get away.'

'Five minutes would be ample,' she said, simply, and held out her hand. 'Good-bye, brother brigand—here's your fee!' She slipped a rope of pearls from her neck and held them in her outstretched hand.

Anthony shook his head.

'No, thanks,' he said, 'but if you'll allow me——'

He stooped and kissed her.

The chauffeur, otherwise Paul, saw the proceedings from the tail of his eye.

'Now I wonder how he'll manage to give his faithful assistants a bonus on that,' he murmured, as he opened out the car.

15: The Seventy-fourth Diamond

The stolid-looking inspector from Scotland Yard eyed the slim figure of the Rajah of Tikiligi with an amusement which he strove hard to hide. The Rajah was young, and in the elegant evening dress of civilisation looked even slighter than he was. He had a dark olive complexion, which was emphasised by a small, black, silky moustache, and his well-oiled hair, black as the raven's, was brushed back from his forehead.

'I hope your highness does not mind seeing me,' said the inspector.

'No, no, I not mind,' said his highness, shaking his head vigorously. 'I glad to see you. I speak English very well, but I am not British subjik. I Dutch subjik.'

At first the inspector was at a loss to put his mission into words.

'We have learned at Scotland Yard,' he began, 'that your highness has brought to this country a very large collection of precious stones.'

His highness nodded vigorously.

'Yes, yes,' he said, eagerly. 'Damn fine jewels, damn fine stones, big as duck eggs. I have twenty!'

He spoke to a dark-skinned attendant in a language which the inspector did not understand, and the man took a case from the drawer of a writing-table, opened it and displayed a brilliant collection of stones which glittered and flashed in the overhead light.

The inspector was impressed, not so much with the value or beauty of the stones as with the considerable danger which their owner ran.

'That is why I have been sent here, sir,' he said. 'I have to warn you on behalf of the Police Commissioner that just now there are two distinct crooks in London who are to be feared.'

'I fear not'ing, pooh!' said his highness, with a lordly wave of his hands. 'This man'—he pointed to his attendant—'is big fellow in my country! He is chief policeman, and he treats bad mans very cruel! He cut off heads very quick!'

He said something apparently in his own language to his attendant, who showed two white lines of teeth in a smile.

'Remember, police officer inspector,' said the Rajah with dignity, 'I do not come to sell. I come to buy—to buy the seventy-fourth diamond for my necklace.'

'The seventy-fourth diamond?' repeated the inspector.

'Seventy-t'ree I have,' returned the Rajah, 'all of great size and beauty. Behold!'

He walked energetically to the table and took up the case again, selecting one large glittering stone.

'I buy one like this,' he said. 'He must be as big, as beautiful, as bright, and I pay anyt'ing—millions.'

The inspector pursed his lips.

'Yes, sir,' he said grimly. 'I dare say. But, at the same time, you've got to look after Benny Lamb, who is in town, and he's a pretty slick fellow.'

'Is he bad mans?' asked his highness, interested.

'A very bad man,' said the inspector gravely.

'Well, cut off his head,' suggested his highness. 'It is very simple.' He shrugged.

'It isn't quite so simple in this country,' replied the inspector, trying not to smile, 'because we have to have what we call evidence even before we can put him in prison, and we have no evidence against Benny Lamb.'

'In my country I kill bad mans very quick,' said the Rajah complacently. 'My country is a beautiful country! I have t'ousands and t'ousands of slaves who work in my mines——'

'Exactly, your highness,' interrupted the detective, 'and that's why the second crook is the most dangerous. He calls himself The Mixer. If he finds that you get money out of slaves he'll come after you, and you'll be very fortunate if you get your diamonds away.'

'The Mixer?' said the Rajah, puzzled.

The detective explained the scope of The Mixer's operations and related certain events of the past. Before he left the Grand Empire Hotel, in which palatial building the Rajah occupied a suite of ten rooms, the detective felt that he had impressed his highness with a sense of his peril.

The Rajah and The Mixer were being discussed in a fashionable restaurant in the West End, where Mr. Benny Lamb, a well-tailored, elegant young man of transatlantic origin, was discussing with two familiars the possibilities of making the biggest coup of the year.

'He's rolling in money, absolutely rolling in it,' he said, shaking his head reproachfully, 'and it's easy for us, Jim.'

Jim, a little red-haired man, sniffed sceptically.

'There ain't any easy money in the world, Benny,' he said, 'but if what you say about the Rajah is true, he's the nearest approach.'

'There's only one thing we've got to watch,' said Benny Lamb seriously. 'I've just had the tip that The Mixer is back in town. You remember that chap who was here a year ago and got away with the bank roll of every crook in town? Well, he's back. I met Baltimore Jones, who's seen him here, and he says The Mixer cleaned him out, not long ago, and left him stranded in Paris—the swine!'

'Will he go after the Rajah?' asked the third man.

Benny nodded.

'He's the guy that will attract The Mixer like a magnet attracts iron filings,' he said. 'I saw him in a box at the theatre last night. He had diamond studs, diamond cuff-links, and I'm damned if he didn't have a diamond watch-strap! It glittered like a Christmas tree, and then some. One of the waiters at the hotel told me that he wore diamond buttons on his pyjamas.'

'What's the plan?' asked Jim, and Mr. Benny Lamb considered for a moment.

'He's here buying diamonds,' he said. 'You wouldn't think he wanted to buy 'em when he's got the whole earth of them, but that's his vice. He's got a necklace at home, according to the accounts I've heard from waiters—I'm well in with the waiters at the Grand Empire—with seventy-three big diamonds, and he's out to buy the seventy-fourth. Now, my idea is that I get a collection of sparklers together and drop in on him and have a little talk. I think I know where I can get the very diamond he wants, but that's beside the point. What I want to do is to see his principal stones, get a few specimens of imitation that look like 'em, and ring the changes when I call on him with the real goods.'

'I know something better than that,' said Jim, and Benny looked with respect, because Jim had flashes of inspiration. 'Work the old "con" trick on him,' said Jim. 'It sounds simple, but those kind of fellows fall for the "con" game quicker than any.'

Benny could not see how the confidence trick could be worked, and Jim explained.

'You go and see him, all dolled up, and take as many sparklers as you can find or get together—genuine ones. Take 'em in a bag and set 'em down careless-like. Tell him you'll call for them tomorrow. These Eastern people like that sort of thing. The next day, when you go, ask to see one of his big 'uns. Tell him you think you can match it if he'll let you take it with you.'

'Bah!' said Benny, contemptuously. 'Do you think he'd stand for that? I thought you were going to suggest something sensible.'

They sat until the restaurant closed before they had formulated their plan. The next day Mr. Benny Lamb drove to the hotel in an elegant car and sent his card to the Rajah of Tikiligi, and the dark-skinned potentate received him immediately, because Benny's card, beautifully engraved, was inscribed with a name which looked at first glance like the name of one of the greatest diamond merchants in Hatton Garden.

He brought with him a respectable package of diamonds, for Benny commanded considerable resources. He had, moreover, friends in the illicit diamond trade who could supply him with an impressive quantity. His highness came from his bedroom into the big sitting-room, attired in a silk dressing-gown. He was chewing vigorously.

'Betel-nut,' guessed Benny, who had some acquaintance with the East.

The Rajah was a little suspicious, or appeared to be, and would not at first talk diamonds.

'I cannot see you without appointment,' he said, shaking his head. 'How I know you are not a Mixer?'

Benny laughed good-humouredly at the suggestion.

'I'm glad you have heard of that rascal,' he said, and then as a thought struck him. 'Has he been troubling you?' he asked quickly.

'No, no, no,' said the Rajah, emphatically. 'I have no troubles. Now, what do you want?'

Benny Lamb plunged into his business without further preliminary. He was a glib, well-spoken and most convincing man, and presently he produced from his bag a cylinder of blue velvet which he unrolled, displaying to the Rajah's approving eyes a number of diamonds of extraordinary size. The Rajah took them up and examined them, putting them down one by one with a little sniff.

'She is no good,' he said, 'and this one, she is no good also.

These are little little ones. They are no use to me. I desire a great one. I will show you.'

He clapped his hands, and his attendant came in, and to him he spoke in a strange language. The attendant produced from a drawer a blue velvet case and opened it, and Mr. Benny Lamb stepped forward and drew a long and ecstatic sigh of admiration. The stones which glittered in their velvet cases were full of beauty and brilliance.

'May I——' He put out his hand, but the attendant closed the case with a snap.

'No, no, you shall bring me some stones like that,' said the Rajah. 'Tomorrow, perhaps, or the next day. At what o'clock will you come, Mister?'

'At five o'clock tomorrow afternoon,' replied Benny Lamb, inwardly glowing with joy.

'They good stones I show you, eh?' said the Rajah with a broad grin. 'What you think they worth?'

'There isn't one worth less than fifty thousand pounds,' said Benny.

'And do you think you can get me one as good?' asked the Rajah eagerly.

Benny did not trust himself to speak. He nodded.

When he rejoined his little gang that evening his plan was cut and dried.

'Faukenberg will have to supply the stones,' he said, referring to the most notorious 'fence' in London, a man who dealt only with the swell mobs and handled property which would have scared a lesser man. 'It must be as near the size of those that nigger has as makes no difference. I tell you he's a pretty shrewd guy that, and if it looked little, as likely as not he wouldn't handle it. Come round to Hodys, and we'll have a drink on this.'

The three men went off together to their favourite bar, and on the way Mr. Lamb gave an account of the interview.

'And he's heard of The Mixer too,' he said with a chuckle. 'That rather seems to me as though that guy is after him. I made a few inquiries. I know some people at the Grand Empire, and there have been one or two mysterious young men knocking around.'

Hodys was crowded, but they wedged their way to the bar, and standing by the marble counter, they had their drinks and raised their glasses in an unspoken toast. Benny was paying for the liquid refreshment, when the barmaid said with a smile:

'Is that your letter on the counter?'

'Not mine,' said Benny, turning. There was an envelope almost at his elbow, and as he picked it up his brow puckered. 'Mr. Benny Lamb,' he read. 'Now who the devil left that here? Did you see anybody?'

His companions shook their heads. They had seen many bodies but nobody of a suspicious character. Benny ripped open the flap, took out a single sheet of paper and read:

You're after the Rajah's diamonds and so am I. There is no reason why we should clash, and it may be advisable for us to work together and share the swag. Will you meet me at the corner of St. John's Avenue, Maida Vale, at ten o'clock tonight? Come alone, and I will be alone too.

'Well, I'm——' Mr. Benny Lamb gasped. 'Well, if that doesn't beat the band! Share the swag, eh? What do you think of that, boys?'

He handed the letter to the men, and they read.

'Are you going?'

'Yes, I think I will,' said Benny after a pause. 'I'd like to have a look at this fellow. We may run against him one of these days and it'll be useful to know who we've got to look for.'

At ten o'clock promptly he was at the rendezvous, and as a neighbouring clock chimed the hour a young man walked across the road and came straight towards him. He was wearing an overcoat with the collar turned up, a soft felt hat was pulled down over his eyes, and as he stood with his back to the street lamp Benny had no opportunity of seeing his face.

'Benny Lamb?' he asked quickly.

'That's me,' said the gentleman in question and glanced round suspiciously to see if The Mixer was accompanied. But apparently he was alone.

'Let's walk up this street, it's quiet,' said Anthony, and side by side, they paced steadily up the broad deserted thoroughfare.

'Now I'm going to come to the point pretty quickly,' said Anthony. 'Are you willing to stand in with me over the Rajah?'

'I don't know what you're talking about,' said Benny Lamb. 'If you're trying to make me confess that I am contemplating a robbery, why, you've made a big mistake, Mister. I shouldn't have come here at all, only I thought I'd like to correct a wrong impression you seem to have got——'

'Cut out all that stuff!' said Anthony, patiently. Are you going to stand in with the swag?'

'Do you think it is likely, Mr. Mixer, that I'd stand in with anybody if I was after the Rajah's sparklers? And I want to tell you this.' He stopped suddenly and slapped the other on the chest, peering into his face. 'I believe you've got into the habit of relieving crooks of the money they've earned. Well, you can get it out of your mind so far as I'm concerned. If I get the stuff from the Rajah I know just how to hold it!'

'I've no intention of depriving you of your hard-earned reward,' said Anthony, sardonically. 'I am only here to make you an offer. Will you stand in half?'

'I'll see you in hell first,' said Mr. Benny Lamb, dispassionately.

'All right,' Anthony nodded. 'Then there's nothing more to be said.'

He was turning away when the other gripped his arm.

'Here, my son,' he said. 'Let's have a look at your face.'

He was reaching up to snatch off the hat when something hit him under the jaw and he went down. He thought at first that Anthony had used a stick, but apparently he had relied upon his fists.

'Get up,' said Anthony, sternly, 'and apologise for taking a liberty.'

Mr. Benny Lamb was in so dazed a condition, less from the effect of the blow than the unexpectedness of it, that he had not even breath for an apology.

Anthony looked at him for a second, then laughed silently, and turning on his heel, walked away. Mr. Benny Lamb made no attempt to follow him. He did not recount all the circumstances of that interview to his companions, because he felt they were not wholly creditable to himself. And he wanted to forget that blow until he could afford to bring it back to his memory. Then he would have an account to settle with The Mixer. Curiously enough, there were exactly twenty-five men in London at that particular moment who had promised themselves a similar treat.

Early the next morning he called upon the redoubtable Faukenberg, who had an impressive jeweller's shop in Clerkenwell. Mr. Faukenberg did not protest against the suggestion that he should loan one of his valuable stones to a crook with three convictions behind him. He was far too sensible a man, and when the story of the Rajah's wealth had been told he had no other thought than the question of profit to himself.

'I can lay my hands on a stone like that,' he said, 'but it will cost you a bit of money, Benny, the loan of it, I mean. It's worth thirty thousand pounds. It was brought to me from Paris by Lew, who touched a French Countess for all her jewellery. I haven't attempted to get rid of it until they've forgotten what it looks like, but it's the very thing for you, and I'm not so sure that you couldn't make a straight deal of it by selling it to the Rajah. He's not likely to read the *Hue and Cry* or know anything about missing jewellery which is wanted by the police. It'll cost you a thousand pounds, the loan for three days, Benny and, of course, I shall hold the money I've got of yours as security.'

'You needn't worry,' said Benny with a grin. 'I shan't lose your diamond.'

He kept his appointment with the Rajah, having first telephoned to the hotel to make sure that the buyer of jewels was accessible, and he came into the Rajah's presence with the diamond in one pocket, and a passable imitation in an exactly similar case in another. The Rajah took the real diamond and examined it.

'Yes, yes,' he said, 'it is a beautiful stone, a very beautiful stone.'

He was evidently something of an expert, for he produced a jeweller's eye-piece and examined the stone critically.

'What do you want for that?' he asked.

'Thirty thousand pounds,' said Benny, and the Rajah looked wistfully at the stone.

'It is much money,' he said, 'and perhaps I do not buy him. No, I do not think I can pay thirty thousand pounds. It is too small, too.'

He handed back the case with a regretful shake of the head. 'You see I have so many bigger.' He said something to his attendant, who again produced the big flat case filled with sparkling stones.

'This one, or this one, is immensely large.' He pointed to one and Benny looked at it. 'This one is of the same size as that which you have brought.' He pointed to a flashing, scintillating thing of beauty which lay by the side of the larger brilliant.

'So it is,' said Benny. He slipped his hand into his pocket, opened the case which contained the fake diamond and palmed it skilfully.

'May I look at this stone, your highness?'

'Yes, you shall look at it. Yes, it is beautiful to see, and it is better than yours, for it is worth forty thousand pounds.'

'Wonderful!' murmured Benny, and picked up the stone.

He was brilliant in his own line. Under the very eye of the

dark-skinned potentate the stone he had taken from the case in his pocket was substituted for the Rajah's property.

'Very beautiful,' he said, gripping the Rajah's stone in the palm of his hand and putting his own back in the case. 'Now, can't I persuade your royal highness to buy this stone?' he said.

'It is not good enough,' said the Rajah, shaking his head. 'Perhaps tomorrow I see you.'

'Perhaps tomorrow you won't,' thought Benny, as he strolled down the marble stairs to the vestibule and sprang into the cab which awaited him.

He drove straight back to Faukenberg, elated with his success. He half expected to see a representative of The Mixer waiting for him on the doormat, but he reached Faukenberg's, and dashed past into the little back parlour where his two confederates were awaiting him.

'Got it!' said Benny, triumphantly. 'Now this is where we make a quick get-away to the Continent, Faukenberg. You look after the stone and market it.'

'What did you do, ring the changes?'

Benny nodded.

'If he had bought my stone it would have been more simple,' he said. 'I could have rung one with the other. As it was, I just had to work it the other way about, take his sparkler and put my beautiful imitation in its place.' He chuckled. 'Here's your diamond, Faukenberg; and it's not worth a thousand, old son.'

'It was worth more to you,' said Faukenberg, calmly, as he opened the case. 'You can't get a stone like that—— My God!' His face went pale.

'What's the matter?' asked Benny, anxiously.

'This—this isn't my stone!' faltered Faukenberg. 'You fool! What have you done?'

'Not your stone?' gasped Benny.

'You idiot!' roared Faukenberg. 'This is an imitation paste thing that you can buy in Bond Street for a fiver! Go back and get my stone!'

Benny had turned pale.

'Are you sure?'

'Go back and get it!' almost screamed the 'fence', and Benny leapt into the first taxi he could find and flew back to the hotel.

His quest was in vain. The Rajah had left the hotel almost immediately after he had gone.

'Are you a friend of his highness?' asked the troubled manager. 'He has not paid his bill this week—he went away so hurriedly and so mysteriously that I'm a bit worried.'

'A friend of his?' said Benny in a hollow voice. 'No, I'm no friend of his.'

'Pardon me, what is your name?' asked the manager suddenly. 'You're not Mr. Lamb?'

'That's my name,' said Benny.

'Oh, then he left a note for you.'

Benny tore open the letter, and his heart sank when he saw that it was addressed in the same hand as that which he had received the previous night. The message was brief:

Thanks very much for the stone and love to Faukenberg.

It was signed 'The Mixer'.

At that precise moment Paul, the 'Rajah's' attendant, in The Mixer's Westminster lodgings, was rubbing the yellow annatto colouring from his face with coconut butter, whilst Sandy performed the same office for Anthony.

'Paul,' said Anthony, evading Sandy's attentions for a moment, 'I forgot to leave the money for the rent at that infernal hotel.'

'Two hundred pounds a week for rooms,' put in Sandy. 'It's wicked. And you've still got three days of the week to go.'

'I'll send the money in banknotes this afternoon,' said The Mixer, 'and I think I'll write to Benny and ask him if he'd like to be my guest there for three days.'

16: Film Teaching by Post

'I notice,' said Paul, curiously, 'the name of Mr. Hickory Bompers on your memorandum pad. Are you thinking of taking a course of film acting?'

Anthony laughed softly.

'I had that idea,' he said. 'There are moments when I rather fancy myself as a movie star.'

He was living in a small house in a very small Kensington square, having taken the premises furnished for three months. He and his secretary had finished breakfast and were standing together by one of the open windows looking across a little patch of green which, surrounded by high railings, was supposed to afford the inhabitants of the square recreation and sylvan enjoyment.

'Seriously,' said Paul, 'have you marked down Mr. Hickory Bompers as a possible source of revenue?'

Anthony nodded, and then asked:

'How did you know that Mr. Hickory Bompers was a teacher of the art of film acting?'

Paul smiled.

'You can hardly escape that knowledge,' he said. 'His advertisements are in all the newspapers; his placards decorate the tube lifts.'

'And he himself is a conspicuous figure in Bayswater circles,' added Anthony.

'Who is he?'

'He's an ex-convict named Griggs,' was the surprising reply. 'Apparently the police don't know this, but I found it out by a curious accident.'

He did not explain what that curious accident was. His was one of those restless natures which was for ever inquiring, inquiring, inquiring. He was on terms of acquaintance with most of the minor crooks of London, though they were ignorant of his identity, and it is probable that he learnt this fact from them. There is a certain type of criminal who is loyalty itself, especially to men of the higher grade working in gangs, and it was quite understandable that Mr. Griggs could continue his services to the cinematic art without incurring that suspicion of the police which is only aroused when direct information is laid.

'Is he going straight?' asked Paul.

'Could Griggs go straight?' smiled Anthony. 'No, he's not that kind; he's just a shifty swindler who's hit upon a method of fleecing a lot of poor gullible girls.'

'What does he do? Does he make much?'

'I haven't troubled to find out about his charges, but he professes to teach film acting by post, and from what I can smell, he's pulling in quite a lot of money. Too much money,' he added, significantly. 'So if you'll dress yourself up as simply as possible, we'll make a call on Hickory Bompers this afternoon, and ask him his terms for personal tuition.'

Mr. Hickory Bompers occupied a large unimposing house in Elgin Crescent: in the meagre front garden was a large blackboard inscribed in gold letters: 'The Hickory Bompers Academy of Cinematography.'

The interior was flamboyantly decorated. The furniture was sparse and of the kind which can be rented fairly cheaply. Mr. Hickory Bompers did not profess to live upon the premises, and his 'Academy' was an academy and nothing else. Therefore it was not surprising that the large room into which they were ushered by a boy in buttons was almost innocent of any type of furniture. The floor was covered with good linoleum and the big yellow folding doors which separated the front room from the back were heavily curtained with violet velvet.

A girl came in and took their names.

'Have you an appointment with Mr. Hickory Bompers?' she said in a tone of awe, as though the name itself struck terror to her soul.

'We haven't an appointment,' said Anthony, 'but we are most anxious to interview him.'

The girl disappeared, and came back after five minutes.

'Mr. Hickory Bompers will see you,' she said, and suggested by her tone that a most unusual honour was being paid to them.

Anthony did not doubt that Mr. Hickory Bompers would see them. He knew that a man of his character did not readily turn away clients with money, and when he was shown into the comfortable bureau where the great man himself sat behind a rosewood desk smoking a large cigar, he had but to take one view of his face to realise that Mr. Hickory Bompers had an eye to the main chance.

A stoutish man, florid of face, his head innocent of hair, he smiled genially and waved a fat hand to a well-upholstered settee by the window.

'Sit down, gentlemen, sit down,' he said, with boisterous good humour. 'You're in luck to get me at an unoccupied moment. Now what can I do for you?'

'My friend and I wish to learn film acting,' said Anthony.

'By post?' asked the other.

'No, not by post,' said Anthony, after a momentary pause. 'You see, we're not satisfied that it can be taught by post.'

'Nonsense,' said Mr. Hickory Bompers, bluffly. 'I can teach you expression, I can teach you how to carry yourself, how to walk, I can teach you all the technicalities of film acting just as well by post as I can *viva voce*. Of course,' he added, 'personal tuition is better for a man who has serious intentions of taking up the cinematographic profession, but naturally,' he coughed, 'that costs considerably more.'

He was looking at them with an appraising eye, evidently

summing them up and discussing within himself the amount they could afford to pay.

'We should prefer the personal tuition,' said Anthony.

'Very good,' replied Mr. Hickory Bompers, opening the drawer of his desk and taking out a book of forms. 'I'll write your name. The cost will be fifty guineas each for the course, payable in advance.'

Now despite his air of confidence, The Mixer, who was a very keen student of men, detected certain signs of nervousness in this jovial soul, and wondered what his trouble was.

'We haven't brought any money with us,' he said, 'but of course we'll bring it when we begin our lessons.'

'That will be a hundred and five pounds in all,' said Mr. Hickory Bompers. 'I prefer payment by cash, by the way, rather than by cheque.'

Anthony nodded.

'What is today?' he asked.

'It's Monday,' replied Mr. Hickory Bompers.

'Well, I'll come on Thursday.'

'Not Thursday,' said the other quickly, 'that would be too late—I mean,' he corrected himself in some confusion, 'that would not suit me.'

'I see,' said Anthony, quietly.

'In fact'—Mr. Hickory Bompers's voice was loud and almost defiant—'I have a very important engagement——'

And here an interruption came. The door opened without any preliminary knock, and a man came in. He was a tall, rough-faced man, who stood for a moment scowling at the visitors and then walked slowly across the room to where Hickory Bompers was sitting.

Mr. Bompers's face lost its genial aspect.

'Well?' he asked, shortly.

'I want to see you,' growled the man.

He was well dressed, but the clothes somehow did not suit the wearer.

'Excuse me, gentlemen,' said Mr. Hickory Bompers hastily, and left the room with the visitor.

Anthony winked at his secretary.

'Thursday will be too late,' he said, significantly. 'I thought as much.'

'What's the idea?' whispered Paul.

'Wait till his nibs comes back, and we'll learn.'

His nibs did not return for five minutes, and then when he did come in he was profusely apologetic.

'Will you make it Wednesday, gentlemen,' he said, 'and don't forget—bring cash. Cheques are no use to me; I have a rooted objection to them.'

'There's one thing I wanted to say,' said Anthony, gently. 'My friend here'—he indicated the astonished Paul—'has written a film scenario, and that is exactly the reason why we want these lessons. We are going to perform in our own rough and ready studio, and we wanted you to put us through a rehearsal.'

'Certainly, certainly,' said Mr. Hickory Bompers, hurriedly. 'Good afternoon, gentlemen.'

They passed the rough-looking gentleman waiting in the passage, and he growled a 'Good afternoon' that was less a pleasant greeting because the scowl had not left his face.

'A strange house,' said Anthony, as they went down the steps and into Elgin Crescent.

They had taken only a few paces when they saw a man crossing the road to meet them, and he was unmistakably a plain-clothes policeman.

'Excuse me, gentlemen,' he said, instinctively choosing Anthony as the leading spirit, 'can I have a word with you?'

'You can have six, my son,' said Anthony, as the man fell in by their side and walked towards Colville Square.

'Are you new clients of Mr. Hickory Bompers?'

'We are,' said Anthony.

'Have you parted with any money?'

'Not yet.'

'Well, take my advice and don't,' said the stranger.

'What's the trouble?' asked Anthony. 'You're a police officer, aren't you?'

The other assented.

'There have been several complaints about this man,' he said. 'People have written in from the country saying that his correspondence course is a swindle—it teaches them nothing, and a few innocents who have taken personal lessons have come away disgusted.'

'Well, I've parted with no money,' said Anthony, 'and it's extremely unlikely that I will.'

He went back to his Kensington home, very silent, as was usual with him on such occasions.

It was not until after dinner, when they were smoking peacefully, that he introduced the subject of Mr. Hickory Bompers.

'Thursday will be too late! Do you know what that means, Paul?'

'It looks to me,' said Paul, 'as though he's going to disappear.'

Anthony nodded.

'To be vulgar but truthful, somebody's blown the gaff,' he said, 'and the tough-looking lad who interrupted our séance with Mr. Hickory Bompers had probably discovered that the house was under police observation and came to tell his partner——'

'Why should he be his partner?'

'He must be a partner. A man like Mr. Hickory Bompers, or Griggs, would not give his confidence to an employee. They're both in this, and both are making a getaway before the police net closes on them.'

'When do you think?'

'On Wednesday night,' replied Anthony, 'Thursday will be too late.'

He spent the next day making inquiries, and all that the police officer told him was confirmed. The most informative visit was the one which he made on the editor of a popular weekly which made a speciality of checking and exposing frauds.

'Hickory Bompers,' said that person with a short laugh, 'yes, he's a fake teacher of film acting. We get half a dozen letters a week from poor deluded girls who have parted with their hard-earned cash, and I have an idea that the police intend instituting a prosecution.'

'But the scheme looks reasonable enough,' said Anthony.

'It is the old, old instance of a crook without knowledge running a business which, in the hands of an expert, could be made into a paying proposition,' returned the other. 'There are hundreds of crook businesses which could be run straight and yield a fortune. These frauds occur because it must have the incentive which only excursions out of the law can give to that peculiar mentality.'

The next morning, at breakfast, Paul put a question which had been worrying him.

'I say,' he said. 'I don't understand that tale you told this fellow about my writing a film scenario. I haven't written a scenario.'

'I've written it for you,' said Anthony. 'It's a wonderfully thrilling drama in one scene.'

'But surely,' demurred Paul, 'a scenario consists of about a hundred and eighty scenes, doesn't it?'

'Not my scenario,' returned Anthony.

He had given Mr. Hickory Bompers his telephone number, and early on the Wednesday morning he received a phone call from that gentleman.

'Mr. Smith?' asked Bompers.

'That's me,' said Anthony.

'About your appointment this afternoon—I gave it to you for four o'clock ; could you possibly come at three?'

'We'll be there,' replied Anthony.

'And don't forget—bring cash.'

'Oh yes,' answered Anthony, grinning. 'I'll bring banknotes, I suppose that'll be all right?'

'Quite all right,' was the hearty reply.

'By the way,' said Anthony, 'I want you to give us an illustration of how one particular scene should be played. Have you a man assistant who could help you?'

'Oh yes,' was the quick reply. 'Don't you worry about that.'

Anthony hung up the telephone and walked slowly into the drawing-room where Paul was playing patience. He looked around the pleasant apartment and sighed.

'I get a bit tired of this continuous moving in and out, round and about,' he said.

'Are we giving up this delightful mansion?' asked Paul, pausing in his game. 'I was hoping that we could last out for another three months without starting somebody in pursuit of you.'

'It was not to be,' answered Anthony. 'You'll have to go round and forage out a furnished flat, preferably in the north of London. There are some nice flats in Finchley. Pay any amount.'

'What am I?' asked Paul, resignedly.

'You're a tea-planter from Ceylon, and you're meeting your brother from South America. Your brother will have a valet with him, and together you are going to take a flat. A service flat for preference, Paul,' he went on, his methodical mind visualising the new change. 'We don't want staff or the bother of housekeeping.'

Paul went.

In the afternoon they drove to Elgin Crescent, keeping a sharp look-out for the officer who had been on duty watching the house. To their surprise he was not in sight. An ominous sign, thought The Mixer. Nevertheless, he mounted the steps carrying a suitcase in his hand, Paul following him with great solemnity, two large swords tucked under his arm. They had the appearance of people who were going to assume some costume for the purpose of making a film, and so the watcher thought, as he observed them from a window in the house opposite.

The rough-looking man opened the door to them. The button boy had been dismissed, thought Anthony.

'What have you got there?' growled Mr. Tinkle (they discovered that such was his name).

'This is for the play: we want to dress for the part. It will give us a little extra confidence,' said Anthony.

Mr. Tinkle muttered something under his breath, and showed them into the cheerless front room.

Anthony had noticed when he came up the steps that the windows were shuttered. Mr. Tinkle explained why when he switched on the light.

'When we give a rehearsal we have to shut those windows, or we'd have half the town staring through. Mr. Hickory Bompers wants to see you, I think,' he added.

Anthony nodded and took from his pocket a bundle of banknotes.'

'I'll go in and see him.'

Mr. Hickory Bompers was glad to see him. Anthony, casting a quick glance round the room, saw that a suitcase stood ready packed; a second suitcase stood open and was almost empty. Behind Mr. Hickory Bompers's chair was a big safe, the keys of which were in the lock.

'Good afternoon,' said Mr. Hickory Bompers, with less heartiness than usual. 'Have you brought the money?'

Anthony laid the banknotes on the table.

'A hundred and ten pounds,' said Mr. Hickory Bompers with satisfaction. 'You'll want some change. I'll give you that after.'

'I'd rather have it now,' said Anthony, 'that'll save me bothering you.'

The man hesitated, then opened the safe and took out a large wooden box. This he opened, and Anthony saw that it was stuffed full of money.

Mr. Hickory Bompers gave him his change, and they went back to the drawing-room, where Paul and Mr. Tinkle were waiting.

'Now this drama,' said Anthony, producing a manuscript, 'deals with the death of two convicts who are overcome by gas when they are making their escape along a sewer. What my friend and I can't get,' he said, 'is the facial expression of two men chained together, hating one another, yet obliged to go on.'

'H'm,' said Mr. Hickory Bompers, dubiously. 'All right; get on with it.'

'Now,' said Anthony, 'you stand over there.'

He took a pair of handcuffs from his pocket.

'Remember you're chained together. That's an essential poin in the story.'

'Can't you do without that?' growled Tinkle.

'Can't possibly do without that. We want to see just hov you'd strain away from each other. You quite understand, Mr Bompers?'

'All right,' said Bompers, with a grin. 'It isn't much for a hundred and five pounds.'

'But we're having other lessons, aren't we?' asked the in nocent Paul.

'Of course you are,' said the other, hastily. 'Your next lessor will be on Saturday. Come on, Tinkle; let's get on with this.'

The two men submitted to the handcuffs being snapped, s that one's wrist was fastened to the other's, though Mr. Tinkle' frown deepened, and he looked uneasy as he felt the cold iro on his wrist.

'Now,' said Anthony, 'I want you, Paul, to stand behin them.'

Paul obeyed, but Anthony gave no further directions; Paul with a rapid twist of his hand, slipped a rope across the con necting links of the handcuffs, knotted it tight, flung the loos ends over the top of the open door and pulled.

'What the hell are you doing?' roared Mr. Bompers. He trie to push forward, but his arm was jerked up by the rope, whic Paul was pulling taut, so that the two men's hands wer stretched up to the top of the door.

'Be sensible,' said Anthony, coolly, and toyed with an autc matic.

'What's the meaning of this?' asked Bompers, his face white.

'It means that we have anticipated the police by a few hours returned Anthony, and watched Paul as he tied the ends of th rope firmly round the knob on the other side of the door. 'I that rope is secure, Paul—I'll see they don't tug too hard a it—be good enough to take the keys out of that gentleman pocket—they're in his waistcoat.'

With his disengaged hand Bompers struck out wildly, bu before he could realise what had happened his arm was caugl and twisted until he yelled. Paul said little, but he could b very prompt in action.

'Here are the keys,' he said, taking them out of Mr. Bompers pocket.

'The money is in a box,' said Anthony. 'I don't know ho much it is, but it looks a lot.'

'You swine!' yelled Tinkle. 'You sneaking dog! Let me get way from this and I'll break your neck!'

'The police will release you when they come,' said Anthony, uietly, 'and I'd advise you both to cultivate the philosophical pirit which is so essential to men who are looking forward to a ong prison sentence. If you give me away nobody will believe ou or sympathise with you.'

'You're The Mixer!' screamed Hickory Bompers. 'That's who ou are. You're the fellow who robs——' He stopped.

'Honest men,' murmured Anthony. 'Say it; you might as ell say it as think it.'

Paul was back now with the box, the contents of which nthony began to transfer to his own and his secretary's ockets.

'We must leave a little for the police to find,' he said. 'If they nd nothing they'll think we're hogs.'

They passed into the passage, leaving two wailing, cursing en behind them, Paul picked up swords and suitcase, and gether they went down the steps towards the waiting cab.

'Drive to Waterloo—fast,' ordered Anthony, as he jumped to the cab. He looked through the rear window of the cab. hat's a police car coming. If they spot us they'll detain us as itnesses, and that will be tragically fatal. Why the dickens oesn't this lazy devil move?'

It seemed an eternity before the taxi whined forward, and had scarcely moved before the car which Anthony had seen ulled up with a jerk and disgorged half-a-dozen plain-clothes en.

Anthony watched them till his car turned the corner of Ladroke Grove and then he sank back with a sigh of relief.

Paul was scribbling notes on the back of an envelope as well s the jerky cab would permit him.

'What are you doing?' asked Anthony, curiously.

'I'm writing a plot, a really good story.'

'Why?'

'I've got a great idea out of this for a film scenario,' said aul with unusual enthusiasm.

Anthony grinned.

'Wait till Hickory Bompers comes out of quod and ask him produce it for you,' he said.

17: The Billiter Bank Smash

It was whilst The Mixer was still living in the small Kensington square that he came home one day with a glum face and threw an evening paper on the sofa of the sitting-room.

'Billiter's Bank has bust,' he said.

'Billiter's Bank?' repeated Paul, looking up in surprise. 'Does that affect you?'

'It affects a great many poor people,' returned Anthony. 'Of course it doesn't affect me. I'm not the sort of person to trust my money to private bankers, especially a fellow with a face like Billiter's.'

'I've never seen his face,' said Paul, interestedly. 'Is it pretty bad?'

'He looks too good to be true,' replied Anthony, epigrammatically. 'Anyway, his bank has bust!'

'What has happened to Billiter?'

'He has vanished like smoke in the air.'

'Taking the liquid assets of the bank, I presume?' asked Paul, and Anthony nodded.

'Yes, he's been gone two days; in fact, it was his absence from the office which first caused alarm and despondency amongst the senior staff. They made investigations, and they found that the vault had been cleared of all currency and apparently Billiter had for the past week been raising money on every security the bank had.'

'Humph! I suppose his nibs is on his way to South America by now?'

'Not he,' said The Mixer, emphatically. 'He's not that kind of man. I only met him once at a City dinner; an oleaginous gentleman who was always smiling. I mistrust those people who are always smiling; they must have a rotten past.'

'Your moralising is always interesting,' murmured Paul. 'What's the exact position?'

'The exact position,' said Anthony, 'is that Mr. Billiter has got away with about eighty thousand pounds, his bank and all the little branches, have suspended payment, and when things are evened up the poor chaps who banked there will probably be paid about three farthings in the pound.'

'Poor devils! Will they catch Billiter?'

'I tell you that fellow is a pretty shrewd bird,' rejoined Anthony. 'He struck me so at the time, and he is the kind of man who would make the most elaborate preparations for a getaway. That's why I say he's not gone to South America, because that's one of the most obvious resorts for absconding bank proprietors, and you may be certain that they've been checking pretty thoroughly. In these days it isn't so jolly easy for a suspect to get away from the British Isles and it's even more difficult for him to get his money away.'

'And you intend to search for him yourself?' queried Paul.

'I certainly intend to find him if I can. It's the least I can do for the poor folk he's robbed. I'm the richest robber in Britain, and I can afford a little of my time and money for a good cause. Eighty thousand pounds isn't a big deficit,' he went on, 'but it's probably only the beginning. When they come to sift the affairs of the bank they may be short a few millions.'

And so it proved, for the next day an authoritative announcement was made that 'so far as could be ascertained' the deficits in Billiter's bank totalled more than a million pounds. The police were searching and they had innumerable clues. The ports and airports were being watched, every great terminus in the country was under constant inspection, but Mr. Josiah Billiter had vanished from the face of the earth as though he had dissolved into the ether. The reports in the newspapers were tantalisingly meagre, and on the fourth day Anthony made a call at Mr. Billiter's expensive flat in Mayfair and interviewed his late housekeeper, a doleful woman.

'Have you come from the police,' she asked, 'or the press?'

'Neither.' Anthony smiled at the antagonistic note in her voice. 'I am one of that small and select circle of people who believe that Mr. Billiter is wrongly accused and that he has fallen into bad hands.'

He had noted one or two paragraphs in the newspapers and particularly had he fixed upon a brief interview which the housekeeper had given to the representative of the *Morning Star*. This had been the theory she had advanced, and on this theory and its exploitation Anthony intended to get into the confidence of the lady. It worked like magic.

'Will you come in, sir?' she said, and led the way through a broad hall to a well-furnished dining-room.

'Perhaps you can tell me when you saw Mr. Billiter last?'

'I saw him on the night before he disappeared,' said the woman, whose name was Mudge. 'He said good night to me, and in the morning I hadn't the slightest idea that anything was wrong until I went to his bedroom with a cup of tea. Then I found the room was empty and the bed hadn't been slept in. I didn't think much of that. because Mr. Billiter was in the habit of going away, though he was very regular as to when he went. He usually left town on Friday morning and came back on the following Monday night.'

'How long had he been doing that?' asked Anthony.

'Oh, for years and years,' replied the woman.

She looked round.

'There is a mystery here, sir,' she said, lowering her voice. 'And I'm going to show you something I found which I didn't show to the police.'

She came back, bearing in her hands a queer-looking box, the top and sides of which were covered with porcupine quills.

'They think they're clever,' the poor old lady tried to sneer, but failed dismally, 'but they weren't clever enough to spot this.'

'Where did you find it?'

'I found it at the back of Mr. Billiter's bureau,' she said, and opened the box.

It was crowded with a miscellaneous and extraordinary collection of articles, and when The Mixer saw the interior he gasped. There were babies' rattles and dummies, there were nurses' caps, little woollen socks, bone rings, and to each was attached a tiny ticket bearing a price.

'Samples,' thought Anthony.

Now why did a banker interest himself in such domestic matters as the provision of babies' etceteras?

'Was Mr. Billiter married?' he asked.

The woman shook her head.

'No, sir. I'm sure he wasn't. I've often heard him say how glad he was that he was a bachelor.'

'Strange! These are all new.'

He looked in vain for the makers' marks. Obviously they came from several firms, because the private markings and the handwritings on the tickets were different. He turned the box out and made a thorough search, but there was no further evidence to connect Mr. Billiter with a love child and Anthony went home that night considerably puzzled. The next morning he got in touch with the auditor who had been appointed by the bank. That gentleman was, to say the least, reticent, but he gave this information, that the bank had no business association with any firm which supplied 'baby goods'.

'That polishes off theory number one,' said Anthony. 'A great many of these banks have some connection with industries and

I thought it possible that the bank may have discounted a bill for such a firm.'

'And may I ask,' said Paul, 'if you think that finding Josiah Billiter will find the money he has taken and if so, do you intend to annex it as usual?'

'Not as usual. This is one of the special cases wherein I do real philanthropic work. The people who are suffering from this failure are the very people who can't afford to suffer. If I can get the money back from old man Billiter, why, I'll be the happiest brigand in the world.'

'I very much hope you get it back,' said Paul. It was the kind of exploit he liked.

The Mixer did some pretty hard thinking. It looked to him as though the saintly Billiter had been leading a double life. Possibly he had raised a family of children, and that would explain his absence from London during the week-ends. But as against this, it was extremely unlikely that he would have so many children that he bought his dummies and rattles at wholesale prices.

'In spite of what you say,' said Paul, regretfully, 'I should imagine he is half-way to Rio de Janeiro by now.'

'I tell you he hasn't left the country,' said Anthony, 'and I have an idea that these rattles and dummies are going to lead me to him.'

The only further information he had secured from Mrs. Mudge was that the station to which Josiah Billiter invariably drove on Friday afternoon was Victoria, and she knew that it was on the Brighton section of Victoria that he had travelled, because on one occasion he had told her that his train had been held up at Three Bridges and Mrs. Mudge, who came from Horsham, knew this part of the country. So wherever Josiah was lay within a triangle, one angle of which rested on Three Bridges, one on Eastbourne and the other at Hove.

'A pretty extensive area to search,' commented Paul, and Anthony agreed.

Apparently the police had a theory which was not very different from the one held by The Mixer, namely, that Mr. Billiter had a large family somewhere in the background.

'The only thing that is absolutely certain,' said Anthony, 'is that he was living a double life of some kind.'

'There is only one kind of double life,' said Paul primly.

'I wish you meant it,' said Anthony. 'No, my theory lies in another direction.'

He spent the whole of two days in a room of the British

Museum searching the files of newspapers which devote space to charitable appeals. Such was his lack of faith in Mr. Billiter's humanity that he could not imagine that this stout and jovial man could be interested even in babies unless there was money behind it. And at last he made a discovery.

Eight years before there had been an appeal for the Alfriston Baby Colony, an appeal couched in the most tender and touching language. From time to time the names of subscribers to this admirable charity were printed, and on two occasions the name of Mr. Billiter appeared against a subscription of one hundred guineas.

Moreover, Anthony noticed that this magnificent donation invariably came when the subscriptions were falling off. It seemed as though it were designed to give a fillip to a lagging charity. He went back home and told Paul the news.

'When you come to think of it,' he added, after he had finished, 'it wouldn't be a bad scheme, for the last place in the world that the police would search or indeed expect to find Mr. Billiter would be a home for abandoned babies!'

'Some babies!' said Paul.

But Anthony's investigations received a check. He came back to the house the next night extremely serious.

'Paul,' he said, 'there's trouble.'

'What is it?' asked Paul.

'Whilst I've been looking for Mr. Billiter, some old friends of mine have been looking for me. The gentleman who taught film acting must have talked to the detectives who pinched him, for I have been watched all the afternoon, and my car has been the particular object of the watcher's curiosity.'

'The car?' asked Paul, quickly.

The Mixer owned a big grey racing car which had served him in good stead, but hitherto it had not been associated with the name of The Mixer.

'That means I have to abandon the car,' said Anthony, 'but before I do, we'll make a call upon this institute at Alfriston.'

They drove down through the lovely Weald of Sussex and passed through Alfriston. This picturesque little village lies away from the railway, and the last person whom Anthony expected to see was the quiet-looking man who had made such tender inquiries at the garage about the car he was now driving.

It may have been a coincidence that he was at Alfriston standing outside the very house in which King Alfred burnt his cakes, or he may have made inquiries at the house in Kensington and learnt of their destination, for Anthony had not warned Sandy to keep it quiet.

'H'm,' said Anthony, and frowned, for he observed that the quiet-looking man was not alone and that he had raised his hand to arrest the progress of the car.

That signal Anthony pretended not to see. He drove on until he came to the institute.

The home was a handsome building of red brick, standing about a mile from the village on the Seaford Road. It looked more like a gentleman's residence with its beautiful gardens and its well-timbered grounds than a place of refuge for innocent childhood.

A trim, neatly-uniformed maid answered Anthony's knock.

'Yes, sir,' she said. 'This is the children's colony. Would you like to see the matron?'

The matron was forthcoming, a stout, somewhat formidable lady in black silk, who regarded the new-comers with disfavour when she found they had come empty-handed.

'We only know Mr. Billiter by repute,' she said. 'He has most generously subscribed to our home, but we have never seen him here.'

This was a facer for Anthony, because she was evidently speaking the truth.

'Would you like to see the institute?' she asked, and to the other's surprise Anthony accepted the invitation.

It was not an uninteresting tour they made through the bright dormitories where children of all ages from a few months to a few years were sleeping or playing.

'How many babies have you here?' asked Anthony.

She told him there were thirty.

'Then this is all?' he said in surprise, indicating the large dormitory they had left.

'Yes, this is all,' she assented.

'But haven't you any rooms upstairs?'

'Oh yes,' she smiled, 'but they are occupied by the staff, by the nurses, myself, and of course Mr. Worthington, the superintendent and secretary.'

'Could I see him?'

'I'm afraid not,' she replied. 'Unfortunately he's suffering from a painful affliction of the eyes which makes it necessary for him to remain in a dark room. But I'll ask him if he will talk to you.'

She disappeared up the stairs and came back in a few moments.

'Have you any intention of leaving a child here?' she asked.

'Yes,' said Anthony, coolly, and indicated the shocked Paul. 'My friend here has a little baby he wants to deposit.'

'Then I think he will see you,' said the woman and led the way up the stairs.

The room in which the superintendent, Mr. Worthington, was lying, was very dark indeed, for the condition of his eyes apparently made it necessary that every blind should be drawn. He was lying in an arm-chair when they came in, a man muffled to the chin, his eyes hidden behind big blue goggles.

'Excuse me, gentlemen,' he said, 'if I do not rise to meet you. Is there anything you want that I can do?'

'I wish to speak to you privately,' said Anthony, and the matron withdrew.

'Well?' asked Mr. Worthington.

'You asked me if there is anything you can do, and I am going to tell you something,' said Anthony. 'You can restore all the money you have taken from the bank which had the misfortune to have you as managing director. You can also put the money you have collected for this home into the hands of trustees who will administer those subscriptions much better than you have done, and as an act of grace to you, I will allow you twenty-four hours to clear out of England.'

Mr. Worthington did not reply. He sat straight and tense, and now that their eyes were becoming accustomed to the darkness they could see the twisted smile upon his face.

'That is a wonderful suggestion,' he said, softly. 'Now suppose——'

'Suppose you keep your hand out of your pocket,' said Anthony, sternly, 'and suppose you strain those weak eyes of yours and take a good long look at my right digits, which at this moment are handling an instrument known as a Browning.'

Mr. Billiter muttered something under his breath.

'Go downstairs,' he said. 'I'll join you in a few minutes.'

'And no monkeying,' warned Anthony.

'I know when I'm beaten,' said Mr. Billiter. 'And to think that for twelve months I have been wandering about in this part of the world with a stick and a pair of blue glasses! You're police, I suppose?—no, you're not,' he added, quickly, 'or you wouldn't let me go. Who are you?'

'I am one of the forty thieves,' said Anthony, pleasantly.

He went down the stairs with Paul, and they waited in the hall. They waited five, and then ten, and then fifteen minutes, when they heard the faint whirr of a car, and ran to the front of the house in time to see the back of their car vanish in a cloud of dust.

'Hard cheese!' said The Mixer. 'I don't think he'll get much farther than the village.'

'Why not?' asked Paul.

'Because there are two Scotland Yard men waiting in Alfriston to interview the driver of the grey car, and though they may know nothing against us, they'll recognise Billiter. This is where we do some mighty quick walking,' said Anthony.

18: The Spanish Prisoner

Walking one Sunday afternoon towards Barnet, and taking a short cut through a broad suburban road, The Mixer broke the rule of silence which governed himself and his secretary in their walks in public.

He stopped suddenly, his eyes lit up and Paul groaned inwardly, seeing what he had found.

'Look at it!' said Anthony, ecstatically.

He was staring at a corner house with a large board erected in the garden to announce that it was 'To Let'.

'It's very dilapidated and miserable-looking, with an ill-kept desolation of a garden, and the architecture hurts me,' complained Paul.

It was certainly not a beautiful house. Wind and weather had discoloured its whitened walls, the barred windows on the ground floor gave it the appearance of a prison, and it looked as miserable as long neglect and unoccupation can make even the most stately of mansions—and this was not a stately mansion, by any means.

'The very house,' said Anthony in an awed voice. 'The very house!'

'Are you thinking of starting a lunatic asylum?' asked Paul, politely, and Anthony grinned.

'That is exactly what I am thinking about,' he said. 'What is it called?'

He went nearer and read the name of the house painted in faded letters upon the sagging gate-post.

'Depe Dene,' he said. 'How lovely!'

He pulled out a note-book and made a note of the agent's name, then resumed his stroll.

'If you take that house I hope you'll arrange to let me live out,' said Paul. 'I really don't feel that I could be of any assistance to you in any scheme which will bring me into that awful barrack.'

'Oh yes, you will,' returned Anthony, confidently, 'indeed you will.'

He declined to discuss the matter any further until they had returned home for tea, and even then his references to the house were oblique and mysterious.

He was dining that night at the Café du Palais in Regent Street, to meet one of those remarkable characters whom he had picked up in his travels. This was Señor Maura, chief of the twelfth bureau of Criminal Intelligence of Madrid.

Anthony had met Señor Maura during his sojourn in Spain, and the visit of the Spaniard to London in connection with an extradition case had given him the opportunity of renewing the acquaintance.

It was a cheerful meal, because Maura had a fund of stories and a remarkable sense of humour. Towards the end of dinner:

'By the way, Señor Maura,' said Anthony, 'I've had a letter from the Spanish prisoner.'

'The Spanish prisoner?' said Señor Maura, and then his face brightened, and he smiled. 'Oh yes, I know who you mean; the gentleman who writes to the unsophisticated Britishers telling them that he is in gaol for robbery, and that the proceeds of that robbery are buried somewhere, and if the dupe will send the prisoner—who, by the way, usually gets an address which is well outside the walls of the prison—a certain sum of money he shall participate in a share of the buried treasure.'

'That's right. He sent the offer to me. I have often wondered what type of criminal works that swindle. He can't make much money out of it. People aren't such fools as to send cash.'

'That's where you're wrong,' said Señor Maura quietly. 'The Malejala gang make an enormous income.'

'A gang?' said Anthony in amazement. 'But I thought the swindle was worked by individuals.'

'It is worked by Malejala, who is the cleverest criminal we have in Spain, and a man whom we have never been able to trap. He is at the head of a big organisation, and covers his tracks so well that although we frequently capture his assistants, we have never yet got a case against him. It is Malejala—who was educated in England by the way—who writes these letters, and you have no idea of the number of people, actuated by cupidity, as well as being bemused by crass stupidity, who send money in order to recover these mythical buried monies.'

Anthony's eyes were dancing.

'What will you give me if I capture Malejala?' he asked.

Maura laughed.

'There is a secret reward of twenty thousand pesetas for the man who exposes Malejala,' he replied, shaking his head, 'but I very much doubt whether it will ever be claimed. Malejala is diabolically cunning. How did they get your name?' he asked.

'As a matter of fact,' said Anthony, frankly, 'it was not addressed to me. The letter was addressed to the man whose flat I have taken, and I opened it by the sheerest accident.'

He spoke no more than the truth. He was scrupulous in such small matters as the personal correspondence of those people whose houses or flats he rented.

'Sunning, that's my landlord, is a shareholder in one or two speculative companies, and I think that your Mr. Malejala makes a systematic search for shareholders in wild duck schemes to try his plan upon.'

'Yes,' Maura went on after a while, 'Malejala makes quite a comfortable income—as a matter of fact he's a frequent visitor to London and spends money lavishly. Moreover, he keeps his banking account with a London bank, which has a branch office in Madrid, so that even if we caught him we could never get the proceeds of his robberies.'

'Does he speak English?'

'Perfectly,' replied the other, and with a courteous little nod, 'as well as you speak Spanish.'

'*Muchas gracias, señor*,' murmured Anthony.

. . . . .

As he had not again mentioned the gaunt house which had excited his admiration on the Sunday afternoon, Paul thought the matter had dropped from his mind. He was annoyed and dismayed when, on Wednesday, Anthony came into their flat flourishing a paper.

'I've taken a house for twelve months,' he announced.

'What house?' asked Paul, apprehensively.

'Depe Dene,' he replied.

Paul groaned.

'I'm awfully subject to rheumatism,' he complained, 'and I——'

'Paul,' interrupted Anthony, thoughtfully, 'I wonder how you would look in a blue dress with a large straw hat.'
'What's the idea?' asked Paul, suspiciously.
'I will explain in as few words as possible,' said The Mixer.

. . . . .

The Señor Malejala had a handsome apartment in the Calle Recelletos. He lived expensively, went everywhere, had a car of his own and although he was not admitted to the best circles, he compensated for that disability by admitting himself from time to time, with disastrous results to the circles upon whose sacred domains he intruded.

He was a regular patron of the Opera and never missed a race meeting at the Hippodrome, and although he knew his comings and goings were watched by an unsympathetic constabulary, the fact did not disturb his sleep at night nor interfere with his enormous appetite.

He had a small office overlooking the Puerta del Sol, where ostensibly he carried on the business of a cork merchant.

To him from day to day came mysterious people who reported the progress of business which had nothing whatever to do with cork trees or their exploitations.

One such came on a hot morning of June, when the street cleaners were flooding the red-hot asphalt of the Puerta del Sol with water that steamed as it fell. This man closed the door behind him and produced from the lining of his hat three letters. The Señor opened and read them, biting thoughtfully at the end of a long thin cigar, pocketed the money two of them contained, and read the third letter again.

The address was 'Depe Dene, Finchley, London', and the letter ran:

Dear Sir,

I have received your moving appeal and I should be most happy to invest a thousand pounds in your scheme for recovering the gold which is buried in Malaga. Though I have some scruples as to whether I should participate in what is evidently stolen property, yet I feel I may put the money to a good purpose——

Señor Malejala smiled. Most of his victims had their own excuses for compounding a felony.

I have no cheque book as my uncle, Colonel Sunning, has taken it from me. I am in the unhappy position of being an heiress with very large sums of money at my disposal in the bank, but for the time being I am under the domination of Colonel Sunning, who keeps me locked up in this awful house until I promise to marry his son, my cousin Felix. He swears that if I do not marry Felix he will say I am mad and get me locked up in a lunatic asylum. Oh, Señor, I hate my cousin Felix! If I could once get out of this place I would put an end to this terrible plot. But although I have offered Colonel Sunning's servant a hundred thousand pounds to assist me in getting away, he is so afraid of the Colonel that he refuses. If I can get a cheque I will send it on to you. If you could by any chance smuggle a cheque to me, I would sign it. You probably know my name. I inherited Sir Veille Mortimer's estate two years ago.

The letter was signed Mary Mortimer. Señor Malejala read it again. He was a methodical, careful man, and within a quarter of an hour he had turned up the files of the English papers and had traced the will of Sir Veille Mortimer. Yes, there it was. The whole of his estate was left to his daughter Mary. There was a headline in the newspaper, a reference to her wealth, and that she was one of the richest heiresses in England—sufficient to make Señor Malejala concentrate his attention upon what might be the greatest coup of his life.

Malejala considered the matter for two days, and at the end of the second day he left Madrid for Paris and arrived in London on a Saturday morning.

Señor Maura, that able officer of police, met his compatriot in Piccadilly and greeted him in that friendly way which police officers have when they deal with the clever men whom it is their business to bring to justice.

'*Buenos dias, Señor Malejala.* What are you doing in London?' asked Maura.

'I have come over to see some friends,' replied Malejala. 'It is a great pleasure to see you, Señor Maura. What good times the criminals in Madrid must be having now that you have left the capital!'

'Some of them have left also,' said Señor Maura, significantly.

The other shrugged.

'It will be little less than a national calamity when you die, Señor Maura,' he said 'O pray the saints that I may never be the cause of plunging our beloved Spain into mourning!'

'And I,' responded Maura, 'pray as fervently that I may

never have to experience the horror of seeing you sit in a chair with the sharp point of the garrotte piercing your neck.'

And with these mutual felicitations they parted. Señor Malejala to pursue his peaceful way to Finchley.

He found Depe Dene without difficulty. It was a gaunt, ugly house, enclosed by a garden of singular rankness, and even as he strolled past he saw a female figure at an upper window. In his enthusiasm he waved his hand to her, and with a dramatic start she stepped back out of sight.

Señor Malejala was a bold man. He believed in taking the bull by the horns, and without hesitation he passed through the creaking gate, along a weed-grown path, to the front door, and rang the bell.

A severe-looking footman answered him. One glance at the interior told the Spaniard that the house was in a state of the greatest dilapidation.

'Does Colonel Sunning live here?' asked Malejala, carelessly.

'Yes, sir,' replied the footman.

'Is he in?'

'No, sir, he is at Newmarket today.'

'I see,' said Señor Malejala, and slipped a five-pound note into the servant's hand.

'I should like to have a few words with Miss Mary,' he said.

'Miss Mary Mortimer?' answered the other quickly, and shook his head. 'I'm afraid I can't let you see her. She's not very well, sir. Are you from the Bank?'

'No,' said Señor Malejala. 'What makes you think I am from the Bank?'

The servant looked uncomfortable.

'Well, sir,' he said, after a moment's hesitation, 'the young lady told the Colonel she had written to the bank for a new cheque-book, and as the Colonel had written only a day or two before, he thought there might be some inquiries.'

The heart of Señor Malejala leapt for joy, and then looking across his shoulder he saw a female figure appear on the landing above. The servant heard its approach too, for he turned.

'Go back, Miss Mortimer,' he said. 'You know the Colonel will not like you coming down. Excuse me, sir,' and he literally pushed Señor Malejala on to the doorstep and closed the door in his face.

So it was all true, thought Malejala, and his dark eyes brightened.

'There is a fortune here for the winning!' said he.

He took up a position where he could observe the house

without fear of detection. Towards evening he saw a car drive up. From the car descended an elderly-looking man, rather bent, who walked with the aid of a stick, and slowly at that.

Now there were two men in the house. An old ditherer, a servant who did not appear to be of very good physique, and the girl. It was easy, thought Señor Malejala, and sought out another compatriot of his, one who dealt extensively in the making and application of certain tools.

That night, armed with a pick-lock, a Browning pistol and one or two delicate instruments, Señor Malejala stepped softly through the garden towards the dark house. Only one light burned, and that in the barred upper window where he had first caught a glimpse of a female form.

He had made a careful reconnaissance of the house during the day, and had decided that the front door was the easiest means of ingress. He had used to very good effect the time he had spent in the hall talking to the servant. There were no bolts, he had noticed, and an absence of the chain which is used in some houses to supplement the locks. To open the door occupied him exactly five minutes. The lock was old-fashioned, and yielded instantly to the queer-shaped instrument he inserted so gingerly.

This was not Señor Malejala's maiden effort as a burglar. In his early days, before he had found an easier and less dangerous method of reaching affluence, he had descended to the vulgar practice of housebreaking, and his earlier knowledge now stood him in good stead. He stepped into the dark hall and closed the door softly behind him, flashing a torch along the passage.

There was no sound, no movement, and he gathered that the household had retired to bed early, for he had seen the light from the basement kitchen extinguished at nine-thirty.

He went up the stairs cautiously, keeping close to the banisters where the chances of a creaking tread were less. And as he crept higher he conjured splendid visions.

Señor Malejala was a bachelor, and was not averse to matrimony provided his bride came to him garnished with riches. He might gain not only a fortune, but a bride, he thought.

The third-floor landing he reached without mishap. Three doors led from the wide landing, and under one of these, that which opened on the left, a light was shining.

He tapped softly on the door.

'Miss Mortimer,' he whispered.

He heard a soft step.

'Who is that?' was the whispered reply.

'It is your friend from Spain,' said Señor Malejala, magniloquently.

He opened the door softly, and the first impression he received was through his nostrils. There was a very strong smell of cigarette smoke, and he hesitated.

'Perhaps she smokes heavily,' he thought.

Another second and he was in the room. He had expected this apartment to be furnished, and his first big surprise came when he discovered that it was entirely bare. Save for two chairs, there was not a stick of furniture in the room, and the 'lady' who had invited him in was not alone. Sitting on the other chair was the servant he had seen that morning, and on the servant's knee rested a large six-chamber revolver, and the hammer was raised.

'What—what——' stammered Señor Malejala.

'Put up your hands, Malejala,' said the 'lady', in a remarkably unfeminine voice. 'Keep him covered. Sandy. And I can take off my wig. . . . Glad I didn't have to go to him and lead him by the hand.'

'I thought that would have been rather funny,' remarked Sandy, grinning.

The woman upon whom Malejala was staring took off her wig with a sigh of relief, and disclosed a very amiable-looking young man, and then the door opened again and the aged Colonel appeared, but he was no longer aged. He was not even wearing his white wig or his silver moustache, and he held himself erect. Malejala would not have known him but for the suit of clothes he wore.

'Malejala, you're for the high jump,' said Anthony.

'Who are you and what do you mean?'

'I mean, my old friend,' said Anthony, most affectionately, 'that for once there is a Spanish prisoner, and you're it.'

It was some time before the Latin temperament of this voluble visitor was sufficiently brought down to the level of coherence.

'Now you've got to be sensible,' said Anthony. 'It is going to cost you six thousand pounds to leave this house, Malejala.'

'Suppose I won't give it to you?'

'In that case we shall bury you neatly in the garden,' said The Mixer '—after killing you, of course,' he added. 'I don't approve of burying people alive. Or else'—he was thoughtful—'I could hand you over to Maura, who's in London.'

'On what charge?' sneered the other.

'I'm not talking of charges,' said Anthony. 'I am talking about handing your body over as a souvenir. Produce your cheque-book, dear boy, pay up and look pleasant.'

'I haven't a cheque-book,' growled Malejala.

'I thought you mightn't,' said the other, and took out his pocket-book. 'Here is a cheque on the London, Leicester and Norfolk Bank, Lothbury Branch ; that is your banker's establishment, unless I am misinformed, and I can add to the information I am now giving you, that you have a balance of eight thousand three hundred pounds in that institution.'

'I'll see you in hell before I sign,' swore Malejala.

'You won't see me,' said Anthony. 'You probably won't see anybody you know unless you take a mirror.'

In the end Señor Malejala paid.

'Don't you ever come to Spain,' he said before he went, and there was an ugly look in his eye.

'Why not?' asked Anthony. 'I love Spain.'

'Don't ever come to Spain,' repeated Malejala, 'if you want to leave alive.'

The Mixer smiled.

'Now in return for your kind words,' he said, 'let me give you a bit of advice.' He tapped the man on the chest. 'Don't you go back to Spain,' he said, emphatically.

Good advice which was entirely wasted on Malejala, and which he regretted ever afterwards, for within three weeks of his return to the capital he was arrested, tried and transported to Ceutra ; for Maura had taken the man's threat to heart and arrested him in his lodgings, and on searching his pockets had discovered them filled with counterfeit Spanish banknotes which had certainly not been in Malejala's pockets before Maura came to his flat and planted them.

19: The Crown Jewels

Sandy had once confided to Paul his belief that if Anthony were in residence at Windsor he would find himself bored within three weeks, and would have given the place away in a month.

But amazingly enough, Anthony had conceived an affection for Depe Dene, that dilapidated house he had taken for no other purpose than to relieve a gullible Spanish adventurer of his hard-won wealth. He had spent nearly fifteen hundred pounds in decorating and furnishing, had had gardeners to clean up the wild vegetation which had overgrown its limited grounds, and had planted himself in the new demesne with every evidence of satisfaction.

Sandy and Paul had followed under secret protest, but were surprised at the extraordinary changes which a few weeks' work on the part of painters, decorators, plasterers and upholsterers had made upon these unattractive premises.

Depe Dene stood on the edge of London, and its upper windows commanded a view across the open country. There were a few other residences in the road. Depe Dene was a corner house; on the other corner were larger premises with more extensive grounds. Grounds which extended, in fact, to the frontiers of a big field which the owner of Shanford had recently acquired.

Anthony retailed this information to Paul, who did not really see that it mattered if their neighbour had acquired the earth.

'I'm afraid you're getting suburban,' he remarked.

'I think it is the duty of a good citizen to be interested in his neighbours,' said Anthony, virtuously, 'and I rather like Dr. van Zile.'

'Is that his name?'

'That's his name and title. He is a doctor who does not practise, being superior to the needs and calls of suffering humanity.'

'By which you mean financially superior?'

'Exactly.'

'He's a Dutchman, I suppose?' asked Paul.

'Go on supposing. As a matter of fact, he's a German. His real name is von Zolle. But as he was born in a village contiguous to the Dutch frontier, he had no difficulty in convincing the British authorities that he was a genuine Hollander. A very interesting man, and as I say, he's bought that big field.'

'I don't think that's very interesting,' said Paul, picking up a book.

'Very well,' said Anthony, patiently. 'Then I'll tell you this. He's had a special power cable laid from the main at the end of the street to his house.'

'That only means that he is going in for electric heating no doubt,' remarked Paul.

'You're still unimpressed? Well, I'll have to continue! He has bought a large searchlight, I saw it being carried into the garden this morning.'

'A German with a searchlight during the war would have been monstrously interesting,' said Paul, 'but as the war ended a long time ago I don't quite see why we should be excited.'

'All right,' said Anthony, 'I will go yet further. He has engaged six prizefighters of low mentality, but enormous force of strength, to patrol his grounds. If you want to know the names of his prizefighters I can tell you.'

He took a little book from his pocket and opened it.

'Kid Magee, Bill Soltz, Johnny Fly of Lambeth——'

At last Paul was interested.

'Why is he having these people to patrol his grounds?' he asked.

'Ah, ha!' said Anthony, triumphantly. 'At last I have broken through the skin of your indifference! Why is he having people to patrol his grounds? What is the answer?'

'Tell me,' said Paul.

'I can't tell you because I don't know,' replied Anthony, disappointedly. 'Only it strikes me as curious, putting all these things together. A searchlight, the purchase of a big field, the engagement of prizefighters—handsome fellows. Mind you, all these lads have been well chosen. They are clean, honest fighters, as straight as a die. Even if he had gone through the country looking for men whom he could trust implicitly he could not have chosen anybody more worthy of his confidence. I propose making a call upon the learned doctor, or the Herr Professor, for I have a feeling that he may be a source of profit and entertainment. Besides which,' said Anthony, 'it is one's duty to call upon one's neighbour and discover his secrets. I wonder what he's afraid of.'

His call was made in circumstances which were not exactly propitious. A heavy rain was falling when he walked across the road and rang at the doctor's bell. The hard-headed man who answered his summons was brusque and almost rude. The doctor did not wish to see anybody. In fact, the sound of the doctor's voice came plainly to Anthony, and it was the voice of a man in a very bad temper. He could hear the thud of his feet stamping up and down some room or other, and the roar of his bull voice, in a language which was certainly not English, shook the very foundations of the house.

The Mixer went back to Depe Dene with something to ponder upon.

'The doctor's in a devil of a temper,' he said to Paul, 'and from what I know of the gentleman, that is an unusual demonstration. He is ordinarily the suavest of individuals.'

'Has the bodyguard arrived?' asked Paul interestedly.

'I should think so,' nodded Anthony. 'I saw some strange hats hanging up in the hall.'

He saw some of the strange owners later, wandering in couples about the doctor's garden, for the rain had ceased, though it was wet underfoot.

'Now I wonder what the devil the game is?'

He locked himself up in his own room, and Paul heard his restless pacing to and fro overhead.

'It is strange,' said Paul, when he reappeared.

'Of course it's strange,' exclaimed The Mixer. 'Here is a perfectly easy-going Dutch doctor, who apparently has no enemies, but who, for no reason that we can gather, engages a body of "minders" to look after him, and has bought an expensive searchlight——'

'And a new field,' added Paul, helpfully.

'Humph!' said Anthony, and again disappeared for private meditation.

'What he would have done if that man had had his house painted, heaven only knows!' said Sandy, when he came in to attend to the fire.

That night, when The Mixer sat at the open window of his bedroom, overlooking the doctor's house, he found a solution to one of the mysteries. He had been there an hour, and he was on the point of rising with the idea of going to bed, when he heard a flutter and a hiss, and immediately from the opposite side of the house a white beam struck up into the air, illuminating the low clouds.

'The searchlight,' thought Anthony.

Then the light began to flicker. Dot—dot—dot—dash—it went; again dot—dot—dot—dash. They were signalling. But to whom? Private aeroplanes wouldn't be abroad on a night like this, and why should they signal anyway? He went outside his door and called Paul up to his room.

'What do you make of that?'

'Good Lord, he's signalling!' exclaimed Paul. 'To whom?'

'Well, it isn't to a plane; look at the wind on those clouds.' He pointed to a circular patch illuminated by the light.

'I should say it is practice,' said Paul, and just then the light went out.

The next day brought no further explanation except that which was offered by one of the doctor's staff who told Sandy that his master was conducting scientific experiments to test the Einstein theory of refraction.

'He's got it pretty pat, hasn't he?' asked Anthony, when this was brought to him. 'A domestic employee doesn't as a rule know the exact terminology of scientific experiments.'

The day was a bright and cloudless one, and he sat up until one o'clock in the morning, but there was no further sign of 'scientific experiments'. The house was dark, the searchlight was not in use. He went to bed, and it seemed that he had hardly closed his eyes before something woke him. It was a drone growing deeper and deeper until it was like the buzz of an angry bee in his ear. He sprang out of bed and walked to the window just in time to catch the last flicker of the searchlight before it went dark. And in that light he saw a great white-winged bird come swooping down from the skies and settle to rest in the field behind the doctor's house.

He tore into Paul's room and shook him.

'Wake up, Paul, the mystery's solved.'

'What is it?' asked Paul, sleepily.

'It's a plane. One which the doctor expected and for which he fixed his searchlight,' said Anthony, rapidly. 'Do you see the idea? He expected it to come by night and the searchlight was to show just where the landing was to take place. First he signalled to the sky, and then probably he flooded the field to give the fellow just enough light to land. I'm going to get into my clothes. Don't go to sleep. I'll have something to tell you when I get back.'

In five minutes he was running up the road which was parallel with the field. There was no doubt about it, there was a light plane in the centre of the field and he could see one or two dark figures moving about it and two others walking towards the doctor's house. One was the doctor; Anthony recognised his walk. The second figure was unknown to him. This man carried a heavy bag and they were talking together in guttural tones.

Anthony slipped through the hedge, and made his way

cautiously across the field to a point where these two men would pass, the man with the bag and the doctor.

He lay flat on the grass and was within a yard of them when they walked past. The bag was evidently heavy, because the doctor asked in German whether he could give the other some assistance and received a curt '*Nein.*'

And now Anthony heard a word which threw an illuminating light upon the whole proceedings. It was the word 'Highness'. and Dr. van Zile's deferential attitude supplied the missing link.

A highness! A German prince in England! What was he doing? And what was in that bag which he insisted on carrying alone? Anthony crept out of the field and fled back to his house.

'I've got it,' he said, going into Paul's bedroom, where the light still burned, and Paul was dozing with one ear open in case of a sudden call. 'The thing is perfectly plain. Now I understand all about the field, the light, and the minders. Dr. van Zile is acting as agent for someone in Germany, and that somebody is probably a prince or a nobleman in touch with one of the late ruling houses, and he has brought with him much bullion,' he said impressively.

'Hence the prizefighters,' nodded Paul. 'It must be fairly valuable loot.'

'And it's loot I'm going to get,' said The Mixer between his teeth.

'How are you going to overcome the resistance of six perfectly good prizefighters?' asked Paul, curiously.

'Where you can't overcome, you under-get,' said The Mixer. That was all he could be prevailed upon to say, and it is possible that the plan he eventually followed was one which he had not thought of at that moment.

As a matter of fact, he sat up until five o'clock in the morning considering and rejecting the plans which his busy brain evolved. There was no law against a man arriving by plane, providing the plane was identified and the usual notifications were given, and he felt convinced that all such arrangements would have been made beforehand by van Zile.

The next day there was no sign either of the visitor or the doctor. The plane still stood in the middle of the field, but there was no mechanic near and its presence did not even excite the interest of the small boys of the neighbourhood, who had seen and heard too many aircraft to be greatly enravished by the appearance.

The day passed, and another day came and yet they made no

sign. The minders still remained in the house or patrolled the grounds, and the same vigilance was displayed by the custodians. That evening the aeroplane left on its homeward journey, so apparently there was nothing illegal in its appearance, and its papers were in order.

'What I can't understand,' said Anthony, 'is why they're keeping the boodle in the house? If the princelet intends settling down in this country, why doesn't he immediately transfer his property to a bank—which has no politics and no racial prejudices, since money speaks all languages.'

He was watching the grounds through a pair of powerful glasses and had been watching all day. Towards evening, when he had grown tired of his vigil, he saw something which was peculiarly significant. Four of the guard were lounging about the garden when they were joined by two of their companions from the back of the house.

Though the day was warm, they were wearing overcoats, and these were new, for the other four came round to admire them. One of the newcomers displayed a cap which had also been recently purchased. Even then Anthony did not realise what it all meant, until one of them disappeared into the house and came back with a brand new suitcase. Then the mystery was solved.

'These two fellows are going on a voyage,' he told Paul, 'and they have been togged up for the purpose. Their natural vanity made them come out and show their pals just how good they looked.'

He searched for and found a copy of the morning paper and turned to the shipping intelligence.

'The *Aquitania* leaves for New York the day after tomorrow,' he said. 'That's it I'll bet you any money!'

He was on the telephone in a minute and had called up a West End shipping office.

'Has Dr. van Zile booked a passage for the United States?' he asked, and after a while the reply came:

'Two cabins and three berths.'

He hung up the receiver with a smile of triumph.

'That's it,' he said. 'Two of the men are sleeping in one cabin and the mysterious stranger is in the other. Now how are we going to lift the crown jewels?'

'How do you know they're crown jewels?' asked Paul.

'They're heavy, for one thing. And although I expect the bag contains a lot of fluid cash, I should imagine that the jewels are its principal contents.'

'Why not try the arrest trick?' suggested Paul. 'Pinch them at the station.'

Anthony shook his head.

'Van Zile is certain to be there and he'd recognise me at any rate,' he said. 'No, that won't do.'

He went down to the City to confirm the telephone news he had had. He was anxious to know the positions of the cabins which the stranger would occupy.

'Mr. van Zile?' said the clerk, shaking his head. 'No, he's not sailing by the *Aquitania*.'

'But you told me he was,' said Anthony in surprise.

'He's cancelled his passage. He's going by the *Ryndam* from Plymouth the same day. It sails from Rotterdam to New York, but calls at Plymouth.'

'Excellent!' said Anthony, but he did not explain to the puzzled clerk what he meant.

He had formed a plan, but if the ship sailed from Southampton it was impossible of execution. Plymouth was the very port he would have chosen, for the ships do not come alongside, but lie out in the harbour and can only be reached by tenders. He went to Plymouth the night before the sailing and perfected his arrangements.

'I've got the motor-boat,' he told Paul, when he came back to the hotel late in the evening, 'and wonder of wonders! The local weather prediction is that tomorrow will be misty. If the mist will only hold I'm all right.'

At one o'clock the next afternoon the boat-train discharged its passengers near the quay and they flocked to the big tender waiting to carry them to the liner now lying at the mouth of the harbour. As Anthony had hoped, the mist remained thick upon the water, and Dr. van Zile with his companions close to the gangway did not recognise his neighbour, though he passed within a few feet. This was due less to the thickness of the fog than to the fact that it gave Anthony an excuse for turning up his coat collar so that only the tip of his nose could be seen. Two of the doctor's companions The Mixer recognised as the prizefighters. Their physiognomy was unmistakable. The third man, and evidently the passenger from the aeroplane, was a tall, dark man with an imperious face and a brusque manner.

Towards him Dr. van Zile displayed a deference which was almost servile, as well he might, for the stranger was the Grand Duke of Hardt-Baden. He was on his way to the west, where there is a ready sale for old jewellery and almost priceless settings.

'You understand, Herr Doktor,' the Grand Duke was saying, 'that the second consignment will arrive in a week.'
'Yes, illustrious highness,' said the doctor, humbly.
'That also must be brought over to New York, and I will meet it.'
The siren of the tender gave a hoot and it began to move out into midstream.
'It is very foggy,' said his royal highness, shivering as he turned up the collar of his coat. 'I wonder what that motor-boat is doing following us.'
He was standing by the rail. The opening through which the gangway had been passed had not been closed, and he was just a little too near. Before Dr. van Zile could answer, somebody bumped heavily against the Crown Prince, and with a cry, but still clutching his bag, he disappeared over the side into the water. Instantly Anthony had flung off his overcoat and dived head first after him. He found the man under the water, and with one quick jerk wrenched the bag from him.
The Grand Duke struck out and came spluttering and yelling to the surface, but the man who had taken his bag in eight feet of water was at that moment being stealthily drawn aboard the motor-launch which, with its engines stopped, was rapidly falling astern.
By the time the prince had been rescued it had disappeared, and none had seen the arrival of its new passenger.
'A transatlantic passenger drowned at Plymouth,' read Anthony in the London evening newspapers. 'I suppose that was me.'

20: The Professor

The Anglo-American Sugar Society was called into existence by the necessities of The Mixer. It was desirable that he should have some ostensible business, and so he had taken a small suite of offices in Broad Street, had furnished it solidly and comfortably, and there, apart from the other uses to which he put it, he conducted, in a haphazard way, the business of a sugar broker.
Paul, before he went into the Army, had had some experience

in the sugar business, so that he was not wholly ignorant of the procedure and routine. Strange to relate, genuine business came their way, so much so that it was necessary to engage a typist.

There was a succession of well-meaning young women, all of whom confessed that they had never seen such a typewriter as Anthony possessed, although he was under the impression that it was one of the best-known models, and who typed with great energy on one-fifth of the fingers with which nature had provided them. They usually lasted four days because they got on Anthony's nerves.

Then came Jane Stillington. It was some time since he had rescued her from the society of Milwaukee Meg and the attentions of van Deahy, but Paul noted from his expression that it could not be very long since she had passed out of his mind, even supposing she had ever done so.

By Miss Stillington's own quiet and obviously pleased recognition of The Mixer it seemed as though the memory of their former brief and exciting acquaintance had by no means passed from her memory, and Paul was not in the least surprised when she was engaged on the spot.

'How is she doing?' asked Anthony, the second day after she came. He himself had been out, and Paul, as manager, had been conducting the business of the firm whilst its owner was engaged upon investigations connected with business of quite another nature.

'I'd hate to tell you how badly,' replied Paul. 'She's such a nice girl, and——'

'Nonsense,' returned Anthony, brusquely. 'Give her time. She's nervous yet.'

'Sentiment in business,' murmured Paul, 'is the foundation of disaster. You told me that when I didn't like to get rid of the last one; told me I was a moral coward or I'd have lifted her out of the chair and deposited her gently in the elevator.'

'Jane Stillington's quite different,' announced Anthony, and Paul, pursing his lips and gazing after his retreating figure, believed that she must be.

On the fourth day, when Anthony contemplated the mutilated letters which he himself had dictated, he summoned up courage to ring for her. If he did not speak to her, Paul must, and he felt that he could do it so much better.

'It's quite all right, Miss Stillington,' he assured her, when she came in, 'but I just wanted to mention . . . er . . . the letters. . . .'

To his amazement and consternation she burst into tears.

'I know I'm terrible,' she said, after she recovered. 'My stuff is dreadful.'

'No, really,' he protested, 'it's just that . . . perhaps . . .'

'I know it is,' she said, ' . . . but I have to do something, and after that experience with Miss Morrison, I've been afraid to take anything like that again. . . .'

Gradually, he drew her story from her.

She had been very well off, her father was a rich timber merchant with a weakness for gambling. He was, however, a cautious man and seldom lost much money, so that when he died with unexpected suddenness she had no fear as to the future. When the will was read it was discovered that he had left her a very small annuity, about fifty pounds a year, and that the residue of his property had gone to 'my friend and companion William Orlando Branson'.

'Branson?' said Anthony quickly, for it was an unusual name. 'Not Crook Branson by any chance? Branson, the man who was fined for running an illegal gambling house?'

'That's the man,' she nodded. 'He's a dreadful person.'

'But how came your father to make such a will?'

She shook her head.

'I'm as much in the dark as you are,' she said. 'This isn't a fairy story, you know, Mr. Smith, and you can make any inquiries you like and you'll find that I am speaking the truth.'

'I know that,' he said, gently. 'Crook Branson! Have you any relations?'

'One sister,' she replied, 'a year younger than myself.'

'Are you both working?'

'No, I'm the worker,' she said, with a faint smile, 'and a pretty bad worker too, you think! My sister Mary stays at home and looks after our flat. She knits jumpers too, and gets twenty-five shillings each for knitting them.'

'And Mr. Crook Branson, I presume, is living in your house and using your—did you have a car?'

'Oh yes,' she said, bitterly. 'My father left two hundred thousand pounds.'

She rose wearily.

'I suppose I'm fired?' she said.

'Not a bit,' said Anthony, with a smile in his eyes. 'You look like being a very paying proposition. At any rate, you stay on indefinitely.'

For some reason she blushed instead of thanking him, and he preferred the blush.

He was light-hearted that night, when he told Paul the story the girl had related.

'Of course, everybody in town knows Crook Branson, and I remember particularly the coming of his sudden prosperity.'

'I heard that he had inherited some money,' said Paul, 'but I thought that was a polite euphemism for his having found a prosperous mug.'

Anthony rubbed his chin.

'My friend,' said Anthony, in his best board-room manner, 'this is a case which requires immediate treatment and adjustment. It gives me a pain in the pit of my stomach to feel that Crook Branson is enjoying money that ought to be'—he nearly said 'mine' but changed the word at the last—'ought to be in the possession of its rightful owner. I am going to hunt up my good friend Inspector Timms, and discover what is known about this menace to society.'

He had scraped acquaintance with an inspector from Scotland Yard, and had found the acquaintanceship a very useful one, for the inspector knew almost every bad man in London, and knew, practically to a penny, what his income was.

'Do I know Crook Branson?' said the inspector with a pitying smile. 'Is there anybody in London who doesn't? He's a bad lot, Mr. Smith, a darned bad lot! We were trying the other day to find out where he got his money. He lives in a big house at Penge, and has a couple of cars. To our surprise, we discovered that he had been actually left this money by some poor fool whom he must have duped into making a will in his favour.'

'He's really bad?' asked Anthony.

'As bad as they make 'em,' said Inspector Timms emphatically. 'In fact, I don't know a worse. He's a man without scruple, without any sense of decency, and even the honour which is supposed to exist between thief and thief is without existence where he is concerned.'

'You relieve my mind. Penge, you say he lives?'

'Yes it's a beautiful house and much too good for Branson.'

'Good-bye!' said Anthony. 'I find myself in complete agreement with you.'

Anthony worked out his plan of campaign as carefully as a director of operations outlines a scheme of attack. Two days later, whilst Mr. Branson was lolling in a deep arm-chair, a whisky-and-soda on one side of him, a box of cigars on the other, his maid announced a visitor.

Mr. Branson was big and rather inclined to stoutness. He had a red face and heavy-lidded eyes. Continuous prosperity and the relief from a certain fear of police interference—which tends to act as an anti-obesity influence—had produced another chin and was on its way to making a third.

He looked up with a pleasant leer at the girl who brought the message.

'Show him in, Joan. Anybody I know?' he asked lazily.

'No, sir. It's a young man.'

'Bring him in.'

The visitor was young but businesslike. From the array of pencils and fountain-pens in the top left pocket of his jacket, he was obviously a slave of journalism and his first words supported this view.

'Good morning, Mr. Branson,' he said. 'I've come from the *Post-Herald*, to have a talk with you.'

'With me?' said Mr. Branson, sitting up in surprise, for he had not previously been honoured by a request to contribute his views on current topics to the daily press.

'We've got hold of a rather queer story,' said the reporter. 'Have you heard of Professor Jelby?'

'I've never heard of him in my life,' said Mr. Branson, shaking his head.

'Well, he's evidently heard of you,' said the other slowly, and Mr. Branson became suddenly serious, for he did not like to hear that people had 'heard of him'. The psychologist could explain this phenomenon by the fact that Mr. Branson knew that nobody could have heard much to his advantage.

'No, I've never heard of him,' he repeated. 'What is he?'

'He was one of the greatest surgeons in the world. His operations were renowned throughout Europe, but unfortunately a few years ago strain and domestic trouble clouded his brilliant intellect, and since then he has been in a mental hospital.

'Good Lord,' said Mr. Branson, politely interested.

'Well, our editor had a letter from him a few days ago,' the reporter went on. 'It was filled with a violent denunciation of you.'

'Of me?' said the surprised man.

'Of you,' repeated the reporter. 'It said that you were the most despicable person in the world and it offered a theory that you had no heart.'

Mr. Branson guffawed.

'Heartless, eh?' he said.

'Literally he meant that,' said the reporter seriously. 'There is apparently a reason why he should have picked on you. The point I want to make, Mr. Branson, is this. The professor has escaped.'

'From the asylum?'

'Yes.'

'How does that interest me?'

'Well, we thought we ought to warn you,' began the reporter.

'Rubbish!' said Mr. Branson loudly, and meant it. 'Those kind of people never worry me. I should say not, indeed! Thank you for coming. Have a drink.'

'No, thank you,' replied the reporter, shaking his head. 'You wouldn't like to tell us what you think about this matter?'

'I could tell you in half-a-dozen words,' laughed the other 'but it would shock your young ears. Why has he got a down on me?'

'Well,' said the reporter, who had been waiting for this ques-tion, 'he says that you robbed his niece, Miss Stillington, or rather the Misses Stillington,' he corrected himself, for he had looked into the shining eyes of Jane Stillington's sister, and been visibly confused. . . .

Mr. Branson changed colour to a deeper purple, and despite his expressed sensitive care for his visitor's feelings, he used half a dozen words of singular violence. The reporter left, and joined the young man who was waiting near Crystal Palace station.

'I don't think you're going to get anything out of that old bird, he's as hard as nails,' said Paul, for he had been the re-porter.

'Did you tell him about the professor?'

'Yes. What's the idea?'

'Did you tell him?' persisted Anthony.

'I told him everything you told me to. Where are we goin now?'

'We're going to lunch with the Misses Stillington. I hear yo took Mary out yesterday, Paul.'

Paul mumbled something.

'I'm going to set Sandy up in that farm he's dreamt of,' sa The Mixer presently. 'Yes—soon. And you . . . you're a mo useful assistant to a crook like The Mixer, but as a partner in respectable business you'd be ideal.'

'Why,' said Paul, 'are you thinking of——'

'I'm thinking,' said Anthony, dreamily, 'how pretty she is.'

'Yes, isn't she?' said Paul, becoming animated. 'I told h yesterday——'

'Told whom?' asked Anthony, coldly.

'Miss Stillington—the pretty Miss Stillington; Mary.'

'The pretty Miss Stillington, my dear man, is our Miss Stillington,' he returned, in so final a tone that the discussion closed.

Between the station and the restaurant where they were meeting the girls Anthony outlined his plan.

'It may and it may not work, but I have had the deed of gift drafted on the off-chance,' he said. 'I found out a lot about Branson. He's in the habit of sitting in what he calls his study until three in the morning, swilling himself full of U.P. whisky and is invariably the last to go to bed. The study adjoins the conservatory. There is a flimsy folding shutter and french windows behind those shutters, all of which can be very easily forced. At any rate, I'm going to take a chance.'

'Where did you discover all this?' asked the other in surprise.

'Whilst you were interviewing his nibs I was being shown round the grounds by the gardener, and the gardener has a grievance and did not hesitate to speak.'

Mr. Branson, as The Mixer had truly said, spent his evenings in the solitary contemplation of his many virtues. He was not the type of man who got drunk. He had lost that gift in his early youth, and was now but a container. Drink made him genial, brought to him the dumb shadows of dead romances and revived pale ghosts of other days, most of which ghosts could not have thanked him for arousing them from a sleep in which they were trying to forget their acquaintance with Mr. Branson.

It was his practice from one till two in the morning to doze away the rough effects of his earlier libations, and he was so dozing when he was conscious of a clicking noise as though a door was being locked. He thought it was the maid, and blinked open his eyes. What he saw brought him to his feet, his face ashen.

Standing by the door was a tall man whose white hair fell in a mane over his shoulders. He was dressed in a black suit which emphasised the pallor of his face; his eyes held an almost unearthly glare.

Mr. Branson looked round. The shutters which closed the conservatory from his study were ajar, and the steel bar which fastened them was hanging down.

'What—what do you want?' he gasped, and his eyes bulged at the sight of the long bright knife in the intruder's hand.

'I am Professor Jelby,' said the man in a hollow voice, 'and if you make a sound I will kill you.'

In the middle of the floor was a long oak table, on which were spread magazines and newspapers. With one sweep the old man sent the contents of the table to the floor.

'Come here!' he hissed, and, fascinated by the snake glare of his eyes, Mr. Branson obeyed with legs that trembled under him and knees that knocked. 'Lie on that table!'

'Why!' gasped the man.

'Do as I tell you.'

Branson hoisted himself up with a groan and lay on the table, and then his left wrist was gripped and he felt a rope slipped round and drawn tight. He was paralysed with fear and dare not move, for he was a trickster, not one of those violent men who live by the exercise of their brute strength in nefarious practices, and he was singularly afraid. The intruder moved to the other side of the table and served the other wrist the same. Then he passed a cord underneath the table and across the man's legs.

'What are you going to do?' whispered Branson, his teeth chattering. 'I don't know what you're about—you oughtn't to blame me for what Stillington did.'

The old man stopped.

'I'm going to cut your heart out,' he said, gently, 'and yet I shall not find it. Such a man as you has no heart.'

'What!' almost shrieked the victim, and then a cloth was bound round his mouth.

A silk cloth it felt, but it was tight enough and painful enough for sacking. The professor picked up his case and opened it. It was full of bright and shining instruments and the frightened eyes of Mr. Branson followed every move.

'First I shall draw a little line down here with the point of the knife,' began the professor in a conversational tone, as with deft and nimble fingers, he opened his victim's shirt.

'Wait, wait!' said the other's muffled voice.

Professor Jelby released the cloth.

'If you keep quiet,' he said, 'I will take this off. But before I operate, tell me how you came to get Stillington to sign that will.'

Mr. Branson thought a while.

'He did it of his own free will.'

'You lie!' hissed the old man, 'and because you lie I am going to look for your heart, for on that I shall see the truth.'

Branson thought rapidly. This man was mad, would carry his threat into execution, and he had the intuition of a madman and knew when a lie or a truth was spoken.

What did it matter if he told the truth? he thought suddenly. Who would accept the word of a madman?

'Here, wait,' he gasped. 'I'll tell you. Stillington was a hard nut. I could never get money from him, and if I ever kidded him into signing a cheque he always stopped it in the morning. It was one of my girls suggested it to me, and with the aid of a crook lawyer we drew up the will, and one night when we got Stillington soused we persuaded him to put his name to the will in the presence of witnesses.'

'That was a crime,' said the professor sternly.

'Maybe it was,' answered Branson. 'I thought he'd remember it in the morning, but luckily he didn't. He was taken ill in the morning and a few days afterwards he died.'

'Is that the truth?'

'That's the truth.'

'Then I'll let you up,' said the professor, 'because I realise you have spoken the truth.'

Branson was amazed. He could not believe his ears, but the cords were loosened from him and presently he sat up with a grunt and slid to his feet.

The professor had laid down his knife and suddenly Branson lurched forward and picked it up.

'Now!' he said triumphantly. 'I've got you! You damned lunatic!'

'You have made your confession,' said the other solemnly.

'My confession! To a madman, without witnesses! Who's going to believe you?'

He heard a noise behind him and swung round. The shutters were opened and a man was standing in the doorway, an open notebook in his hand.

'The reporter!' he gasped.

'Not the reporter,' said the other with a wan sad smile. 'I am Inspector Timms, from Scotland Yard, and I am going to take you into custody for conspiracy to defraud.'

Mr. Branson went white and sank into his chair.

'I see,' he said, huskily. 'The whole thing was a trap! But you've got to prove it! That confession was got from me under threat. That's no confession; I know enough of the law to tell you that.'

'Unfortunately,' said the suave Paul, 'one of your girls, as you call her, has already confessed.'

'Grace!' said the other, startled, and cursed. 'I knew she would.'

'Grace it was,' said Paul. 'What am I to do with this man, please?'

'Here, wait, wait,' said Mr. Branson, 'if you'll give me a chance of getting away I'll make restitution.'

'You can make it now,' said the professor, who had removed his wig and was cleaning the paint from his face with a pocket-handkerchief.

He took a paper out of his pocket and flung it on the table.

'There is the deed by which you assign all your property received from the late Joseph Stillington to his two daughters in equal parts.'

'Suppose I don't sign?'

Anthony's eyes narrowed.

'I am not acting a part with you now, Branson,' he said, 'and I tell you that if you do not sign you will be sorry I did not operate!'

A minute later the deed had been signed and duly witnessed.

'Repudiate this tomorrow,' said Anthony, 'and I'll tell you what's coming to you. This man is not an inspector any more than I am a professor.'

'Who are you?' asked Branson.

'I am known as The Mixer, and I think I have gone just about as far as I can, and I am not at all anxious to go to prison, particularly as I find my bank balance in a condition most conducive to virtue. I have arranged to leave this country in a month, and I am taking with me'—he paused—'a wife. You, therefore, will realise,' he went on, 'just how vital it is to me that you should not cut up rough tomorrow.'

The eyes of Mr. Branson flattened and he smiled.

'I see,' he said.

'So therefore I'm going to watch you tomorrow and the next day and yet the next day, and at the first sign that you are betraying me I shall step up to you and shoot you through the spinal column. Is that clear to you?'

Mr. Branson tried to speak, but failed to find words.

'I shan't betray you,' he said at last, and meant it.

Moreover, he kept his word.

Below and on the following pages are other Arrow Books which will be of interest:

THE BLACK SPIDERS

by John Creasey

The island of Canna: twenty years before an earthquake had struck, splitting one of the mountains, rupturing the solid rock, opening up buried strata. And more than just rock had been revealed.

Spiders.

Swarms, hordes of deadly, venomous spiders had been let loose. Spiders whose bite was deadly and terrifyingly quick to take effect.

This was the lethal horror that Department Z faced when they found that they had to deal with a vicious maniac. A maniac whose crimes started in a lonely cottage in the south of England.

A KIND OF PRISONER

by John Creasey

Ryall of Department Z was kidnapped. Judy, his beautiful wifo, was the victim of a murder attempt.

And that was just the start of it all. Suddenly all hell broke loose. Department Z and its personnel had been attacked before many times. They expected it. But this time it was something more. Someone was trying to destroy Department Z. Destroy it totally. Smash it so finally that it could never be put together again.

And no matter what precautions were taken, every plan, every move that its operatives made, seemed to be known, countered and exploited beforehand.

Either there was a traitor loose within the Department, or the kidnapped Ryall was having all the secrets of the Department systematically squeezed out of him. And until this was discovered, the Department would not be able to plan or operate.

THE INFILTRATOR
by Andrew York

Jonas Wilde: codenamed Eliminator, a part of a very small and very deadly section of the Security Services. A man trained to kill. A man used to operating alone. An exposed, isolated job and a job only made tolerable by the knowledge that backing him is an organisation both tightly-knit and totally professional. A job in which a man can have no friends, can trust no one except fellow section members.

It is the section that decides his targets, plans his routes, provides for him. The section programmes him, defines him, motivates him. Without the section he can have no separate existence.

So when without warning the Elimination Section ceases to function, Jonas Wilde faces the most dangerous situation of his life. The physical danger is acute, but physical danger he is used to, can handle. Worse is the mental and emotional danger: the dilemma of not knowing who he is fighting and why. Of not knowing whether there is any point in fighting, whether there is anything left to fight for.

ASHES TO ASHES
by Emma Lathen

Over the last ten years, Emma Lathen has received more than her fair share of complimentary press notices. The climax came when C. P. Snow, writing of a recent book in the *Financial Times*, pronounced her 'probably the best living American writer of detective stories'.

As always, her protagonist is John Putnam Thatcher, and this time it's the wind of change in the Catholic Church which becomes a whirlwind round the Sloan Guaranty Trust, Thatcher's Wall Street firm.

The Sloan is backing Unger Realty Corporation's plans, to the tune of four million dollars, for a twenty-storey apartment house. The property is now occupied by St. Bernadette's Parochial School, which has faithfully served three generations of local Catholics, but which is now broke. Joseph, Cardinal Devlin, is only too happy to get it off his hands. Not so a group of irate parents who have served a subpoena on the Cardinal. A nuisance suit against the Roman Catholic Church is not likely to bring that august institution to its knees, but a murder rapidly changes the situation from a local battle to headline news.

And then the radical Catholic organisations move in: the Mothers for Birth Control, the Council of Concerned Laymen, even the extreme ecumenicals who combine Catholicism with Buddhism. The Parents' League do their best to resist these unwanted and embarrassing allies, but the affair keeps on throwing out new shoots: a series of bomb scares paralyse the Sloan and much of downtown New York. . . ..

FINISH ME OFF

by Hillary Waugh

The hotel room was expensive and elegant. The girl was expensive and elegant. And dead. As was the man with her.

Lieutenant Frank Sessions of the Manhattan Homicide Squad had another case.

The girl was a call-girl. That was quickly established. The man, a client. But who had the murderer been after? The girl? And then the man just because he was there as well? Or the other way round? Or were they both the victims of a puritanical fanatic with the self-appointed task of cleaning up New York?

The key witness was the girl's partner in expensive prostitution. And she seemed unwilling to say anything. It was lucky that Frank Sessions liked women because he soon realised that he was going to have to spend a lot of his time getting to know this one very well.

'30' MANHATTAN EAST
by Hillary Waugh

Monica Glazzard was dead. However it had happened, it would have been big news, would have been of particular interest, to the nation in general and to the authorities in particular.

Whenever someone famous—particularly a nationally-syndicated newspaper columnist—dies, a little more care than usual is taken. After all the public is watching.

The cause of death? Apparently suicide. An empty sleeping-pill bottle beside the bed. But Lieutenant Frank Sessions of the Homicide Squad was called in just in case. A particularly scathing gossip-columnist will have a particularly large and dedicated collection of enemies.

Then the discrepancies in the evidence started to show up. Little things, but a number of them. The sort of things that worried a professional such as Frank Sessions.

At least he didn't lack for suspects—quite apart from the dead woman's public victims. The secretary; she had lied about her alibi and had helped herself to her employer's jewellery. The daughter; an unhappy girl who hated her mother. The gigolo; he seemed incapable of telling the truth about anything at all.

Yet as the case developed it was to have the homicide department at full stretch before arriving at a climax which proved a big double surprise.

THE SHADOW GUEST
by Hillary Waugh

Strange, how Angela Whelan had been attracted to the house right from the start. Standing alone on the Sussex cliffs, unlived in for years, bleak and damp, it seemed an unlikely place to exercise such a strong pull.
But, if it was what she wanted then her husband Howard was prepared to live there. Just over from the States, they had to find somewhere quickly. Living in London, hardly seeing her husband who was desperately busy supervising the government contract that his firm had won, loneliness had driven Angela to the edge of a nervous breakdown. Now, with a psychiatrist's help, she seemed to be better. Maybe the peace and quiet of the country would complete the cure.
But soon Howard was uneasy. His wife's nightmares were recurring and intensifying. Disturbing laughter in the night. The sound, but only the sound, of an appalling car crash, the repeated impression of a man standing on the edge of darkness outside. And Angela's frantic opposition to the suggestion that they should leave. Ghosts? Or the delusions of a mentally sick woman? Howard realised that, whatever the cost, he had to settle the issue once and for all.